Caroline de Costa is an obstetrician and gynaecologist and professor at James Cook University in Cairns. She is the author of three novels in the Detective Cass Diamond series, *Missing Pieces* and *Blood Sisters* teaming with *Double Madness*, which was shortlisted for the 2016 Sisters-in-Crime Davitt Awards. She has also published a prequel to the series, *Hidden Lives*, with Boolarong Press. Caroline has been acclaimed for short crime-fiction, winning the Scarlet Stiletto Kerry Greenwood Award in 2019 for *Screwed*, and was highly commended for *Combustible* and *Love in the time of coronavirus* in the 2020 Scarlet Stiletto Awards.

Double Madness

Caroline de Costa

First published in Australia by Margaret River Press in 2015

Second published by:
Boolarong Press
38/1631 Wynnum Road
Tingalpa Qld 4173
Australia.
www.boolarongpress.com.au

A catalogue record for this book is available from the National Library of Australia

ISBN: 9781925877946 (paperback)

Cover and text design by Anne-Marie Reeves
Edited by Deb Fitzpatrick
Proofread by Kabita Dhara
Typeset in Adobe Garamond Pro 12pt

Printed and bound by Watson Ferguson & Company, Tingalpa, Australia

For Jane Patrick, with thanks for everything

I wish to acknowledge the traditional owners of the land on which the town of Cairns stands, and of the surrounding country and sea. My fictional work is set on your land and seas. I hope I have treated this country, you as Elders and Owners, and your ancestors, with the respect due to you.

Delusion – a false belief based on incorrect inference about external reality that persists despite evidence to the contrary.

Diagnostic and Statistical Manual of Mental Disorders – American Psychiatric Association, 2000

Folie à deux – Induced Delusional Disorder

A. A subject must develop a delusion or delusional system originally held by someone else.
B. The two people must have an unusually close relationship with one another, and be relatively isolated from other people.
C. The subject must not have held the belief in question prior to contact with the other person.

Diagnostic criteria in *International Classification of Diseases* (ICD-10) – World Health Organisation, 1994

The intervention most likely to be helpful (in *folie à deux*) is separation of the subjects.

Wehmeier, *Psychopathology*, 2003; 36: 37–45

Cairns, Far North Queensland, 27 February 2011

If it hadn't been for Cyclone Yasi, it would have been much, much longer before anyone found Odile Janvier.

Yasi had roared into town around midnight. When she reached the rainforest on the mountains to the west of Cairns, she let rip. She plucked giant paperbarks from the earth like a child picking daisies. She tossed branches from high in the canopy onto the forest floor below. She swept great piles of timber down the mountainside, carrying tiny animals far from their loved ones and carving deep gullies in the mud.

Sheltered by an old fig, her back against an ironbark, Odile Janvier was protected from the worst of Yasi's wrath. Her dark hair was slicked wet but stayed tightly pinned back above the perfect arches of her eyebrows. A Hermès scarf fluttered wildly. Her pearl necklace and earrings were undisturbed, as was her shirt of peach silk by Gerard Darel. So, when an oyster-coloured dawn broke through the treetops, she was still there.

If it hadn't been for Tim and Chris arguing about whether to take the back road from Davies Creek through to the Copperlode Dam, it would have been much, much longer before anyone found Odile Janvier.

The road was a dirt track that wound through old rainforest, pristine and unpeopled. It was water catchment land, closed to the public, but Tim's brother Kieran, who had once worked for the water authority, had shown it to them, and how to get in on a sidetrack. Ignore the signs, he'd said.

They were coming back to Cairns on a Sunday evening, three weeks after Yasi. Just the two of them, the kids left with Chris's parents.

'We could take the forest road,' Chris said to her husband. 'We haven't done it in ages. We can stop at the café near Lake Morris for a coffee, see how high the water is in the dam, before we go down the other side.'

'Love, after Yasi, there'll probably still be trees down. It'll be a mess. We won't get through,' Tim countered. He tilted his head sideways like he always did in an argument.

'Mmm,' she said, turning directly towards him, her eyes wide open, her own strategy for getting her way. 'You always say you like that drive. The car's done it heaps of times. And there's two hours of daylight left.'

After a few moments he gave in. 'We can just go and see how it is,' he said. 'Turn back if the road's blocked.' She was right: he loved that drive through the steaming forest, so grand and yet so intimate. Loved the big-dipper descent on the other side, with its views right across Cairns to the ocean. The rain had eased up and the air was clear.

When the biggest storm ever to hit the Australian coast had been brewing out in the Coral Sea – category five, the highest risk – there had been panic down south in Brisbane, where people were still mired in floodwaters of their own. In Cairns, the engineers couldn't promise that the hospital could come through a Cat. 5, and there were 230 patients inside. The Premier ordered them all evacuated and the hospital shut down. The entire staff worked for twenty-four hours solid before Yasi's arrival. Tim's task was to triage the pregnant women. Imminent labour and an impending cyclone were a potent mix. He and his team induced labour for some women, caesared others, and sent as many as possible home. The rest had to be airlifted to Brisbane. In scenes not witnessed in Far North Queensland since World War II, army corporals in jungle fatigues, every last cop in the place, and medical students high on excitement helped ferry stretchers into ambulances and out to the airport for the trip south.

Outside the hospital, the sky grew lower and darker every minute. In the emptying wards, every television showed the weather, and every computer was tracking Yasi. On the screen the cyclone was half the size of Queensland. The small red circle at the centre was the most dangerous, moving slowly, deliberately westward. Though nobody said so, they were all hoping that red circle would turn south. Not that they wished any harm to the people of Innisfail or Cardwell, who'd already been through Larry five years ago; they just wanted that eye to shift away from Cairns. People hugged each other before going off to sandbag their homes. They'd heard it was going to be bigger than Hurricane Katrina in the US and there was a rumour that the army had flown in 10,000 body bags.

At home, Chris and the girls moved furniture and toys off the veranda, taped windows, and shopped for whatever was left in the supermarket (tinned turkey and condensed milk). Chris put a casserole in the oven so there would be something to eat when Tim came home – who knew when the power would go? She pushed family photos into storage boxes together with her most treasured pieces of china, and stashed the lot in the boot of the car. You had to accept that if you lived in a Queenslander, with timber walls and floors and an iron roof, that roof might go in a big blow. And if the roof went, everything went.

Tim had come home exhausted just as the first winds arrived. They moved with the girls into the under-the-house, where solid concrete blocks sheltered the laundry and the playroom. Matty's dog was tied up where he couldn't get at Dora's rabbits, whimpering in their cage on top of the washing machine. As night fell, they lit candles and listened to the radio on batteries and the booming wind outside, the four of them wrapped up together in sleeping bags on the floor.

Then, as she reached the coast, Yasi relented and turned south, coming ashore at Mission Beach. Cairns and its suburbs were spared the worst, although Yasi did not neglect them entirely. At Tim and Chris's house, she tore the blinds from the front veranda and dropped them fair and square on top of

Mt Whitfield. She uprooted the lipstick palms along the front fence and hurled them into a swimming pool three blocks away. As Tim and Chris and their children huddled together the old Queenslander sighed and groaned above them like a labouring woman ready to push. There were sudden sharp bangs that Tim couldn't identify, that later proved to be the barge boards on the side gable detaching themselves.

When it was light, the wind dropped. Tim clambered up the flooded back stairs and saw that his house still had a roof. On the veranda was a disorientated tree python, as unhappy as Tim at their meeting. The snake slid hastily through a gap in the stairs and vanished into the gloom of the rain-sodden garden. At that same moment a police car pulled up at the gate.

'Mobile phone towers are out, Doc,' the cops said. 'The hospital's reopening and they need you back at work. We'll take you; the road's not in great shape just now.'

'OK,' he answered. 'But my wife's not going to be happy.'

It seemed to Tim that day that every pregnant woman in North Queensland had held off overnight. He and Henry and Susanna did fourteen emergency theatre cases in 24 hours before he could finally crawl into bed.

So they'd been delighted when Chris's parents turned up on the first flight from Sydney once the airport was reopened, to help clear up, and then offered to stay on so that he and Chris could have a weekend together on the Tablelands.

On their way home now to Cairns, they passed the Davies Creek picnic ground, heading south toward the Water Board fence. Chris took a quick look around as they reached the gate marked 'Closed To The Public'. Tim nosed the Toyota through the scrub covering the sidetrack, then onto the dirt road beyond the gate. Of course it was mud, not dirt, now – ponds of mud, lakes of mud, a vast, quivering mousse of mud stretching far into the bush. But in the big Toyota it was an easy drive for the first few kilometres, winding through flat rainforest country. Splintered branches and piles of wet leaves lay on the road but no trees had fallen across. The late afternoon sunshine filtered down between the tree trunks to alight on a thousand raindrops on a thousand viridescent leaves, so that the forest sparkled in every direction. Huge spiders were busy recasting their webs high up between the branches. From the car's CD player the mellow notes of the oud of Joseph Tawadros spread out to entertain them in their work.

The road headed down towards a creek crossed by a narrow wooden bridge. The water swirled just to the top of the planks and the trunk of an ironbark had fallen partway across, its feathery topshoots trailing in the stream. Tim stopped the car and got out. His boots squelched as he tested the timber of the bridge, felt the current, measured the distance around the obstacle.

Leaning out, Chris asked, 'Is it OK? We can go back if it's not.'

'I don't want to go back,' he said, getting into the car again. 'We can make it alright.'

He put the Toyota into low gear then edged forward. The front wheels rolled onto the bridge and Tim slowly manoeuvred around the treetop. There was a sudden lurch as the planks gave way beneath the weight of the car. It plunged a metre onto the creek bed and came to a shuddering stop, nose down, just as the American bass player in the Tawadros band reached his crescendo.

'Shit!' He turned off the ignition and, abruptly, the music died with it. 'Can you climb out the window and get out onto the road?'

She was already doing this. 'You come too!' she said. 'Right now! That current could take it away any moment.'

Tim grabbed his mobile, climbed across to the passenger seat and in a few seconds they were out on the road, wet but unharmed. Brown floodwaters eddied about the car and forest flotsam began to pile up against the doors.

'Sorry, sorry love,' she said. 'It was a stupid idea.'

'No, it's OK. I agreed to come.'

'So …' she asked after a moment, 'What do we do now?'

'I think – give Kieran a call.' Tim flipped open his mobile and punched in his brother's number.

'Hi Kieran, yeah, good thanks. Um, spot of trouble, mate. Up on that Davies Creek road, you know the one you showed us. Why what? Yeah, yeah, right, I am a silly bugger. Because about five k's down the track, you know that little bridge, well that's now an ex-bridge, and the car's fairly in the middle of it. Gave way when I was crossing. Yeah. Luckily it's only about a metre deep, otherwise we'd be halfway down the mountain by now. Yeah, it's going to need a tow, at least to get it out, and given how water's pouring over the bonnet maybe more than that. Yeah, yeah, I know it's water catchment ... yeah, well nothing I can do about it, I'll just have to wear the fine. Yeah, no, you never said a thing about it, we just decided to wander in here today, Chris and me... Yeah, that'd be great. We'll walk back toward the main road and I'll keep my phone on.'

He shut the phone and looked at Chris. 'He's coming up but he doesn't have the Pajero, only the Camry, so he can't get right in. He wants us to walk back to the gate. Plus he's going to get onto someone he knows in the Water Board and do some fast-talking. Because a towie will need their permission to come in here. And I don't think we should try to take anything out of the car, not even that CD you like. The bridge is too likely to break up completely and that current's quite strong.'

She looked at the flooded creek again. Hell, they really had been lucky. 'We'd better start walking,' she said. 'At least we haven't come far. By the time we get back to the gate Kieran will likely be there.'

He took her hand for a moment as they made their way up the shallow slope and onto the flatter track leading back to the picnic ground and the highway. A fragile mist hung between the trees deeper in the glades of the forest. As they rounded the bend an echidna came snuffling out of the shrubs at the roadside, black and white spines erect. He raised beady eyes above his long pointed nose, examined them carefully, then returned to his search for ants beneath the vegetation. They stopped for a moment to watch him.

That was when they noticed it. The smell. Chris was the first to turn her head towards the bushes at the side of the road.

Tim knew the smell. You didn't forget it. He'd talked to pathologists he'd worked with about the smell and they all had the same reaction: morose recognition.

He'd first come across it as a junior doctor in Port Moresby. The Boroko cops had asked him to look at a fellow who'd been pulled out of Waigani Swamp. After some weeks at the bottom. They needed a doctor to be sure he was dead, they said. There'd been other occasions too, before he'd started his obstetrics training and had been working in general practice in country towns where doctors had to get involved in these things, and the smell had been there too. Now that he spent his days delivering mostly healthy babies to mostly healthy women in an immaculate hospital he didn't come across the smell. But he hadn't forgotten it. He clutched Chris's hand again and he could feel the goose pimples spreading down his back.

'Urgh, a dead animal,' she said. 'A tree kangaroo?'

He shook his head slowly and handed her his mobile. 'I don't think so. It's coming from beyond that big fig. Can you hold this? Give me a minute. You stay here. I'm going to take a look.'

As he stepped off the road into the bush the echidna took fright and scuttled away on short stumpy legs. Chris watched Tim push his way past ferns and low palms until he vanished around the side of the fig, climbing over its wide buttress roots. She realised she was trembling. He was gone for perhaps thirty seconds. Then he reappeared, and ran stumbling towards her. When he reached the road he was white and shaking. He crouched down in the mud and vomited.

Chris reached out a hand to his shoulder to steady him. With the other she flipped open the phone and hit redial.

'Kieran!' she said, and she realised her voice was wild, hysterical. 'Kieran! We don't only need a tow truck up here. We need the cops.'

That afternoon, Detective Senior Constable Cass Diamond sat at her desk in the Cairns Criminal Investigation Bureau. The CIB, Cass had been pleased to find, was on the top floor of the Police Department building in Sheridan Street. Like her boss, Detective Inspector Leslie Fernando, Cass had dragged her desk next to the window, so that between compiling reports of gunshot wounds and composing allegations of serious bodily harm she could look up for a moment and contemplate the view.

This view was like nothing she'd ever had at any of her many and varied workplaces down south. Admittedly, as views went up here in Far North Queensland, Leslie's was much better, taking in extensive swaths of the Coral Sea. But Cass's view was of her own personal mountains, often mysteriously wreathed in cloud, framed within the window space like the pages of a picture book. One particular mountain was a perfectly symmetrical cone, just as she remembered from a book Jordon had loved as a child. (And now he had climbed that mountain, Walsh's Pyramid, almost as soon as he'd arrived in Cairns, just before Christmas.) On that mountain, she imagined, there would be the spirits of the ancestors whose country it was, guarding the rainforest and the creatures within it.

In those mountains, in fact, had been found the subject of the file she was now working on. According to his grieving mother, who'd reported him missing the previous September, Wayne was a sweet boy who at twenty-eight was spending a few months between proper jobs, had never touched drugs in his life, and wouldn't harm so much as a moth. According to others, who were not grieving, Wayne (aka Jumbo) was a 150-kilogram small-time dealer, in e and weed mostly, who'd double-crossed several people in his time, and finally paid for it. But none of these people, who were all seeking to use this information to their own advantage with Detective Diamond, knew who or where or when, or indeed anything about what had actually happened to Wayne. Or if they did, they declined to impart that knowledge.

Hoping to be led to bigger fish, Leslie had ordered an extensive search for Wayne but it was only after weeks of fruitless inquiries that an anonymous call to Crimestoppers brought his team to the bottom of Heales Lookout in the mountainous rainforest south of Cairns. There they found their man. Others had been there before – probably honey ants first, then bigger ants, flies, spiders, maggots, crows, cane toads, rats and feral cats. There was little more than bones and hair, with a few strips of blackened flesh and rotting fabric. The smell had gone; Cass had been glad of that. Wayne had been identified by DNA samples from his toothbrush. The way some of his former associates spoke of him, Cass had been surprised to find he even used a toothbrush. The pathologist who performed the autopsy, Dr Leah Rookwood, had drawn attention to the stoved-in top of his skull, and multiple fractures elsewhere, but she couldn't say whether he'd been alive or dead when these happened, and, whatever else had come his way, Wayne had definitely fallen a long way down a mountain. He'd last been seen leaving the Redlynch Tavern by car; it was said he'd then been dropped off at home. His DNA was found in that vehicle too but its owner freely admitted he'd given him a lift. He'd just never seen him again.

The car owner was but one of the 116 people Cass had interviewed in the weeks since she'd begun this job. Few of these 116 had been attractive personalities and on one occasion she'd needed her skills in martial arts to deal with two she'd been trying to bring in for questioning from the Redlynch Tavern. She'd formed the definite impression that Wayne Buscati was not a person she would ever regret not meeting. However, not one of her interviews had brought her any closer to knowing who killed him. The Coroner would probably return an open finding.

It had been a long afternoon. Unless there was the sudden announcement of a serious new crime needing her urgent attention, Cass would be off-duty in an hour, when her colleague Drew Borgese would take over. She was planning to drop in at home, see what Jordon was doing this evening, which was probably hanging out with one of his new friends, and then go for a run along the Esplanade. She'd found it was cool enough by evening to run the five kilometres from her unit in North Cairns down to the Pier and back. Then she'd jump into the pool in the unit complex before dinner. Which tonight was likely to be pasta. By Lean Cuisine. Again. Her fridge was a temple consecrated to convenience foods.

At thirty-four, Cass was trim and compact. Today's tan trousers and white shirt fitted her perfectly. She'd been running and working out regularly, ever since the day she'd left Rufus eight years ago, and it showed. In that time she'd shed ten kilos and was now a stable sixty-one. That same day she'd cut her waist-length hair short, very short, so that now it sprang in curls from her head, black with red glints from her Irish grandmother. It was also the day she'd started her application to the Police Academy.

Cass had imagined that in Far North Queensland more people would recognise her for what she was. She'd been wrong; it was the same as Sydney. Some people thought she was Italian, others West Indian, and once in Cairns Central a complete stranger had addressed her in Tamil. She'd had a conversation with Inspector Fernando about this and discovered that he'd had the opposite experience. He'd been born in Sri Lanka. He told her how sometimes people would look at him, obviously asking themselves, is he or isn't he? Then when he opened his mouth their faces cleared and you could see them thinking, no, he's not. He's educated; he can't be.

'And what about Drew' he'd said, pointing at Detective Sergeant Borgese. 'He's always being asked by kids to sign autographs because they think he's a Yank playing for the Taipans.'

'Yep,' said Drew, 'I always give 'em a big smile when I sign, and tell 'em to keep practising.' Drew was nearly two metres tall and skinny with it. Too skinny, in Cass's opinion. He'd spent all his life in Cairns but one grandmother had been Fijian and had married a ship's captain and come to Far North Queensland. Drew's skin was the colour of a ripe kiwi fruit, his face sprinkled with darker freckles passed down by the other grandmother, a Welsh woman who'd married an Italian and moved to a farm outside Mareeba. Between them, the grandmothers had contrived to give him fuzzy gingerish hair, cut short, Cass had noted, in classic detective mode.

Cass's own skin was the colour of almond peel. In Sydney she'd met white women who had themselves sprayed this colour at enormous expense. Someone had once even asked her where her tanning salon was. Cass had responded with a perfectly silent gaze. Slowly realising her mistake, the woman had blushed with confusion.

Cass typed away at her report. She was almost finished. She was considering whether to go downstairs and get another coffee. Just one shot this time, she thought, conscious of the day's caffeine intake so far. Her New Year's quota, she'd promised Drew, would be four a day. But all four today had been double shots.

Downstairs, she was likely to run into someone for a chat, so that was appealing. People were friendly here. Within six months she'd got to know just about everyone working in the building.

Not that they were unfriendly down south. But there had been problems. Dubbo had been her first posting after she graduated from the Academy. A lot of people there had known her dad in the old days. Or had at least heard him sing. Some were critical of what they saw as betrayal. 'You were doin' good, girl, why'd ya join the cops?'

She'd learned to smile and shake her head at this. Occasionally, when it was a serious question, say from a reporter on the *Dubbo Weekly*, she'd waffle on about 'one way to make change' or 'we need more of our people on the ground.' She knew that she really believed both these things, even though the most compelling reason, when she'd first applied for the place at the Academy, was to stick it to Rufus.

The difficulty with being a copper had been her family. They were spread right across the state. Many she knew intimately, had known all her life. Others – aunties, uncles, cousins – just turned up for Christmas or funerals, or appeared from distant parts to stay for weeks that turned into months. No problem with that. She'd had her share in return, in what her mother called her 'gap years'. And after those years, after Richie's death and the realisation that she alone was responsible for Jordon, she'd finally got herself back on track, thanks to one auntie – her dad's sister, Nellie – who literally shook her when she was nineteen, and said, 'Girl, you gotta go and do something good with your life, not just hang about with the kid.'

Because of who they were, these family members often found themselves in confrontation with the law. Mostly just in small ways. Then they would turn to her for help. When she could help that was fine. She'd guide them through the paperwork, point them in the direction of the free legal service. But most times there was nothing she could do. They had to go to court, maybe serve time. Those things were hard.

Cass had thought to make a new start in Queensland. She'd had to spend more time in uniform there before she could be considered for detective training. For this she'd been posted to Logan. Not a good place for Jordon, her mum said. And she was right. Six weeks into the job, Jordon, fourteen, was picked up by a patrol car late at night, when he was supposed to be sleeping over with a new friend.

Mum and Mo had stepped in then. They'd taken Jordon in for his final high-school years. The same years and the same school that Cass herself had dropped out of. Dungog High. Jordon had been happy to shift to the sprawling mudbrick cottage in the bush outside Newcastle, with Gran and Mo and the four aunts and uncles who were his own age. Not to mention Richie's family, who were spread throughout the district. Cass commuted home whenever she could.

After Year 12, she'd expected he'd want to stay down south, where his friends were. But he'd come up here instead of going on schoolies' week. That had surprised her. He'd taken a look around. 'It's cool here, Mum,' he'd said. Next thing, he had a job at Wok in a Box, and was thinking about the university at Smithfield. A science course. He had the marks for it.

The first time he'd come in to pick her up after work, because she'd lent him her car for the day, the desk officer, a chatty woman called Di, said, 'You don't look old enough to have a son of eighteen!'

'No,' Cass said, 'I'm not, really. I wasn't.' She'd been a week short of her sixteenth birthday when he'd arrived in Blacktown Hospital in Sydney.

Di listened to this, cocked her head and said: 'Well he's

turned out a credit to you, love.'

Cass saved the report and sent it to the printer. She logged off and was about to go in search of that coffee when the desk phone shrilled. The very same Di from the front desk.

'Detective? A bit of excitement for you. Dead woman up in the Davies Creek area, reported about half an hour ago by a passing traveller. Informant's a doctor from up at the hospital. I know him. He's quite sure she's dead, no need for emergency services. Tied to a tree.'

'You mean the woman? Tied to a tree?'

'Yep. Apparently. The doc said he didn't stay long at the site. Well, I don't blame him. Seems his car broke down and he was walking out to the main road.'

'Where's Davies Creek? Is it far?'

'It's up on the Tableland. National park. Not all that far for a crow, a bit south and then directly inland. But it's all state forest. There's no direct road from here to where the lady is. Seems like the folk who found her were taking a shortcut on a private track. I've known a few people do that; it's very pretty up there on the range. There's a squad car going out from Mareeba, but they're going to want you up there, and Drew, and the scenes-of-crime officers.'

'What kind of age is the woman?'

'Dunno – the doc didn't say. He sounded pretty crook. Well, you would; something like that really spoils your day.

Mixed up in drugs like that other bloke Buscati, I'd say she was. In fact I'd bet the farm on it. Nasty though, dying up there. Whatever she'd done.'

'So how do I get to this place, Di, if it's so far off the beaten track?'

'It's a toss-up – take the Kuranda road and turn south, or the Gillies road up the range and turn north. I reckon Kuranda'd be better – too many turns on the Gillies, and it'll be getting dark. You'll need a LandCruiser from the pool. And I'll organise a plain vehicle to bring the body down to the mortuary when you're ready. Get yourself a takeaway coffee. It could be a long night.'

Cass paused just long enough to text Jordon. *Sorry will be late called out new case spag in fridge cu later luv mum#*

She grabbed her jacket, tucked the phone in the pocket, and made her way downstairs towards the car park. On her way she'd pick up that coffee. With three shots.

Cairns, 30 January 2011

Three weeks earlier, on a Sunday, at around eight in the morning, Dr Henry Jolley had glanced at his reflection in the bathroom mirror, then, with his old horse-hair shaving brush, begun lathering his cheeks. He'd never liked that spray-on foam that passed for shaving soap these days. Happily, the soft, faintly perfumed genuine article his father had always used was still available in Sydney. He always stocked up when he went down south.

He stepped back and squinted to get a better view. Once or twice he'd tried shaving with his glasses on, but the soap had smeared the lenses. He picked up the old Gillette razor, and began the job.

This was a good time of day for thinking. Beneath the lather, Henry often found he saw the problems of life with a new clarity.

But no problem had ever been as difficult as the one he now wrestled with.

This damn situation! This … this woman he'd got entangled with. He'd stepped straight into her trap, and yes, it was only with hindsight that he could see that. At the time, who would have thought such a thing could happen? Would any other man in his early fifties have acted differently? Thought differently? Yet there it was. The threat loomed over him from one month to the next, and he could see no escape. Apart from just continuing to pay.

And now, Henry thought, guiding the razor, it's just got worse. I could not possibly tell Susanna what I've done. What I've committed to.

Susie, she'd said he could call her. But he preferred her full name. He said it softly now – Su-san-na.

Earlier that week he'd supervised her in a difficult hysterectomy. She'd done it beautifully. He'd left her to close up the abdomen, and wandered into the tearoom, where he'd found Tim.

'She has the makings of a very good surgeon,' he'd said to Tim.

'She has,' Tim had agreed. He cleared his throat. He hadn't failed to notice that Henry's concern for their senior registrar was becoming more than professional.

'She's also a very attractive woman, Henry.'

Henry sat forward, interested. 'She is indeed. She is. Do you think … um …'

'I think you should go for it, Henry.'

'But she's a registrar, and I'm her supervisor. And, at my age …'

This was fast becoming the most intimate conversation Tim had ever had with his older colleague.

'She's a senior reg and she'll be finished her training in June,' he ventured, tilting his head to look directly at Henry.

Henry nodded, though thinking more of Susanna's

enticing Chilean accent and her green eyes above her surgical mask as she calmly handled the instruments. And the slight glimpse he'd had of cleavage beneath her scrubs as she'd bent to insert a catheter.

Warming to the topic, Tim went on: 'She lives at Trinity Beach. You could ask her out to L'Unico. She's in her forties and divorced; she can look after herself and say no if she wants to.'

Henry emptied the soapy water from the basin and replaced it with fresh. It wasn't as easy as Tim made out.

He couldn't possibly tell her his secret. It was so tawdry. So nasty. What it said about him. A serious breach of the doctor–patient relationship. And a married woman. Though none of that really summed it up.

But how could he pursue a relationship with Susanna, and not tell her? He knew that, ethically, morally, he could not, and in a town the size of Cairns there was always the possibility he would be found out anyway.

Henry rinsed in warm water, splashed with cold, reached for a towel. And observed that the smoothest shave could not conceal the furrows deepening at the sides of his eyes. Ah well, he had made the right decision to leave Sydney five years ago, leave the comfort of the big city hospital and try to do something worthwhile up here in the bush. In just a few more years he'd be retiring. He hoped to feel then that he had made some contribution.

None of this helped solve the immediate problem.

At a party just before Christmas, he'd run into that detective. Inspector Leslie Fernando. They'd found themselves standing alone on the balcony of their hosts' hillside pole house, looking over a damp green garden stretching down to Lake Placid. With his second Scotch in hand, Henry had decided to sound out Leslie on the possible criminal aspects of his problem. In a red batik shirt and chinos, his hair now streaked with silver, Leslie exuded an air of relaxed authority. Henry decided to make it sound like something that had happened to another doctor, a long time ago, in another state. A misunderstanding by a patient, he said.

'This is just a rumour?' asked Leslie. 'You don't know who this woman is? You've no evidence?'

'Well. They, she, the woman … could have been a patient of mine at some time. Not here in Cairns. Elsewhere.'

'But no hard evidence? No videos, threatening notes, anything like that?

Henry took a gulp of Scotch. 'I can't exactly say that, no.'

Leslie had looked at him closely. 'If there is something, don't tell me anything about it! Unless you do want to pursue this case. One thing, I suppose, if you know who these people are, you could make some discreet inquiries. See if there has been any trouble in the doctor's family – a divorce say, resulting from this, ah, this misunderstanding. And yes, in answer to your question, if there were a complaint the police are bound to investigate.'

'I see,' Henry had said.

Now Henry pulled on trousers and shirt for a quick ward round, and made a decision. It was by no means a solution, but it was at least a plan.

He was meeting Tim this evening. They planned to go over their perinatal figures for the previous year for the annual report. The cyclone was also on its way. At some point he'd mention Susanna. Tell Tim a bit about the problem. Choose his words carefully. Misunderstanding. Compromise. What did Tim think he should do? Could Tim help him, help him find a real solution – with Susanna. But also with the real problem.

The real problem. That was something else he would have to deal with today. Again, dammit. It was the last Sunday in January; the day that the Controller insisted on receiving payment. He wanted it placed under cover of darkness, not during daylight hours. He? Well, Henry had always assumed that the Controller was a man. But as to his relationship with the woman, Henry didn't know. He felt his blood pressure going up just thinking about it and tried to calm himself. But hell, sometimes he felt he could bloody well kill someone to get out of the spot he was in.

Henry took a deep breath, and ran a comb through his hair. There was still plenty of it left, thank God, even if that was more salt than pepper now.

From a drawer he took a plain buff envelope and, opening his wallet, checked that his ATM cards were there. He needed to withdraw twenty $50 notes during the course of the day. This evening, around eight o'clock, he'd be pushing the stuffed envelope through the letterbox of that strange backlane unit.

As he'd done every month now for nearly four years.

Cairns, 28 February 2011

Late on Monday afternoon, following the discovery of the body in the forest, Detective Inspector Leslie Fernando called a meeting of the team. Before signing off on a media release he wanted a complete rundown on everything known so far about what they were calling the Davies Creek case. Which, despite the flat-out efforts of Detectives Cass Diamond, Drew Borgese and Troy Barwen, was not all that much. And what they did have was mystifying rather than helpful. There was so far no clue at all to the woman's identity.

The three detectives sat around their boss's office while he got himself comfortable on his desk in front of them. Behind him the Coral Sea glimmered in the late afternoon sunshine. Gulls whirled and swooped outside the window. Leslie was smoothly shaven, in grey trousers and immaculate white shirt. On day one of her job, Cass had mentally filed his hairstyle under traditional-short-back-and-sides.

Now Cass sat to attention on an upright chair, her laptop open on her knees. Across a low armchair on the other side of the room uncoiled the full length of Detective Sergeant Drew Borgese, all 195 centimetres of him, like a python resting on a riverbank. His arms dangled down to the floor on each side of the chair, fingers drumming a silent rhythm on the carpet. Drew was leading this case, and Cass had already discovered that the ex-basketballer's permanently laid-back take on the world concealed a sharp mind and a sympathetic personality. What's more, he'd lately been delegating important parts of cases to his younger female colleague.

Detective Constable Troy Barwen sat astride a typist's chair, leaning forward on the chair's back, which rolled under his weight. He was short and solid, with hair cut in a flat-top, and large brown cocker-spaniel eyes. Looking at him now over her laptop, Cass reminded herself that dogged persistence was a useful character trait in a detective, and that his earnest contributions to their conversations enhanced their team efforts.

'So fill me in,' said Leslie.

'Well Sir,' said Cass, 'the body was found yesterday afternoon by a doctor – Dr Ingram. He was driving back from the Tablelands with his wife. His car broke down and they were walking back to the main road.'

Leslie straightened up suddenly. 'Tim Ingram?' he asked.

'Yes. You know him? He seems a sensible kind of guy,' Cass answered.

Leslie nodded. 'I met him in a case a few years back. He looked after a woman in a rape and serious bodily harm. That Chinese girl dragged into a car at Smithfield. Interesting that he found this woman.'

'Well, we'll talk to him and get a statement, of course,' said Cass. 'But it does seem he just happened to be there. His wife wanted to drive along that road, he said.'

'I might talk to him myself,' Leslie said. 'Go on.'

Cass and Drew had reached the Davies Creek turnoff little more than an hour after the call had come through the previous afternoon. At the gate to the water catchment area they'd found a crowd. Tim Ingram was a tall, fair, youngish man, with tired eyes. His wife, Chris, was beside him; Cass had immediately liked her calm presence in the rather frenzied scene. With them was Tim's brother Kieran, who'd come to bring the couple back to Cairns, necessary given that their vehicle was going nowhere immediately, at least under its own power. Also present were four uniformed men from the Mareeba station, scenes-of-crime officers, two four-wheel drives, and a number of interested bystanders who'd been barbecuing at Davies Creek picnic ground. As the Cairns contingent arrived, a tow truck pulled up and the driver jumped out, eager to see what was happening.

It was decided that Tim, Chris and Kieran would go along the forest road with the police and the towie: Chris and Kieran to help deal with the stricken Toyota, and Tim to direct the police to the corpse.

'You don't need to look at it again,' Cass had told Tim in the back of the LandCruiser. 'You only need to show us where it is, and give us a statement a bit later on. I can understand it was shocking, even for a doc.'

'Yes,' he'd said, 'it was. But no worries, I'm OK now, though I'll be happy to just have to show you where she is. It was so unexpected, and on top of the car going into the creek.'

Darkness was falling as the convoy made its way slowly along the road, churning up great gobs of mud which spattered the windscreens of the vehicles behind. The forest canopy hid the setting sun and the trees were blurred in the gloom. Only the pale trunks of the paperbarks stood out, ghosts among the shadows. By the time they reached the spot where Chris and Tim had seen the echidna they all needed the flashlights that the Mareeba police produced.

Cass knew it would be a long time before she forgot the sight of that body in the middle of the rainforest. It was one of the grisliest scenes she'd ever encountered. The dripping eye sockets, the strangely bloated flesh that still seemed to keep the shape of the woman's face, the gaping rictus of her open mouth. Above all, the smell. Not just the clinging stench of putrefaction, which she had braced herself for, but another more penetrating and somehow horribly sweet smell that she had never before encountered. Despite the darkness there was also the buzzing of flies, many of them close relations of the maggots that could be seen feasting on the corpse as she and Drew flashed their torches up close. Within minutes, powerful spotlights were set up and the site was lit with an awful clarity. It was, Cass had thought, like a stage set. Designed around a giant doll, broken and grinning horribly, tied to the trunk of a small tree. Around that tree were the buttress roots of a huge strangler fig which merged into the outer darkness of the theatre wings. And they all had their roles in the play, as they gathered and sifted through the evidence, took photos and made notes, sidling around the silent central character of the drama.

'The body was tied very firmly to a tree,' Cass now told Leslie. 'A tree that was in the shelter of another much bigger tree, so it was almost like a cave, one of those big figs. The pathologist said she must have been there during Yasi. She was not too far from the road but very well hidden from it. In a place that you'd have to think had been chosen carefully. She would have been sheltered and protected from the cyclone by the size of the fig tree. Her hands were tied behind her back and also behind the tree. I would say that in life they were tied tightly. With the ... decay of the body, much of the tissue was gone and the knots were loose against the wrists but they were still very tight in themselves. The same with the legs: both ankles had been firmly tied.'

'With rope or wire? Any clues there?' asked Leslie.

'No – with scarves. Silk scarves!' Cass said. 'Hermès. French. Four of them, altogether.'

'I had a look at the Hermès website,' she continued, 'not having ever had a Hermès scarf myself. They sell in boutiques in Sydney and Melbourne, for $550 each. Of course you can also go to Paris if you want a greater choice.'

Leslie looked perplexed. 'You're telling me that someone tied up this woman with thousands of dollars' worth of luxury silk scarves? Couldn't she just have untied them or ripped them off?'

'Well, yes to the first part of the question, and my guess is that she was alive when it happened. There's fraying of the silk as though she's tried to rub them against the back of the tree. But they're strong, like parachute silk, and don't tear easily, as you'd hope for $550. Or maybe something else happened to her as well.'

The team, detectives and scientists, had begun work at once. But the gloom of the forest at night meant the proper search couldn't start until daybreak.

Once begun in earnest, it had continued throughout the day. The scientific staff had taken shots from every side before carefully untying the corpse and placing it in a body bag in the transport vehicle. This had then been taken to the hospital mortuary. Drew had given himself the task of following the body through and attending to confirm identity, and watching as Leah Rookwood performed the autopsy. Cass had spent the rest of the day trying to identify the victim and Troy had stayed at the scene in the rainforest.

'There's no sign of any major injury,' Drew reported to Leslie. 'At least, no blows to the skull or lower body, like Wayne Buscati had. No evidence of a gunshot wound. Leah will have a more detailed report ready for us very soon.'

'So,' said Leslie slowly, 'is it possible that somebody, or more than one, tied her up there and just left her to die, slowly, from dehydration and so on?'

'Yes. Terrible to think of,' Cass said. 'The water authority fella said that a few of their vehicles had gone along that road since Yasi, clearing large branches, but the road wasn't blocked, so they'd have had no reason to stop for long. And it seems the bridge where the doc broke down held during Yasi, but the heavy rain afterwards wore away at the timber. Driving a car onto it was the final straw.'

'The woman looks to have been in her forties or early fifties,' said Drew, still dangling his arms in his corner chair. 'But we have no idea who she is. No ID, no possessions on her at all.'

'She might be a tourist,' added Barwen. 'French, maybe. As well as those scarves she was wearing foreign clothes.'

'A black lace bra from Intissimi,' explained Cass. 'Also very expensive, believe me. A silk designer shirt from Paris, ditto as to price. A Donna Karan skirt. But no undies. One Christian Louboutin shoe. I had to google Christian. When I found his site I could see why we'd never crossed paths before. Our lady had chosen his Bianca range, which sell for $795 a pair. All his shoes have red soles, which apparently justifies the price. What's more, she definitely did not walk in those shoes to where she was found, at least not along that road. The heels are skyscraper high. So maybe she was carried there.'

'Cass has found absolutely no record of any woman like this missing from anywhere in Queensland or the rest of the country right now,' Drew said.

'That's right,' confirmed Cass. 'I checked everywhere. No guests missing from any Cairns hotels or resorts anywhere in the state. No reports of anything at all. I called the French Embassy in Canberra as well as Interpol. Description doesn't match anyone listed with them. The French suggested talking to the Swiss and Belgians. Another blank. You'd expect a woman like this to have someone missing her somewhere. More than that, she should have family and friends banging at our door, wondering where she is.'

'Leah Rookwood put the death at about four weeks ago,' said Drew. 'Just before Yasi. Although she's also taking samples of the bugs that she comes across in tissue remains, the larvae and pupae and so on, to get an accurate time of death. She said it's complicated by the weather up here even at the best of times, the heat and the humidity. And the best of times it has not been.'

The ground around the site had been searched, netting a Chanel Rouge Allure lipstick and a powder compact. These were very close to the road and partly buried in mud. A team of police and emergency services volunteers was methodically combing the wider area. Tim's Toyota had been hauled out of the creek and taken into Mareeba, and the water authority had decided that in the circumstances Tim's presence on the land could be overlooked.

'The lipstick and compact have no prints on them,' Cass said. 'Not surprising, if they've been lying for weeks in the mud, including through the cyclone. Close to the road-edge, like she might have been sitting in a car there doing her face, before whatever happened to her happened. Or maybe they were knocked out of her bag. Would you believe, the shade of lipstick is called Incognito! Kind of a dark red. Would have gone well with the colour of the shirt. And her fingernails and toenails, what I could see of them, were painted the same colour. This woman had style.'

'And money, it seems,' Leslie pointed out. 'Or access to it. So why hasn't she been missed? She doesn't sound like the run-of-the-mill North Queensland drug-dealer's partner. Even though it can't be far from where Wayne Buscati was found, this sounds very different. Completely unrelated, I'd say. Have you looked at the scarf angle? What about these big-city boutiques you googled?'

'Already taken care of,' replied Cass. 'I've asked Sydney to get the store to run a check on possible customers. They sell them online as well as in-store. I've given them details of the four scarf designs. They feature a lot of horses' heads and gold chains. That might ring a bell with someone, or there might be a computer record.'

'Brisbane is working on a comfit drawing for us,' said Drew. 'It should be ready tomorrow morning. It can go nationally then. Someone *must* know who she is.'

'So this woman,' Leslie said slowly, 'was in no way dressed for a walk in the rainforest, even a short one. Yet somehow she either agreed, or was forced, to go to this remote spot, in high heels.'

'Or maybe she was dragged,' said Cass. 'But there's so much dirt and mud on her, plus the decomposition, it's no longer possible to say whether she was dragged, maybe with her hands already tied. Presumably she was brought along the road in a car or at least a vehicle of some sort. Three or four weeks ago only four-wheel drives would have got in there. Apparently very few people go along that road, even from the Water Board. The killer, or killers, must have known the road and the area.'

'Though,' said Drew, 'we can't say yet that someone *intended* to kill her. We also don't know yet if she was raped, or sexually assaulted in some way.'

'Um, OK.' Cass looked dubious. 'Then let's just say that someone who wanted to be playful persuaded her to let them tie her tightly to a tree in the middle of nowhere, and then pushed off and forgot to come back.'

'Well, not very likely,' Drew conceded. 'But, well, we all know there are people who like to tie each other up, for whatever reason … and it can go wrong … the silk scarves give it a bit of a twist, especially with the missing underwear. But without knowing who she is or where she comes from we can't even begin to speculate about what's happened.' The phone at his elbow rang.

'Borgese here. Hi Leah! Right, thanks, we'll be there first thing.' He hung up.

'Leah Rookwood will have a first report on the autopsy ready by 8 am tomorrow. You can go straight to her office then, Cass.'

'I could come along …' Troy Barwen started to say, but

Leslie shook his head. 'You need to carry on with supervising the site search,' he said. 'And Drew, what about checking the airport? Get the CCTV footage of the week before Yasi and look for a woman like this.'

Barwen sank back into his chair with an expression that reminded Cass of the pet wombat she'd had as a child when he was locked up for the night. Drew briefly caught her eye, and shrugged.

On Cass Diamond's second day with the unit Drew had walked in on a conversation Troy was starting with the new detective. He was explaining to her how he enjoyed long walks on the beach, and solving crosswords. Drew was in time to see Cass swivel around in her chair and say: 'Barwen, I'm happy to work with you in any way we're asked to, but I absolutely do not mix my professional and personal lives.' Then she'd snapped her chair back to fix her gaze on her computer screen.

'We'll put out a media statement, Sir,' Drew said now. 'A short statement. Body of a woman found yesterday in dense rainforest outside Kuranda. Not yet identified. Caucasian, thought to be in her late forties or early fifties. We'll say we believe she may be a European tourist. May have been dead for up to four weeks. Cause of death not yet known. Police inquiries proceeding, etcetera. If any member of the public can provide information about her identity, kindly call this number. Or Crimestoppers.

'And we'll meet here again tomorrow morning,' he finished. 'Around midday. Unless something turns up before then.'

Cairns and Hobart, May 2009

Some two years earlier, on a May evening, Dr Trevor Symonds had sat sprawled at his surgery desk, idling through the pages of the newsletter that always accompanied his copy of the *Australian Medical Journal.* The journal itself was getting too damn hard these days, Trevor thought. Once, he'd been able to read it all, when things had been pretty much confined to the diseases and molecules and drugs he'd learned about in medical school, and in his few hospital years afterwards. Now there were biochemists and geneticists and every other kind of young hot-shot expert discovering new enzymes and new hormones and inventing new drugs to treat the diseases they'd created. Sometimes, now, he managed to read the abstracts at the top of the articles. After all, he told himself, it's the top line that counts, ha ha!

Besides, he was planning to go to the College conference in Hobart next week, and he would certainly go to some of the lectures there. For one thing, he needed the attendance points to keep up his registration to practice. Mainly, though, it would give him a chance to catch up with some of his old mates. The ones who'd moved into general practice in other states. Johnnie Flanagan, for one, and Martin Scott. They'd always been good blokes. Not likely to take him to task, no matter what they might have heard about him and Lyndall.

And they'd be wanting to let loose a bit, have a few drinks, play a few games in the casino, ha ha! Yes, he was looking forward to it.

You only had to sign in at the conference each morning, anyway, to get the attendance points, and all the talks were summarised in a folder they gave you the first day. Certainly they *should* give him something, for the nine hundred bucks he'd had to shell out.

He turned the page, glanced at the headline: 'New Infection Control Measures to Affect All General Practitioners by 2012'. Christ, more rules, more rubbish. He scanned the article. It seemed that, on top of everything else, he was going to have to invest in a brand new computer-controlled autoclave to sterilise his surgical instruments, at around $20,000, just because his current model didn't have laser-controlled follow-through systems to record and print out details of every single item going into it. All these regulations, they were just getting too much. His old steam steriliser worked perfectly well. If it ain't broke don't fix it, he thought, ha ha!

Suddenly his attention was caught by a photo at the bottom of the page. 'Former infection-control nurse Joy Bulmer,' ran the caption, 'now in charge of marketing for Ascham Medical, will be at the College's Hobart meeting to demonstrate the new range of fourth-generation autoclaves.'

Joy Bulmer! He'd often wondered what had happened to her. It must be eleven, no, twelve, years. He studied the photo carefully. If that was taken recently she wasn't looking too bad. She'd always been a bit plump. Podgy even. Size 16, Lyndall would have said, though not disparagingly. Of course, she'd never met Joy. Lyndall. Better not to think of Lyndall. Lyndall was always size 10, back to size 10 within weeks of the kids' births, he remembered that. No, better not to think of Lyndall. In the photo Joy's hair was streaked blonde, as it had been when he knew her. Her pubic hair was dark brown, though, he knew that, ha ha! She'd kept her name ... perhaps she'd never married? Though you never knew these days. And she was going to be at the Hobart meeting!

Trevor lounged in his chair, stretched his legs, and thought back to his days in Weipa. A mining town, two hours' flying time away, always in need of doctors. He'd started off just flying up for the day once a fortnight, helping out the single doctor in the public hospital. Then, as he got busier, once a week. Joy was the head honcho in the hospital then.

First of all it was just one or two drinks together in the pub before his flight back, no harm in that. Then he began to think there was enough work for two days – he could go up at lunchtime on Tuesdays, stay at the Albatross, come back to Cairns on Wednesday evening.

But of course the real reason for the overnight stay had been Joy. Not that he hadn't been getting on with Lyndall. That was one of their better patches. But a bit of variety never did any harm, he'd thought. Joy was a jolly sort of girl, didn't seem to be looking to settle down or anything like that. Taking the Pill, so he wasn't the only one. Lyndall never twigged, not that time. Weipa, he told her, it's as dry as a lizard's back. It never occurred to her he might be going there for sex.

And Joy had been willing, more than willing, from that very first night. Here I am alone in a strange place, he'd said, I need you to show me around. After a steak and a few beers they'd gone back to her flat next to the hospital. He'd given her ten out of ten for her pelvic floor muscle control. Of course she'd never had kids. Lyndall by then was a bit slack in that department, after two forceps deliveries, not her fault of course, but a bloke did appreciate a bit of tightness when he could get it. And, later, Joy started doing things he'd never even thought of suggesting to Lyndall. Momentarily, the image of Joy's ample buttocks, milky-white in the dying light, came to mind.

It had lasted several months. Each Tuesday, by the time the plane had crossed the mountains and was heading north-west over the grey-green countryside, he was already in a state of semi-arousal and had trouble concentrating on his afternoon's surgery.

But then she'd got difficult. True, he had hinted, just hinted, that his marriage was packing up and he might shortly be separated. When he'd said he couldn't meet her in Cairns, she seemed to realise the separation wasn't going to happen. Asked more questions. Started to insist on condoms. Talked to a mental health nurse who worked with Lyndall.

So that one Tuesday it was all off. Joy had called him a lot of unfair names, he remembered. Said he'd lied to her; of course that wasn't true. So he gave up Weipa altogether, switched to Cooktown. No obliging blonde nurses there, unfortunately.

Well, he wouldn't mind seeing her again. Especially now, with Lyndall gone. Just for old times' sake. Enough water's flowed under the bridge, he told himself, for her to be pleased by a chance meeting. And Hobart seemed the perfect place for that. At coffee and lunch breaks there'd be a crowd around her stand. All the chaps were going to have to buy these new sterilisers. They'd be wanting to look. He'd be able to locate her, look at her in a crowd first, then wander up and seem surprised to see her. 'Bubbles', that was what she'd liked him to call her, as they'd rolled around her queen-sized bed. He'd remember that, ha ha!

In the following week, before the Hobart conference, Trevor Symonds thought quite a lot about Joy Bulmer, and in the plane on the way down to Hobart, he thought about her even more. The sound and movement of the aircraft recalled his Weipa trips, and there was that familiar surge of excitement in his loins. He thought how good it would be to get into bed with someone he felt physically familiar with. Like Lyndall. But it was no use thinking that. I might be losing my touch a bit, he told himself, maybe drinking a bit much lately too. Not surprising, being left like this, what do you expect? Looking for new women at this stage of my life, I shouldn't have to do that.

Arriving in Hobart, he took a taxi direct to Wrest Point. The convention centre was the site for the conference, located within the casino and next to the hotel. At the casino bar he found both Johnnie and Martin and their wives.

After some initial pleasantries and backslapping and do-you-remembers, he told them about Lyndall. There was an awkward silence. The women exchanged knowing glances, and Trevor remembered he'd never liked those two. Just wait till tomorrow, I'll meet up with Joy, he told himself, and to cover the silence said loudly, 'It's my round'. But after two drinks Johnnie and Martin and their wives excused themselves, and Trevor was left to drink with two blokes from South Australia whose names he couldn't recall, and who'd left their wives at home, and who, like him, wanted to celebrate a bit.

The next morning he woke with one hell of a headache, and found he'd been sleeping in his only decent pair of trousers, which were now crushed and smelling of stale booze. He had to put on an old pair of corduroys, and a shirt he didn't know how to iron, and he didn't get down to the conference until after eleven. Coffee was already being served in the sponsors' display room, which was crowded with his medical colleagues. He couldn't even get near the Ascham stand, and then he had an argument with the smartarse redhead who was running the registration desk – nice legs and a low-cut top showing lots of cleavage, but a real little Hitler. She said he couldn't sign in for the first morning session and get his College points because he was too late.

So he had no chance to look for Joy then, and because the redhead was watching him so intently, probably to see if he really was going to attend the lectures in the second session, he had to finish his coffee and go into the conference hall, instead of idling inconspicuously among the stands of blood-pressure meters and urine-testing kits, trying to get a look at Joy.

At that moment Joy Bulmer was in front of the mirror in the pink-marbled ladies' room of the Wrest Point Convention Centre, touching up her makeup in preparation for the lunchtime rush of potential Ascham customers.

Alone in front of the glass, she studied her reflection. All in all, she felt happy about the way she looked. Happier than she'd ever been when she'd been married to Barry. Barry Snodgrass, who'd hassled her constantly about her weight, especially after Brendan was born. It was true, she had put on a bit during her marriage, now fitted more easily into a size 22 than a 20. But in Ascham's corporate outfit of stylish navy skirt and jacket, teamed with a blouse patterned with tiny blue sterilisers, she looked good, she knew. Authoritative but still feminine. Today, knowing how conservative most of her medical clients were, she'd added a double row of pearls and her smart but sensible Diana Ferrari navy heels. Indeed, her size was an asset in her job, not the liability it might be in some other businesses or organisations. Selling sterilisers and surgical instruments, Joy had found, meant meeting directors of nursing, infection-control supervisors, meant talking to a lot of women who were physically big as well as having big personalities. Women who were used to running their own show, to holding the purse strings. They could relate more easily to Joy than to some stick of a twenty-year-old. Ascham knew well what a prize they'd got. Her sales last year had outclassed everyone else's, and she'd been rewarded with a lovely holiday in New Zealand for herself and Brendan.

Life had indeed taken a turn for the better since her divorce from Barry. She'd been fond enough of him when they'd married, and thought she could learn to live tolerably with him. But then Barry had become so boring. He never wanted to go out. He hadn't much liked her going back to work even once Brendan was in primary school. He didn't like her friends or her socialising. Joy liked to be busy, to be where things were happening. She liked the atmosphere of hospital work, of being part of a team. Liked working hard, then relaxing completely when she went off-duty. Lunches on Fridays that lasted till tea-time, bottles of champagne. That was how she'd earned her nickname, 'Bubbles'.

One Friday, Joy came home by taxi, having left her car in the station car park. She knew she'd had more Seaview Brut than was good for her, and she was late collecting Brendan from after-school care. Barry arrived home to find his dinner not ready. He had shouted at her, had said she was extravagant. Even though she paid half the mortgage and all the housekeeping before spending anything on herself.

They'd had a huge fight and Joy had taken Brendan to her mother's, as she'd done several times before, only this time she didn't come back.

Brendan had been unhappy and withdrawn at first. When he realised he could take Joy's maiden name – drop the hated Snodgrass and become Brendan Bulmer – his unhappiness disappeared almost overnight. And his mother was more than ready to revert to Joy Bulmer.

After her divorce, Joy took a course in infection control. She found a short maternity-leave replacement post, and was looking around for something permanent when the job with Ascham came up. She wouldn't have been able to do it if she'd still been married to Barry. So much travelling. But living with Mum, who at seventy was still fighting fit and a formidable bridge player, Joy could go off at any time and leave Brendan happily at home with his nana. And go off she did, all over Australia, talking up Ascham's products and accumulating frequent flyer points.

What's more, she'd found she was getting more sex than ever before. It had been surprising to Joy how many male doctors, nurses and theatre technicians were available, even though she'd put the weight on. Maybe even because of that. Here, in Hobart, she knew she'd have offers. A few men from previous flings might be around, too, without their wives. Joy was finding that she liked things this way. Some drinks, dinner, bed. Joy had done with commitment, thank you, and she always remembered to pack protection.

Joy applied L'Oréal's Pearly Pink to her lips, took a last contented look at her reflection and dropped the lipstick into her bag. She made her way past the papier-mâché potted palms, false rocks and waterfalls decorating the casino that completely obscured the cool beauty of the Derwent beyond the windows. Beyond some fake Mexican cactus she could see the Ascham stand. It did look striking. She, Jill and Melanie, Ascham's permanent reps in Hobart, had spent the previous day setting it up, using ribbons and crepe paper in Ascham's brand colours, and their efforts had been worthwhile. The new model DSK 440 steriliser was steaming away at the front, with its special glass door that Joy herself had thought of, so doctors could see the instruments sparkling inside while the microbes perished. Health departments everywhere were insisting on these new all-in-one, computer-controlled, laser-printing sterilising systems. This was good news for Ascham. In the morning coffee break Joy had taken the names of at least twenty doctors who wanted to place orders. A huge number of Ascham's brochures, designed by Joy herself, had been picked up, together with all the free Ascham pens and notepads. Joy lifted more boxes of pens from behind the stand and began to spread them out, waiting for Jill and Melanie to return from their coffee break.

Trevor sat fidgeting through the morning session of the conference. The talk was way over his head, a talk about some bug called *Clostridium difficile*. When question time came, Trevor bumbled along his row of seats and out the door. It was half past twelve. He could just, casually, find the bar again. Have a quick gin and tonic before lunch, to steady himself. Maybe a double. And he could look for Joy.

From behind some rubber Mexican cactus he peered across at the Ascham stand. There were three women behind the stand in the Ascham corporate uniform. He sidestepped into a display of gynaecological speculums and found a point behind a cardboard cut-out illustrating the latest insulins, from where he studied the Ascham set-up.

All three women, he saw, were blonde. He pushed his bifocals more firmly onto his nose to get a better look. Two, he could see, were under thirty. Not bad-looking, the two of them. But Joy must be forty by now. At least.

The third woman he could see only partially. She was busy talking to a GP he knew vaguely, a man from the Gold Coast. She was mostly concealed behind a pile of boxes. That could be Joy. She turned her head and he thought yes, she looks quite like how I remember her. He was about to move casually forward when the woman stepped sideways and more fully into view, and Trevor Symonds realised it couldn't be Joy Bulmer after all.

She'd been a biggish, bubbly girl in Weipa. But she wasn't – she couldn't be – as fat as that. That must be someone else.

Disappointed, Trevor retreated back past the gynaecological display and its surprised attendant, past the cactus, away from the world of medicine, and on to the welcoming ambience of the bar.

Having set out her brochures, pens and pads, Joy was busy again with enquiries even before the doors of the conference hall opened for lunch. Out of the corner of her eye, Joy had noticed a man behaving rather oddly. Kind of skirting around Ascham's display. Almost how some men looked outside adult shops, she thought. Of course Ascham had some rivals in the marketplace, but it was hardly likely that Surgical Standards or Australab would have reps behaving like that. Between chats with clients Joy took a better, more focused, look at the man. A doctor, possibly, but with a slightly different air about him. That sense of professional authority, of being well cared for, so familiar to Joy, was somehow lacking. This man looked rather seedy, a bit frayed at the edges.

Come to think of it, he looked a bit like … Terry? Trent? No, not Trent; Trevor, that was it. Trevor Symonds. A doctor Joy had had a bit of a fling with when she was working up in Queensland for a while. It had been in a small mining town, not much social life, so she'd been glad of the diversion. She'd dumped him though when she found out that he had two small children, and that his wife, a psychiatrist, was working full-time and having to manage the kids on her own while her husband chased skirt around the countryside. Before she'd agreed to anything in bed, he'd told her he was divorced. It wasn't that Joy had been interested in any kind of long-term relationship with him. She just didn't believe in getting involved with married men.

No, that couldn't be Trevor Symonds, he'd only be in his late forties by now, and this man looked at least sixty, and showing it.

Joy returned her attention to her client, a Gold Coast doctor with two practices, who was interested, most interested, in installing the new sterilisers in both his practices, and when she looked up again, the strange, seedy man had gone.

Cairns, 1 March 2011

Questions came flooding in from reporters, once the police media release had gone out on Monday evening. Detective Borgese would not comment on whether there were similarities between this case and the still-unsolved death of Wayne Buscati. He simply repeated that police inquiries were proceeding.

Police inquiries were indeed proceeding. At eight on Tuesday morning, while Detective Barwen trudged through the mud of the Davies Creek National Park and Detective Borgese sat at his desk trawling through databases and organising a search for middle-aged-but-stylish European women who may have entered the country through Cairns Airport, and not yet departed it, Detective Cass Diamond sat in the office of Dr Leah Rookwood.

Piles of journals and patient notes were strewn across the office. On Leah's desk stood a small glass jar compressing a very large tapeworm, and above the coffee machine was another jar containing a human hand. Fortunately, that machine was turned on. Cass always needed the coffee but as well the aroma helped counter the pungent fumes of formalin preserving Leah's specimens.

Cass was also glad that at the centre of the discussion were Leah's laptop photos of the remains of their unidentified victim, meaning that today she did not have to enter the mortuary itself. While forensic pathology was an important adjunct to any detective's career, she felt she had seen quite enough of the dead woman in the past two days.

'Fascinating,' Leah said. 'Adipocere. I don't often see it.'

To Cass's raised eyebrows she explained: 'Saponification. The flesh literally turns into a kind of soap. Instead of just putrefying. With putrefaction, there's decomposition and decay, due to bacteria – mostly from the bowel, but also bugs brought by flies and a whole raft of other insects. With adipocere there's hydrolysis, breaking down of the fat in the subcutaneous tissues. Then, aided by water and heat and some bacteria, the tissues form a soap or wax. See here,' she said as she scrolled through the photos, 'her cheeks and buttocks have this greasy soapy greyish-yellow appearance. They haven't decomposed and liquefied like the contents of her skull or the liver and bowel have.' Helpfully she clicked onto her photos of these organs, which were indeed quite fluid.

'So what does that tell us?' asked Cass, moving her gaze to a point just above the computer.

'Well,' said Leah, 'not all that much. That there has been abnormally hot wet weather on the Tablelands for the past few weeks! Heat and water are needed for adipocere. It doesn't help very much with fixing the time of death. Although most books agree – I've just been having a look – that it takes weeks not days even in the most favourable circumstances to produce adipocere. So she's been dead at least four weeks.'

'Is that what the smell is?' asked Cass.

'Indeed it is. My lab technician's been complaining bitterly. He prefers standard decay. It's partly ammonia but there are other chemicals in it. Sickeningly sweet, isn't it? It does go away or at least become acceptably sweeter with the passage of time.

'The benefit of adipocere in this case is that it tends to hold together other decomposing tissue like muscle, so there is some preservation of her facial structure. So we have more idea of what she looked like in life than had she undergone straightforward putrefaction. That's helped do the comfit picture for the media. There's also some adipocere around her abdomen that is cancelling out some of the loss of tissue from putrefaction. So she's kind of the same shape that she was, and is fitting into her clothes. Whereas in these pictures of her lower limbs you can see that the skin has just sloughed off in sheets along with her toenails. The same thing on her hands; no chance of fingerprints.

'So … bone structure Caucasian. Age – I'd guess forty-five to fifty-five but if she was on hormone replacement she might be older, it maintains bone density and skin quality. Those designer labels suggest a woman who took every precaution against the changes of ageing. Hair grey at the roots but coloured not long before her death.'

Cass nodded. She'd noted this at the site.

'No fractures,' Leah continued. 'There was some fraying of those scarves around her wrists as though she might have struggled a bit, but no evidence of bony damage. No marks or grazes on the skeleton consistent with bullet or knife wounds. No injury consistent with wounds by firearms or knives within the skull, thorax or abdominal cavity, although the organs are in an advanced state of decay. No bullets or foreign bodies anywhere in those cavities.'

She looked up at Cass. 'I presume your people haven't found anything at the site suggesting she was shot?'

Cass shook her head. 'They've found practically nothing apart from some makeup and lipstick that were close to the body. And cigarette butts, although they could be from anyone.'

'The items of clothing, although very dirty and wet, don't show any sign of damage from an instrument or firearm,' Leah went on. 'In fact all the buttons on the shirt were intact and done up to a level above her breasts, and the skirt was zipped up and in place around her waist. No knickers though and the bra fastenings undone. Very expensive jewellery, I'd say, that interestingly wasn't taken from her.'

She raised an eyebrow at Cass. 'Pearl necklace and earrings. Solid silver bangle on her right arm, no helpful identifying marks on this, and Bulgari watch on her left. Still going and telling correct Cairns time and date when handed to Drew yesterday – not much use to us in establishing time of death. Again, not a cheap item.

'From what remains of her I would say that she was in good general health. One hundred and sixty-three centimetres tall. From various conversion tables I've worked out that she weighed about 62 kilos in life. Consistent with her wearing size 8 Australian, maybe 10, which is equivalent to European 36 to 38, which is what she was wearing. Quite petite by most Australian standards.

'She coloured her hair a very dark brown, which suggests that's what it was in her earlier life. Eyes – well, from what remains, under my microscope, I'd say they were brown. Most remaining skin very necrotic and peeling; what there is of it looks light brown, olive. Can't say if it's natural or if she was suntanned or had one of those fake tan jobs – she does seem the kind of woman who might have been spray-tanned.

'Bilateral breast implants – the silicon kind, not saline. They're an American make but that means nothing. Most European countries would import them from the States. They're certainly registered for import here. I checked on the company website and this type's been available about ten years. So she's had a boob job in that time, either for the first time, but more likely, given her age, to replace earlier implants that were leaking or just old.

'Teeth in very good condition – or at least, mostly porcelain. She's had a lot of expensive dental work. Caps or crowns where her own teeth remain. So if we can find her dentist, identification would be definite.'

'Could be somewhere in Europe, judging by her clothes,' Cass said. 'Although fashion's global now. They sell the Hermès scarves in Sydney and Melbourne.'

Leah nodded and went on: 'She's also missing her gall bladder so she must have had surgery, a cholecystectomy, at some point. There's no evidence of any major animal interference with the body, so it's not that the organ has been taken away. It's been surgically removed, although the site of the scar on the body surface has completely disappeared with the post-mortem changes and the weather and exposure. The uterus is slightly better preserved than other organs. That's what we usually find, because it's protected in the pelvis and it's a dense fibro-muscular structure. It has a scar, probably a caesarean scar. So this is somebody's mother.'

She paused a moment, then added: 'Of course we'll test what remains of vaginal secretions for evidence of sexual assault. I note that her legs were tied to the tree though. Her thighs must have been close together when she was first bound up. But she could have been raped, given how tightly her hands were tied.

'It's all very weird. And although it doesn't bear thinking about, with no sudden cause of death clear so far, it does seem she might just have been tied up like that and left to die. Which might have taken a while, depending on how hot it was there. You said it was shaded; that would have prolonged things. In open sunlight, without water, she would have died of dehydration much more quickly. And even in the shade she might have very quickly become confused and then unconscious.'

'Toxicology?' Cass asked.

Leah nodded. 'Yes, I've sent samples for drugs and poisons,' she said. 'The adipocere means we have more tissue for that, which is good. I've asked them to run the tests urgently.'

While she talked, Leah was studying Cass. She'd liked this woman from their first meeting, in the initial stages of the Buscati investigation. At that meeting Leah had noted Cass's name. She had asked where Cass came from and when told New South Wales, north of Newcastle, she immediately asked, 'Are you related to Lexie Diamond?'

'His daughter,' Cass had answered, with some surprise. 'You knew Lexie?'

'No, but I loved his songs,' Leah said. 'Still do. I have lots of those old cassettes from the 80s, when I was a student, and all the CDs that have been re-issued. And I heard him once in Brisbane. That would have been just a couple of years before ...'

'Before he died,' Cass finished for her. 'Yes. I was eight then .'

'So your mother is Suzanne?'

'No.' Cass had smiled. 'My dad, well he was a product of the sixties, y'know, he liked to spread the love around. My mother is Alice, she's American but she's lived in Australia for yonks now. White American, as I guess you can see. She was never married to him.'

'But you have your father's name?'

'Yes. Mum wanted me to have his name, well his stage name, the one everyone knows, not his Aboriginal name. She wanted me to have that identity.'

'So did you see him much, when you were growing up?'

'Oh yeah. He was around a lot, up until the time he got sick, despite all the other family and kids he had.'

Two wives, three other long-term relationships, eleven children. Or so his family had thought, Cass had explained to Leah. When, about two months before he died, it became clear that the liver cancer that had made its first appearance when he turned fifty was winning the battle, Suzanne, the second and still incumbent wife, had got together with Venetia, the first wife, and Mary, an early love. Together they planned a Sunday picnic to which all of Lexie's children were invited. This was to be at the house on Port Stephens, with its rambling bush grounds, that was Lexie and Suzanne's home, and where in the last months of his life he lay in bed on the veranda. Still smoking, still drinking – and why not? Cass had said to Leah, who nodded her agreement. The media had cited his drinking as the cause of the liver cancer. In fact, he'd contracted hepatitis as a child, living in a tiny lean-to outside Moree. Like so many Aboriginal kids.

'But,' Cass had told Leah, 'as well as the expected five women and their eleven kids, three other kids turned up. Including Patrick, who was just four then. The others were in their teens.' Each with a mother and each with such clear facial features and broad Lexie smiles that there was no doubting their paternity. Lexie had greeted them all, quite unsurprised and seemingly intimately acquainted with what each was doing.

'So you have, what, thirteen brothers and sisters?' Leah had asked.

'More,' Cass had answered, 'because my mother had four more kids after me, though Lexie wasn't their father. I grew up with all of them; the youngest is fifteen now. And I have dozens of cousins, and uncles and aunties spread right across New South Wales.'

Now, as she talked about the autopsy findings, Leah watched Cass making rapid notes on her laptop. She doesn't miss a thing, Leah thought, and she always looks stunning. Not a trace of makeup when she's at work apart from lip gloss, but her skin is perfect, she has the figure of an athlete and that fantastic springy, glossy hair. She must cause a stir down in Sheridan Street every time she moves.

Cass looked up. 'The strangest bit about all this,' she said slowly, 'has to be the scarves.'

Leah nodded. 'Yeah. I'd have to think there's some significance in them. Significant to the person or persons who tied her up, and maybe to the woman as well.'

'I've tried the Hermès stores,' Cass said. 'They still have to get back to me but if that gets us nothing I'll try all the retailers.'

She sat, thinking, for a moment. Then said slowly to Leah: 'Would a *tourist* bring *four* silk scarves on a trip to Cairns? All in the same kind of design. Four?'

'I see what you mean,' said Leah. 'Maybe if she was going to spend a lot of time in the casino or something? But what you're thinking is – she's more likely to be local?'

'Yes,' Cass said. 'And to have got to that particular spot, someone needed good local knowledge. To get onto that road. Maybe not the woman herself. But whoever took her there.

'Like the doctor who found her – he knew how to get in through the bush.' She stood up, thinking of how Tim Ingram must have known about that rainforest road for quite a while. She picked up her laptop and phone.

'Thanks for that, Leah. And for the coffee. You'll send through a copy of your report?'

'Yes – later today. The body will stay here for the moment of course. No-one has claimed it yet, anyway.'

'We'll put the comfit image on the evening news,' Cass said, as she moved towards the door, thinking again about those scarves. 'Someone has to know who she is.'

Cairns, February 2009

Two years earlier, Dr Lyndall Symonds had sat rigid, facing Dr Jane O'Malley across the desk in Jane's surgery.

'Shit, Jane, the bastard mustn't even use condoms!'

Jane, her personal doctor but also Lyndall's friend, reached out a hand. Jane had not been looking forward to this encounter. Just that morning, she'd received the report of the Pap smear she'd taken for Lyndall the previous week. Lyndall, who'd never had anything wrong with her Paps before, had put off having this done, for two and a half, then three years. The results had been unexpected: high-grade changes, together with the presence of the wart virus. Jane had called Lyndall that morning, sounding as light-hearted as she could, but Lyndall had not mistaken the urgency of her message, and had made an appointment for that afternoon.

'Lyndall,' Jane began slowly, 'let's take things one at a time. All this is common. The wart virus is common. You know that. Some types are associated with the development of cervical cancer. But you haven't got cancer. You've got pre-cancer, it seems, on the basis of the smear, but that's a completely curable condition. That's the whole point of Pap smears, to pick up things before they become serious.'

'And what do I have to do, who do I have to see, in this town, to cure my … pre-cancer?' demanded Lyndall.

'Everyone we know will know now what they always suspected: Trevor Symonds sleeps around as well as drinks too much. He doesn't worry that he gives … his wife … this … disease!' Tears of rage welled up.

Jane said gently, 'I do understand how you feel … but we need to do something about the Pap result. You'll need some treatment. You could go down to Brisbane, keep it away from here, but really there's no need for that. Why don't I send you to see Henry – I know he's a friend, but he'd be very good and helpful. He'd manage it very discreetly for you.'

Jane bit her lip, then continued: 'You said you didn't know, weren't sure …' Her voice trailed off. She had no particular interest in gossip, but she'd heard Trevor's name linked to a member of the hospital theatre staff, as well as a medical secretary. She just hoped both those women had regular Pap smears.

'Jane,' said Lyndall, 'you know, and don't know. Since I had the kids it's been the same – late nights "working back at the surgery", weekend calls that take three hours, conferences away on his own. By the time I realised what might, well, what was happening, it was already too late. It was a pattern, between us as well as for him. Even though we'd still been having good sex … it wasn't that he was missing out at home, as far as I could see. I'd find out what was going on, get more and more fed up, we'd fight, not speak for a week or so. Often it seemed to me that the affair would break up in that time, almost as if he wanted to finish it but needed to provoke me to do it. Then we'd have another almighty row, which usually ended up, well, frankly, with us having sex, and me forgiving him all over again, without anything really changing between us. Until the next time. And it's been like that for nineteen years.

'But it was always … understood, though we never actually talked about it, that he'd use condoms … elsewhere. He didn't want to, with me, once I'd had my tubes tied.

'I had the kids to think of. Each time I've thought of leaving him, I've said to myself, just wait, Lyndall, until the kids finish school. Well, Jane, just today, on my way down here, I've realised that's *now.* David's already moved out, and Nic's starting uni this year. Driving along, I just felt so angry … I hope his prick gets warts all over it and falls off! I suppose you don't know how long I've had the virus?'

'No, I don't. Certainly it's been some time, maybe years, and it's taken a while to bring about these changes. It's not only hard to say when it might have happened, it's pointless.'

'Well,' said Lyndall, 'I've had an affair, too – only one – since I married the shit. With the kids' music teacher.' She laughed, briefly. 'When Trevor was working up in the bush and having an affair with a nurse there. It was, um, twelve years ago. And we always used condoms. Anything from then would have shown up long ago, wouldn't it?'

'Probably,' Jane nodded.

Lyndall realised that in asking this, she did want to know the answer. But she also wished, somehow, to show Jane that she was not completely defeated by the day's revelations. She'd been able, once at least, to give as good as she got. Driving down to the surgery that day, her mind in a turmoil, she had thought, among other things, of Bernard. Fondly.

He had been four years younger than her, but infinitely more experienced. She remembered the initial boredom of those Tuesday afternoon piano lessons. His patient French accent: 'Now, Dav-eed, just try again slowly … drop your hands like leetle parachutes … Nic-o-la … you must practise more … make your fingers like a too-nel for a train …' Bernard's own fingers were long and slim. One Tuesday, Lyndall had watched them sliding over the keys and, unaccountably, imagined them stroking her clitoris. She'd raised her eyes to Bernard's face, and had seen, amazingly, that the thing was arranged between them.

It had been easy to leave David's music books behind so that Bernard had to bring them around later that evening. Trevor had that nurse he was seeing up in Weipa on Tuesdays, and always stayed there overnight. He imagined Lyndall didn't know. But of course Lyndall always knew. Good God, didn't he realise that her whole working life was about understanding how other people behaved and thought? She knew him better than he knew himself.

Lyndall had told Bernard about Trevor, that first night. The children were only mildly curious to see their music teacher there, and David was pleased his books had been returned. Lyndall had put them to bed while Bernard drank brandy in the living room. Then she'd led him by the hand quite deliberately to the bed she shared with Trevor. She'd been anxious about a new man, after having had the children, both forceps deliveries, about how much she'd stretched inside, about the sagging of her breasts. But Bernard had been tender, appreciative, cuddling her in ways that Trevor never had, and had soon introduced her to the delicious pleasures of anal sex, while his fingers played arpeggios just as she had imagined.

Each Tuesday for several months she'd put the kids to bed and ring Weipa to check that Trevor was still there, before Bernard arrived. She hadn't dared to go out with him, to risk getting a babysitter and being seen with him around town. It had been as much to prove to herself that she too could still do it, was still attractive, as the delights of the relationship itself.

After they'd made love he would ask her about her work. She'd tell him about the cases she'd seen that day. A pregnant woman with an acute psychosis who'd been picked up off the Bruce Highway by the police: naked, on all fours and barking like a dog. With the right drugs and therapy she'd been restored to sanity and would be able to take her baby home. A cane farmer gone broke who'd tried suicide with weedkiller. He'd been in intensive care for two weeks with poisoning. Now Lyndall was helping him through the depression and out onto the other side, hopefully to some semblance of normal life again. Bernard listened intently, as Trevor never did, and asked gentle questions about the lives and families of these people she talked of so affectionately, about which parts of their brains produced these dramatic actions, and why. He himself believed strongly in the power of music to calm mental distress. As a student in France he had regularly played piano for dementia patients in a locked ward. He remembered elderly women with tears in their eyes clapping for a Strauss waltz as if they were at the opera.

It had all ended abruptly. Trevor seemed to split up with the nurse without the usual tantrums, and suddenly he wasn't going to Weipa anymore, just up to Cooktown for the day. She managed one final evening with Bernard; he was going back to France soon anyway. They'd crept back into the music school after it had closed and lain on the floor behind the grand piano. Afterwards, he had cut off a lock of her dark hair as a keepsake, and laid it between the pages of his copy of *The Well-Tempered Clavier*.

She still had his mother's phone number, in Clermont-Ferrand, on a slip of paper in her best handbag, at the very top of her wardrobe.

She'd never dared to suggest anal sex to Trevor. He'd be shocked. He was really very conservative in his sexual tastes as well as his political opinions. And he might wonder where she'd got the idea.

For years Bernard had stayed dormant in her mind, to be awoken only very infrequently and then for only very short sessions, usually when Trevor wanted sex but she was not aroused. The memory of Bernard was always effective.

That memory had been jogged, briefly, when she'd met another Frenchman in Cairns. In fact, he'd become her patient – something which happened entirely by accident, and only because she was required by the Children's Court to see his son. He spoke English with the same accent and nuances as Bernard had; the two were about the same height and had the same olive skin.

There, Lyndall quickly found, the resemblance ended. One Frenchman was not in fact the same as another. Michel Janvier turned out to be a very difficult case and Lyndall did not enjoy having him as a patient. Even though his consultations were infrequent, she was afraid they might never cease. She could never solve his problem. And while there was absolutely no physical attraction for her, she was aware that Janvier was one of those patients intrigued and excited by his increasing dependence on a woman psychiatrist, so that she was always careful to keep both a physical and an emotional space between them. The buzzer for her receptionist was close by on the desk during their fifty-minute sessions.

In fact, after Bernard there'd been no-one else, no-one for whom she'd felt the slightest flicker of interest. And in those times when she and Trevor had been getting along together, patches which in recent years had been less and less frequent, the sex, Lyndall thought, had been the best part. But it was over now. Absolutely.

She would move out of the house by the end of the

week. She would go through with treating this Pap smear problem, get over this surgery, and then she would organise a divorce.

When Lyndall saw Henry the following week, he was as understanding as Jane had predicted. He had no intention of mentioning Trevor. But Lyndall was forthright. After a tense few minutes during which her innermost parts were surveyed and a sharp instrument used to extract a biopsy sample, she dressed herself and sat opposite him at his desk.

'I'm leaving him, Henry,' she said. 'It's something that's been coming for years, and it's finally at a head. To find this level of carelessness has made me decide to end the marriage.'

'You don't think the situation might be helped with some counselling?' he asked.

'For me, no. It's too late. I just want to leave, while I can. And for Trevor? He comes from a set mould. Private school, rugby, university, you know. All his friends are the same: doctors like him. He's never mixed with people who don't share the same opinions, the same politics. That's what medical school does to a lot of people, in my experience, men especially. First selects them out, then preserves them. He'd never accept attempts to change him. He's sure he's perfectly all right the way he is.'

'The drinking has become a problem?' It was a rhetorical question. Henry had seen it himself.

'Yes. When we first met I was really swept away by him. I was still a student, and here was this dashing surgical registrar, quite a bit older, interested in me. He already drank a lot at parties. I didn't drink at all then, so I was always able to drive him home. He wasn't aggressive when he was drunk, just embarrassing, and the next day he'd be apologetic, and charming all over again.'

She paused, then said: 'I guess the pattern was there even before we were engaged. He'd be making passes, touching up other women, talking about scoring, if he'd been drinking, even when I was there. Other girls in my company laughed it off. One or two, I realised later, tried to warn me. But I was very naïve. I thought it was incredible that I'd managed to land this big fish. And – the old story – I thought it would be different once we were married.

'But in fact as soon as we were married he dropped out of surgical training, didn't pass his primary exam. Too much socialising – said he didn't want the surgical lifestyle anyway. There was always bravado.'

Yes, thought Henry, bravado. He was aware of at least three rumoured affairs in Trevor's recent past, even though the subject interested him little. Always a lot of swagger, name-dropping, fairly tasteless jokes in the theatre change rooms. Not apparently anything to do with Lyndall herself, who was a jolly nice woman, Henry thought. And still damned good-looking. He preferred brunettes to blondes, any day. No, it must be rooted in Symonds' upbringing.

'I think,' said Lyndall, 'that it's all part of the same problem. His father was always a heavy drinker, though not, as far as I know, a womaniser. But his father had an excuse: the war. He was a prisoner of war, came back from Burma a different man, they said, well of course he was lucky to come back at all. So Trevor grew up thinking that drinking like that was normal. The answer to all life's problems. That's what he does now whenever anything's too hard. Henry, you only see him drinking socially, and that's bad enough, but on a daily basis, it's been affecting his practice, his judgement about patients, and how he relates to us, his family.

'I think, also, it's what gives him the … nerve … to go after other women. I never know who knows what. People seem to drop hints and then, when I try to follow them through, they clam up. It seems that everything is more noticed, and more criticised, because he's a doctor. He's been the GP to so many people, so it's somehow more surprising, more shocking, in a town this size, than it would be in a big city.'

She added: 'I even worry, sometimes, that he might have an affair with a patient, or have tried to. I worry that his judgement is getting more and more erratic.'

'Have you any evidence for that?' Henry asked. Lyndall looked up suddenly. Henry's manner seemed to have changed. Did he know something she didn't? As she gazed intently at him Henry's neck flushed a deep scarlet.

'No,' she answered slowly, 'it's just something I've grown concerned about. Do you … is there something you know about?'

Henry seemed to gather himself, and shook his head.

'No,' he said, 'it's just that if such a thing did happen he'd lose his registration. If there was a complaint.'

'Well, exactly,' said Lyndall, 'and much more than his registration. But,' she stood up to leave, 'I'm no longer worrying about Trevor. I'm doing what I'm always telling my own patients to do! Changing my life, acting for myself. And do you know what, Henry? I think I'm going to enjoy it!'

Her immediate future was full of plans. First this surgery. She had complete faith in Henry for that. Then a definitive move. For the moment, she and Nicola were staying with friends, leaving Trevor alone in the house. She had told him, tersely, about her Pap result the previous week, once she had the car packed and a place to go. Soon she must find a flat for herself; Nicola wanted to move to a student house out near the university. She must increase her consulting hours and look at taking on more private patients. There would be lots of expenses in the coming months and she would no longer take any of Trevor's money. For the first time in her whole life, Lyndall would live on her own.

But at some point, she knew, there was something else she would be doing. She would be taking down her handbag, finding her French phrasebook, and trying, just trying, the number in Clermont-Ferrand.

Cairns, 1 March 2011

Back at the station Cass grabbed more coffee, and a cheese sandwich she'd brought from home. She texted Jordon – *hi don't forget take back those dvds overdue ru in for dinner 2nite ?? luv mum#* – then sat down to run through the responses she'd got from the Hermès stores interstate. The stores all had very good records of who their customers were, and there was no purchase of the four designs she'd specified from any of the stores by a single customer during the past five years, no match to any woman who might be their corpse.

Her phone pinged and there was response from Jordon – *u said u will watch hurtlocker again & u didnt watch sherlock holmes yet. U mite get clues from jude law #.*

OK, she replied, smiling, *but take the others back.*

Two fruitless hours followed as she called one city store after another from the list of retailers Hermès had supplied. There were a few customers in Cairns but they'd all bought only one scarf and none seemed likely to be their victim. Frustrated, she went in search of another double shot, then sat at her desk, searching for inspiration from the silken fibres of these damn scarves.

Whether it was the rising caffeine levels she couldn't say, but certainly one idea came: silk. Those scarves were made of the finest silk. They would have needed to be cleaned …

and she doubted their owner would have trusted them to the washing machine. So maybe she sent them to the drycleaners.

Cass swallowed the dregs of her coffee then took the stairs two at a time down to the ground floor. She didn't need a car, it was just a five-minute walk to Cairns Central Laundry. So intent was she on her mission that she completely failed to see Troy Barwen returning from lunch, crossing the foyer in the opposite direction. His injured gaze followed her as she went rapidly out the door and turned left into Sheridan Street.

Fifteen minutes later she was back in the building and in Drew's office. A grin spread wide across her face.

'The benefits of the sporting life!' she said mysteriously to him, then added: 'And networking! Or at least, netball-working.' She smiled. 'I've just been to the drycleaners. Their headquarters across the canal, you know, they have depots all over Cairns. To ask about Hermès scarves. An Indian family has taken over the business, and I play netball with their daughter. Luckily Sharmila is there just now.

'I gave her a description of our woman, minus the gruesome bits. After a minute Sharmila said: "That sounds like Mrs Janvier!" Sharmila says she's a very smart woman who owns a lot of scarves, always very dressed up. Said she must have an important job to dress like she does in Cairns, but she doesn't really know all that much about her.

'One other interesting thing – Sharmila and her mum both remember her because although she brings them a lot of work she never gives her phone number. Again, they think this is because she's someone important who has to protect her privacy, but they're sure she lives locally, at least part of the time.'

'Janvier?' said Drew slowly. 'Now why does that name sound familiar? Do a search of our databases, Cass, and then we'll take it from there.'

'I'll get onto it straight away,' Cass said. 'And I'm thinking about why, if she lives in Cairns, she hasn't been reported missing sooner.'

Cass went back to her desk and began to trawl the police databases. An hour later later, she called Drew and Troy into her office. She had several printouts ready and photos on her screen.

'We have an Odile Janvier resident in Cairns,' she told them. 'And bingo! She's French. At least, born in France. Fifty years old. Born Odile Marie Lebrun on 22 June 1960, in Nantes, France. Married a Michel Janvier in St André, France, in 1982. Acquired Australian citizenship in 1985, in Brisbane. Height 164 centimetres, hair dark brown, eyes brown, no distinguishing marks.'

They studied the photo from Odile Janvier's driver's licence on Cass's laptop. It had been taken in 2002. She was heavily made up in the photo, and so did not greatly resemble the corpse, but there was an overall similarity, and the descriptions matched. She was a stylish woman, Cass thought, but there was something quite malicious in the look she gave the camera.

'You'd think a woman with family overseas might be on Facebook,' Cass said. 'But she's not, at least not under that name.' Cass flicked to another photo.

'Her husband,' she continued, 'is, or perhaps was, Michel Philippe Janvier. Aged fifty-five. Also born in France, in 1955. Acquired Australian citizenship in 1978. Gives his occupation as 'businessman'. His current business is said to be Kwality Kleening, with an office at 11E Falmouth Lane, Portsmith.' In his photo Michel Janvier was unsmiling, olive-skinned, with blunt, smudged features.

'Their home address, it's in Cairns?' asked Troy.

'They're not in the phone book,' Cass said. 'So I went through Telstra. There's a Michel Janvier living at 11 Paradise Close in Earlville. And the electoral records show an Odile Janvier living there as well. Also, Michel is down as having previously had a business number at that Portsmith address. But he had the phone disconnected about five years ago. The bill for Earlville is overdue. It should have been paid two weeks ago. The Telstra bloke was very helpful.'

Cass turned to Drew. 'You said you recognised the name. We have records of our own for two other Janviers. Dominic and Damian. Brothers. Previously living in Cairns, in Smithfield. But not here now, apparently. Maybe the children of Michel and Odile, who don't have any convictions themselves.'

'Yeah, that's it!' exclaimed Drew. 'Janvier – now I remember! When I was still in uniform. Two kids, both dealing drugs in school, especially the older one. Went to a couple of schools, expelled from them both, I think, maybe even three schools. About ten, twelve years ago.'

Cass pulled up Dominic and Damian Janvier from the police database.

'Dominic was born in 1985,' she said. 'First came to the attention of the police when picked up under-age in a club in 1999 – at 2 am. He was fourteen. He had a small amount of cannabis and e. Returned home to his parents who didn't seem too concerned about it, according to the reports. At sixteen, charged with possession in the Children's Court, sent to Townsville. Seen by a psychiatrist. Dr Lyndall Symonds. She spoke of his difficult life with his mother and her evidence was taken into account by the court. A further charge when he was eighteen, possession, in Sydney. Just cannabis. Went to jail for six months. Next heard of in northern New South Wales, possession and supply. Twelve months. Time reduced for good behaviour. Finally, in 2009, convicted of robbery of a pharmacy in New South Wales and now serving a longish spell in Wellington Gaol.'

'Well, if the woman is Odile Janvier at least we can conclude that Dominic hasn't killed his mother,' remarked Drew. 'Although we should check that he's still inside, and has been, at least since Christmas. He might have been paroled. "Difficult life with his mother" in the psych's report – that's certainly interesting.'

'As for Damian Janvier,' said Cass, 'he was born in 1986. So he's a year younger. Was in the Children's Court in 2001 when his brother was also charged, but after that Damian seems to have kept out of trouble. He's not recorded on the electoral roll in Cairns at the moment. There is however a Damian Janvier listed with Telstra, living in Tasmania. Has a Tasmanian driving licence. He's on Facebook too. He's working as a chef in a restaurant in Hobart.'

She opened Facebook and brought up the entry for Damian Janvier.

'Since we aren't his friends we can only see what he puts on his home page. He lives with his girlfriend Katie. That must be her there.' There was a photo – an open-faced young man with dark, gelled hair styled in a faux-hawk, his arm around an attractive blonde in her early twenties, both of them in chef's outfits and standing in a restaurant kitchen. 'They work in the same place. Music tastes: U2 and Beyoncé. He also likes bushwalking and fishing.'

'Right,' said Drew. 'Cass, you and I'll go to Earlville. Troy, take Constable Garth and check out Portsmith. We'll meet back here later.'

Cairns, August 2009

Two years previously, on a sunny Tuesday morning, Dr George O'Malley stood at the glass doors of the hospital's operating theatres, dressed in blue surgical scrubs, watching the progress of Dr Arthur Geoffrey Mellish down the corridor towards him. Dr Mellish was a short man, with a neat little pot belly, sparse gingerish hair combed carefully over his bald spot, and a narrow, straggling moustache. Today he wore a short-sleeved light-grey safari suit with his College of Surgeons tie, white brogues and black socks, an outfit that reminded George irresistibly of Mickey Mouse.

'Whadda you bet, Nimal,' he asked his colleague Dr Jayasinghe, who stood beside him, 'that Aggie asks us about the batting order? And I don't mean what's happening in England.'

Nimal smiled. 'Yes, George,' he said, 'Dr Mellish is a sporting man.'

The theatre doors parted and Mellish marched in. 'Morning, George,' he said.

'Morning, Arthur,' responded George, who had been the anaesthetist for Mellish's regular operating list for three years now. It was, he had said to his wife Jane, one of life's many burdens that he had to bear. Jane had laughed and punched him on the arm.

Nimal spoke up: 'Good morning, Dr Mellish.'

Mellish turned. 'Oh, morning, Jayasinghe. Got a list of starters for me, have you?' Behind Mellish's back George rolled his eyes at Nimal.

'Yes, Sir. One gallbladder is cancelled; the second, Mrs McNamara, she has a respiratory tract infection.'

'Ah! That narrows the field a bit. Though the bowel resection could take time, tumour might have spread a bit. We could be on a sticky wicket there.'

'Yes, Sir. It is a pity her general practitioner did not refer her earlier, Sir. I understand she'd had bleeding for six months. Her GP attributed it only to her haemorrhoids and did not investigate …'

'Yes, well,' Mellish considered, 'Dr Symonds, he's her GP, isn't he? He's an old friend of mine. I might have a word with him. He does refer me a lot of patients though. Got a few problems lately, Trevor Symonds. Spending a bit too long at the nineteenth hole … But yes, if he'd sent her along sooner, her outlook would have been better.' He took a quick glance at the operating list.

'Very good,' he said, 'let's tee off. While we've got the wind behind us.' Dr Jayasinghe nodded gravely but without comment. From the age of five he had been accustomed to listening to the English news of the BBC World Service with both his parents. His English was as fluent as the Singhalese he spoke at home. The mixed metaphor rankled. But he needed the support of Dr Mellish. Badly.

Nimal Jayasinghe was working as a surgeon, but his job was a temporary one. He had trained as a surgeon in his native Sri Lanka, and worked as an army surgeon. But this work was not recognised in Australia. Nimal needed to work under Mellish's supervision for another five months, and have his boss's approval, so he could register fully as a surgeon in Australia. Then he needed to find another job for next year, preferably here in Cairns. Mellish, he knew, had clout with the committee of selectors for these jobs.

Without Mellish's approval Nimal could only continue to work in Queensland in the far west of the state, in an 'area of need'. He himself would not mind that. But his wife, the pretty, pouty Premala, would not want to go. She would like to stay here in Cairns, to have a nice house here, and a second baby. He did not want to have to tell her they were going to Weipa, or Mt Isa.

Mellish headed toward the surgeons' change room. 'Be a good chap and get the ball rolling, will you, Jayasinghe. Open the abdomen and hold the fort while I just have a cup of coffee …' In the change room he found Gerry Wheeler, the orthopod. Gerry was gloomy – in London, Australia was already five wickets down for 99.

The patient safely asleep, George sat down beside her and began to read the day's paper. It was a sore point with him that Mellish allowed no music in theatre during surgery. Every other surgeon had his or her own favourites so George enjoyed a wide range of musical tastes during the working week. Except on Tuesday mornings. Now he peered from time to time at the readouts on the anaesthetic machine as Nimal painted the skin of the patient's belly with iodine, then took a scalpel and opened her abdomen layer by layer. The familiar smell of burning flesh filled the theatre as he plied the diathermy probe, sealing off small bleeding vessels so that hardly a drop of blood was spilt. With warm, moist sponges, he packed organs out of the way, giving a clear view of the operation site. As he finished these arrangements, the theatre doors swung open and Mellish entered, drawing on his surgical gloves.

'Ah … Jayasinghe, good lad. Now we can hit the ground running!' Mellish said. George suppressed a snort and buried himself in the paper.

Nimal Jayasinghe knew all about hitting the ground running. As surgeon to the Army of the Democratic Socialist Republic of Sri Lanka, he had parachuted, with a full pack, into the northern town of Jaffna, besieged then by the Tamil Tigers. Two crates of surgical equipment were parachuted down from the same flight. It was only the second time he had been in an aeroplane.

The duty sergeant had laughed at Nimal's trepidation, agreeably shaking his head in the way of Sri Lankans who hope to oblige.

'Most people,' he offered helpfully, 'learn very quickly.'

Nimal twisted his ankle hitting the rubbish-strewn beach, but still he ran, off the exposed sand, towards the cover of the shell-damaged streets of the town, towards military headquarters and the hospital. He tied up the ankle and began to operate. Arriving in the early morning, he had by lunchtime carried out three laparotomies, patched and plastered a shattered arm, and performed an above-knee amputation.

Now he played a secondary role as Mellish assessed the spread of this colon cancer. The lymph glands which lay around the blood vessels supplying the bowel, to which the cancer would spread first, were firm. Each one must be found and removed. Mellish reflected a moment.

'Well, Jayasinghe, we'll just have to try to clear everything out here, and if it does spread to the liver she can have chemotherapy. The late diagnosis has really got her between a rock and a hard place.'

'Indeed, Sir,' agreed Nimal gravely, 'she is between the devil and the deep blue sea.'

Mellish nodded. It was, he thought, much better to have this chap assisting him than one of those damnfool registrars they kept sending him. In the last few months there'd been three of these, including two women. He'd sent them both packing. By Jove he had. Surgery was no place for women, thought Mellish.

Floating down towards Jaffna, the devil and the deep blue sea had come briefly into Nimal's brain. The blue sea was Jaffna Lagoon; if the wind blew him too far south, and into it, he would disappear beneath the foam, weighed down by

30kg of pack, the harness, and his army boots. The devil was the Tigers, the snipers in wait at the perimeter of the town. It would only need one accurate shot … And once on the ground, though the fear was less, damped down, it was always there, every day: the fear that the Tigers would overrun the town, bomb and blast their way in. A fear Nimal remembered as located accurately, anatomically, in his own bowels, in the descending colon, the sigmoid colon and the rectum, to be precise.

After four months, the Sri Lankan Army had broken through and relieved Jaffna, and Nimal had moved back to the relative safety of the military hospital at Anuradhapura, further south. He was happy to be there. His parents, teachers originally from Colombo, had moved to a small town in the North Western Province, within sight of the great rock fortress of Sigiriya, and he was able to visit them when he had leave. But around him, he could see, the whole country continued, literally, to be sandbagged against terrorism; the sandbags were spilling open, and behind them all the infrastructure of the society – the hospitals, schools, post offices, sewage works – was rapidly crumbling in the muggy heat.

Nimal had lived with the war since he was seventeen. He bore no particular animosity toward the Tamils. Several of his best friends at school had been Tamils. Nimal would like to have stayed in Sri Lanka. But even without the war it would be difficult to establish himself in private practice without contacts. Nimal was a scholarship boy. His parents were on meagre salaries. They had no car, lived in the schoolhouse, owned only a small grove of coconuts. Nimal had been happy when his Colombo uncle had approached his parents with the proposal from Premala's family, to receive in return her gift of permanent Australian residence. He hoped to be able to bring his parents to Australia, and really wanted to raise his children here. And Premala was really very pretty. He thought of the soft crescent of her right breast, fitting above the fold of her sari. Though here she mostly wore trousers, Western dress.

More than anything, for Premala – to keep her respect and affection – he must get this job. He had worked conscientiously all year, more than was required of him, in order to impress Mellish. This ran through his mind now as he held retractors, exposed the operation site, mopped up blood, and cut the ends of his boss's stitches.

Mellish laid clamps on the bowel. He isolated the tumour, found and extracted the many lymph nodes. He welded the two cut ends of the bowel back together with the technological marvel of the staple gun. He spoke little as he worked.

He would have liked to discuss the cricket with his assistant. After all, he thought, the chap is Sri Lankan. He must have some interest. The Australians are really taking a hammering and England had made 332 in their first innings. But Jayasinghe seemed lost in his own thoughts, although he was certainly following the operation, Mellish couldn't fault him there. Mellish was never quite sure, really, what to say to these Asian chaps.

At last, the seam across the bowel complete, the final lymph node plucked out, Mellish straightened up.

'Well, Jayasinghe, game, set and match, eh? Just close her up for me while I dictate some notes. Put in a drain. And I might have another cup of coffee while you open the batting on the gallbladder, eh?'

'For Chrissake, Nimal,' said George, after Mellish had bowled out of the theatre door, 'we'll be a while getting organised in here. Don't let him bully you like he does the registrars. Go get a coffee yourself, and something to eat.' And Nimal, grateful, took this advice, but returned in time to set up the next case.

The patient's gallbladder would be located through a telescope passed though a tiny cut in her belly. The telescope transmitted pictures onto the medical video screen which the staff were wheeling into place – moving smartly, for they had all at some time felt the sharp edge of Mellish's tongue. All the surgery would be done watching the screen, not the patient.

Again Nimal prepared the abdomen with iodine, draped the site. Introduced the telescope and displayed the distended gallbladder on the screen.

'Tally ho!' Mellish cried as he returned and began the main part of the operation. As he selected his instruments, watching the screen, locating and dissecting the thickened wall of the gallbladder from its bed in the liver, he thought again, briefly, of Jayasinghe. They puzzled him, these Asiatics. The man was a good doctor, he would say that. Quite competent with his hands. But … too quiet, too self-effacing. Not a rugby player. Mellish did not know how to begin a conversation with him. And Arthur Mellish did nothing these days that he was not completely sure about. Mellish wondered – but only for a moment – if Jayasinghe was married, if he had children. One of those arranged marriages, perhaps? Mellish's thoughts moved on to a favourite theme: how the town was changing. When he and Winifred first came here, thirty years ago, it was a good place for an Englishman. Doctors were respected. Everyone who was anyone knew everyone of importance in the town. Of course, there were always the Aboriginals. And of course, he'd always been ready to look after them as patients. But they weren't a bother. They didn't even hang around in the parks then, just stayed in their own communities. And apart from one Chinese restaurant there were no Asians that he could recall. Now there were Japanese and Greek and Thai restaurants, Vietnamese hot bread shops and Chinese grocery stores. And he even had a black man giving his anaesthetics now, though George O'Malley was technically Canadian and married to an Australian. Of course, he wasn't a racist, but he didn't know what to make of it all. Why, just last week he'd dropped by his drycleaners – he'd been going there for thirty years – and found it taken over by Indians. Not that they didn't do a good job on his trousers. But it wasn't like when old Bob, who'd been his patient, was running the place. The pace of change, Mellish told himself, is too rapid, we need to keep the ball in our own court, or we'll be outnumbered by these immigrants and refugees. Bringing all their families in, too, he knew that for a fact. Jayasinghe, for example, how many relatives had he brought into the country with him?

The size of the town now had, however, made it possible to conceal the only occasion on which he had strayed from the narrow path of marital fidelity. Really, that had been one from left field. He could never have anticipated it. The damnable events that had followed it, though! He'd really taken his eye off the ball there.

Of course, the woman was a foreigner; couldn't be trusted. But he'd been off his game, letting that happen. Sometimes he felt so angry he wanted to track them down, the woman and the people with her, so angry he wanted to … to strangle them all with his bare hands, thought Mellish. Fortunately, as long as he kept paying, no-one would have the least idea. Not his colleagues, not his secretary, and most of all, not Winifred.

With a flourish, Mellish withdrew the detached gallbladder from the patient's abdomen, and prepared to leave the closing-up to his assistant. But before he could leave, emboldened by necessity, Nimal Jayasinghe spoke. George lowered his paper to listen to this exchange.

'The Selection Committee, Sir, I believe it is meeting next week. I have given your name as a reference, Sir, as you told me, but I'd be grateful, if you were able to … to speak on my behalf …'

'Well, Jayasinghe, I'll certainly see what I can do. Your work has always been quite satisfactory. But of course, the field is wide open, and there are a lot of candidates.' He didn't need to specify: Australian candidates.

'Oh, thank you, Sir.'

Walking towards the change room, Arthur Mellish thought that he would really like to go into bat for Nimal Jayasinghe. But he'd bumped into Wally Miller, head of the Selection Committee, at a drinks party just last Friday, and Wally had told him exactly who would be shortlisted for the Cairns jobs next year.

First, Jimmy Marston's boy. Jimmy was a urologist on the Gold Coast, and was in medical school with Wally. Then Terry Abbott's son. Terry had a big practice north of Brisbane and sent his sons to the same Brisbane boarding school the Mellish boys attended. And Sara Waterhouse. It was important to interview one woman, Wally said, even though we wouldn't employ her, and Sara's a bright girl, her father's a chest physician and a professor. So there wasn't any way Nimal Jayasinghe was going to fit into this scheme of things, though Mellish was not going to tell him so. He'd promised Wally he'd keep it under his hat. The interview and selection process must be allowed to run its course, and Dr Jayasinghe informed, regretfully, by post, of the Committee's decisions.

Arthur Mellish meditated for a moment on this. Then thought, oh well, he's not behind the eight-ball, he can go and work out in the country. It's not as if he's between the dev— it's not as if he's up the creek without a paddle. He'd probably like it out there. And if he does have a wife, she'll probably be quite happy, used to the climate, and so on.

With that, he dismissed all thoughts of Dr Jayasinghe, and, throwing a theatre gown over his surgical blues, headed off towards his consulting rooms, and his lunch.

'Well Nimal,' asked George when Mellish was gone, 'do you think he's bowled you an easy one?'

'Ah George,' said Nimal, rapidly inserting clips to close the patient's incisions, 'I don't think so. I think he just bowled me a googly.'

Cairns, 1 March 2011

Paradise Close was a small cul-de-sac on the hill behind the Earlville shopping mall and number eleven was at the very end of it, where the street opened into a turning circle.

Drew Borgese slowed the unmarked car as he pulled into the street and he and Cass looked around. To their left were numbers one, three and five: all low-set bungalows, unfenced and with tended gardens. Despite Yasi there was an abundance of palms and tropical flowers in these gardens. On their right, numbers two, four and six matched their neighbours across the street. Further down, number seven was a vacant block, neatly mowed, although number nine, also not yet built on, was head-high with weeds. Blocks eight and ten were occupied by a comfortable old Queenslander in the middle of a sprawling garden.

'That's the original house,' Drew told Cass, nodding at it. 'I remember when this was all sugarcane.' A giant purple bougainvillea had taken over the left side of the old house and now seemed responsible for holding it up. The result was that number eleven was quite isolated from its neighbours. The isolation was increased by the wall of white stucco that ran right around it, cutting it off from the rest of the street and from the vacant land behind it. A black roller door, firmly closed, seemed to be the only way in, at least at the front.

Three children on bikes outside number five wheeled around to watch the strangers. Drew parked the car and he and Cass got out and surveyed the property. The house itself was quite silent, the only noise the chatter of the children in the street. There was no letterbox. The grass in the nature strip was recently mowed. Cass noticed that the grass in front of number nine was similarly mowed, despite the wilderness on the block itself, as was the grass in front of the old house. Neighbours must have done the lot, if the inhabitants of number eleven weren't responsible, and in the last few days.

In the absence of a doorbell Drew banged on the roller door. 'Hello! Mr Janvier! Mrs Janvier!' His cries echoed inside the garage beyond. It was possible to see partly over the front wall. The roller door led directly into a double garage attached to the house, a single-storey white stucco bungalow. Sliding glass doors, closed and with blinds drawn behind them, led onto a neglected garden. There were small palm trees along the side wall of the property and Drew pointed to the many palm fronds that had been blown into the front yard. It seemed this had not been cleared up since Yasi.

Cass made her way around the left side of the property, at the very edge of the weeds on number nine. Full-length drapes completely covered what must be the side window of the living room but further back a slatted timber blind gave a partial view into the kitchen. No occupant could be seen. The kitchen led onto a back patio and a swimming pool. The pool was filled with debris, palm fronds and tree branches, and thick green slime covered the surface of the water. Several potted plants lay on their sides.

Drew put his head around the front corner. 'Anything to see from there?'

'Not a thing. Living room and kitchen, pool. All looks untouched since Yasi at least. Lots of muck in the pool. The house looks empty.'

'I'll take the other side and meet you at the back.'

'OK.'

The wall continued around the property, rising to a height of about two metres at the back, so Cass could see nothing more than the roof of the house and the top of what looked like a garden shed close to the back wall. There was another roller door in this wall, and it wasn't responding to Cass's efforts to open it.

Drew appeared, and also gave the door a tug, but it didn't budge.

'Did you find anything?' she asked.

'The garage leads straight into the house. Two rooms at least on that side, probably bedrooms, windows shut and blinds drawn, and a bathroom, opaque glass window. Judging by the width of the house there's another room in the middle at the back.'

He measured the height of the wall with his eyes, then jumped up and grabbed the top, easily pulling himself up so he had a view of the whole back of the house. He'd lost none of the strength of his basketballing days, Cass thought, eyeing him.

With a jump she did her own chin-up. He looked approving but made no comment.

'Ah,' she said. 'Broken window. Could be evidence of a crime.'

'Yep, indeed it could, Diamond. We'd better go in …' He called again. 'Hello! Anybody home? Mr Janvier! Mrs Janvier!' He dropped back down onto the grass beside her.

'Y'know, our street is just like this,' he said to Cass. 'In Brinsmead. You've been there. Only there's no walled fortress like this one. In our street everyone knows everything about everyone else. Including my wife.'

'Yes,' answered Cass. 'I always think it seems like a great little community. Leila and your kids always have people dropping in. She always knows what's going on.'

Drew nodded. 'So I think we should check out the neighbours here.'

At that moment two small figures on bikes came from around the corner.

'They've gone away,' said the first one. 'Before the cyclone,' said the second.

'My mum said they must've gone to France,' said the first.

'Is your mum home?' asked Cass. 'Where do you live?'

'Number five. Yes she's home.'

'Are you the cops?' A third excited small figure had made an appearance. 'Cos you look like you are. Did they steal something? Are you going to put that crime-scene tape around the place?'

'Yes, we are police but, no, there's nothing wrong. We're just trying to locate these people. Can we see your mum?'

Drew and Cass followed the children back into Paradise Close. By now four more kids on bikes and skateboards had appeared to watch the action. From the front door of number five emerged a young woman in shorts and T-shirt, feet bare.

'Ma'am, I'm Detective Diamond. Cairns CIB. And this is Detective Borgese.'

'Is there a problem?' countered the woman. A normal response for unexpected meetings with police, Cass thought.

'No problem, Ma'am. We're just trying to locate Mr or Mrs Janvier, who we believe live in number eleven. The house looks as though no-one has been there recently.'

'Janvier,' the woman repeated. 'I've never known their name, even though we've lived here four years. I just know that they're Odile and Michel. They keep very much to themselves.'

'Have you seen them recently?'

'We've been talking about that – because of the cyclone, y'know … they weren't here then. A couple of the men from the street did take a look over the wall to make sure the house was closed up before Yasi arrived, and everything looked all right. Maybe the last time we saw them was a week before that. We think they must be overseas. The yard looks terrible, trees down and so on, and the pool's full of slime, but not really knowing them, y'know, well, no-one feels able to get into the yard and clear it up for them. We mowed the nature strip, my husband did, but that's all. It's funny, other times they've been away they've always got a garden service to come in. They both seem really neat and fussy. Always want the garden to be perfect.'

She looked suddenly perturbed. 'I hope nothing's happened to them?'

'We're just making some routine inquiries,' Drew answered. 'Do you know what he does? Mr Janvier? Where he works? Or his wife?'

'He's a businessman. She told me that once. But I don't know what, exactly, or where. She's a teacher somewhere – she told Mrs Berry, the old lady across the road. She's been here sixty years. Her family had the cane farm before the land was divided up. Mrs Berry told me Odile taught in one of the high schools. I don't know where. None of ours are in high school yet.'

'Did – does Mrs Janvier have her own car?'

'Oh yes! A red Honda Prelude. And he has a four-wheel drive, a white Mitsubishi.'

'And when they're here, they go off to work each day?'

'Mostly they go out late morning I think. I don't often see them. I go at eight to drop the kids to before-school care because I work mornings. In the evenings I might see them pass by usually around our teatime. She's in and out during the day. I've always thought she must work part-time.'

'They have children?'

'No. At least … no, I'm sure they don't. I've never seen any. They have very few visitors and no-one who looked like family. And, y'know, she's not really, well, maternal … she's so elegant, that French thing. Always high heels and suits, and matching bags, and silk scarves, even to go to the shops.' Aha, thought Cass, though she said nothing. That sounds like our woman.

'Does anyone in the street collect their mail for them?' Drew asked.

'They've no letterbox!' The young woman looked at him slightly oddly – Cass could almost see her thinking: he's a detective, and he didn't see that?

'They have a post-office box,' explained the woman.

'Do you know which post office that's at?' asked Cass.

'No, sorry. I really, y'know, hardly know them even though they live right there. They just make clear they want to keep to themselves. I might go six months without speaking a single word to her although we always wave if she's driving past. And you can see – the house has a wall around it; it's not like they want to chat.'

'Have you ever been inside the house?' Cass asked.

'Never.'

'And her husband? Does he mix with any of the men in the street?'

The woman hesitated. Then said: 'No. Not at all.' Cass waited for her to speak again, and after a moment she said,

'I guess I would say … that he seems like he's under her thumb. He does all the shopping – I see him in the supermarket quite often, on his own. I've never seen her in the supermarket, ever, though you can see her in dress shops, in Cairns Central or Abbott Street.

'And he seems to do most of the housework … from what you can see over the wall.' She blushed at what she'd said, then laughed. 'Oh, I won't say we don't talk about them in the street. We do. He never speaks to anyone, just drives straight past. At first, people here thought he was up himself, now they just think, well that's how he wants it. But he's often out in the garden and usually he keeps it perfect. That's why it's so surprising the place is such a mess now. But … I do hope nothing's happened to them?'

'We're just making some inquiries. Thank you for your time – can I ask your name?'

'Wendy. Wendy Egan.'

Drew and Cass walked towards the car. The children had drifted away.

'That broken window …' began Cass.

'Yep, I think we should go in through the back. Less public, though I'm sure we've got the whole street watching anyway. Let me do it, and I'll open up for you if I can.'

Behind the house, Drew pulled himself up and over the wall. From the inside he opened the small roller door and Cass followed him in. Through the broken pane of glass they could see a bedroom in considerable disorder.

'Police! Hello!' Drew called, and again his voice echoed through an empty house.

He carefully put a hand through the broken pane, undid the lock, pushed up the window and climbed in.

'Go around to the kitchen door and I'll let you in if I can.'

The door was bolted top and bottom but had not been deadlocked. Drew opened it and Cass stepped into a kitchen that seemed quite unremarkable apart from the smell of rotting fruit. There were fitted timber cabinets, a microwave and oven, all quite clean. No dishes in the sink. A 2011 calendar with French country scenes hung on the wall, open at January. A digital wall clock read 11.15 but Cass's watch read 3.22. The dishwasher was at the end of its cycle, its orange light glowing, and the timer on the microwave was flashing zeros. So the power had gone off with Yasi, then come back on, but nothing had been touched since. The fridge was purring, but its contents told the same story – there was mould covering butter, cheese and milk. On top of the fridge was a fruit bowl containing rotting pineapple and oranges.

The living room was also tidy, with television, DVD player and stereo all in place, and speakers mounted high on the walls. There were a few framed prints, ornaments on shelves, copies of *Vogue* on a glass coffee table.

Across a short passage on the garage side of the house were two rooms. One was a bedroom with a single bed made with military precision, a wardrobe containing male clothing, shoes precisely arranged and shirts and trousers hung according to colour. On the bedside table were a couple of books in French: a thriller and some science fiction.

The second bedroom was larger, but it contained no bed and had an adjoining dressing room. Instead the whole area was taken up with clothes racks. In fact the room was packed with clothes – meticulously arranged women's clothes. Dresses, skirts, shirts, pants, shoes, handbags and scarves were sorted by type and colour.

'She must work in the fashion business, not a school,' said Drew. 'Or at least, worked …'

Cass was looking at it all, puzzled.

'No,' she said, lifting up one after another of the items, 'they're all size 10 or thereabouts. And they've been worn, though they're in good nick. I think these are all hers.'

He looked amazed. 'Surely no woman in Cairns needs a wardrobe like this?'

'All very good brands,' Cass was checking. 'Like what our corpse was wearing. And the shoes and accessories are all coordinated too.' There were large mirrors on two walls and a third mirror had a dressing table in front of it, covered with pots and tubes of makeup. 'There must be at least sixty lipsticks alone,' she remarked. 'This woman is serious about her appearance. Was serious. If it's her.'

The final bedroom, with the broken window, was separated from the others by a bathroom and laundry that were well kept and contained little of interest. On the bedroom floor was a sprouting coconut, obviously from the tree outside, the culprit that had broken the glass during the cyclone. The wind and rain had got in. The carpet by the window was wet and mouldy and there was a pool of mud by the queen-sized bed. Bottles of makeup had been sent flying from the dressing table and cushions tossed about.

And spread wildly about the room were several items that Cass pointed out to Drew: Hermès scarves.

Cairns, February 2010

Jane O'Malley sat at the desk in her surgery looking across at a new patient, a five-year-old girl named Kianna. The family had come up to Cairns from Brisbane about eighteen months ago, Kianna's mother, Samantha, said. Previously they'd been patients of Trevor Symonds but for various reasons had decided to change.

Jane noted that for some reason the mother seemed very nervous.

Certainly the child had been through a lot in her five years. At the age of six weeks, she'd been diagnosed with hydrocephalus. Though her brain was normal, the fluid around it could not drain away. She spent four weeks in the Children's Hospital in Brisbane having a shunt put in. And had been in and out of that hospital numerous times since.

'I can see it's been a difficult few years for you,' Jane said to Samantha. 'But she's been fine for the past two years, is that right? You take her down to Brisbane to see Dr Skeggs, I see. He's been happy with her, it seems. He last saw her six months ago.' Jane knew Joe Skeggs, a paediatric neurosurgeon, a kindly man with six kids of his own. 'So why have you brought her along today?'

'It's her teacher, really, that's worried,' Samantha said. 'She's just started school this year, you know, she started off sitting at the back of the class but the teacher moved her to the front next to the whiteboard. I didn't think there was anything wrong, she's as good as gold at home, no problems, but the teacher spoke to Brian, Kianna's dad, told him she was concerned about Kianna's eyesight. Brian wanted to take her to our GP … to … to Dr Symonds. But I said, I don't want to go to Dr Symonds anymore, I hear Dr O'Malley's very good.' As she said all this she shifted in her chair and fiddled with her car keys.

Jane smiled at the little girl. 'Do you have trouble watching TV at home, Kianna?' she asked. 'What do you watch?'

'Um … the Wiggles … but I have to sit up close or I can't see it,' Kianna said, as Samantha shuffled her feet uncomfortably.

'Just pop up on that bed for me, pet.'

Jane picked up her ophthalmoscope and looked deep into Kianna's eyes. The optic nerves were swollen and cloudy.

'OK, Kianna, you go and play in the toy room while I talk to Mummy,' Jane said.

Kianna gone, she said: 'Samantha, she'll need to go down to Brisbane again to see Dr Skeggs. Urgently. I think the shunt is blocked somewhere, maybe just partly, and the fluid is building up and pressing on the nerves at the back of her eyes.'

'So … she'll need another operation?'

'I'm afraid so.'

'And … if I'd taken her sooner, back to Dr Symonds … would it have made a difference?'

'I can't answer that yet, until we know what's wrong … but possibly, yes. I'm sure he would have referred you earlier if he'd looked in her eyes and seen what I've just seen. Unfortunately when you made the appointment, being a new patient to us, no-one realised that it was urgent.'

'Oh, she seemed well,' said Samantha, adding vaguely, 'and I was busy with things, you know …'

Jane bit her lip. There was more to this than Samantha was letting on. Why had she taken so long to bring Kianna to a doctor, and why had she changed doctors?

'While I'm here,' she said, 'before I ring Dr Skeggs, I'll just make a note of her last boosters – the shots she had before she started school. Dr Symonds gave her those, I suppose?'

Samantha flushed. 'No … no … I haven't taken her back to Dr Symonds for some time.'

Jane took off her glasses, pushed back her fair hair, and studied Samantha's face carefully. 'Well, it's important to do these things. Kianna needs all the routine health checks as well as her special care.' And, warming to the subject, she added: 'What about you? Are you looking after yourself? Have you had a Pap smear, for example?'

Samantha's response was to burst into tears.

'Samantha, what's the matter?'

'Promise, promise, you won't tell? I'd feel so much better, talking to you … to someone.'

'Of course,' responded Jane. 'Whatever you tell me is confidential. Is it a problem with your relationship, with …

ah,' she consulted her notes, 'with Brian?'

'No. It's … Dr Symonds. He wanted … to have sex with me.'

For a moment Jane was speechless. Trevor. Lyndall's husband. Well, soon to be ex-husband. She knew him well. She and George tried to avoid him these days, although in the past they'd been much closer friends. Now that Lyndall had left him, Jane was in Lyndall's camp. As were most of the town's medicos. She knew what people said. She knew what Lyndall herself had said. She knew about the practice secretary everyone said he'd had an affair with, and a few stories about nurses. But patients? Even when Lyndall had suggested it was possible, Jane had thought he would have had more sense.

Delicately, she asked Samantha if she wanted to tell her any more.

'He was our GP when we first moved here. I had to see him so often – with Kianna, her having the shunt, and having to be so careful every time she got a cold or something. He always seemed so, well, cool, controlled, and, well, being a doctor, knowing so much, you know. I guess I just, sort of, got a crush on him. Only he never did anything, said anything then.

'Then about a year ago I found a lump in my breast. I went straight along to see him.

'He was great, really reassuring, calmed me down, said he was sure it was just a cyst, not to worry, but he would organise for me to have a mammogram and an ultrasound straight away. Which he did. Then he sent me to another doctor – Dr Mellish – to put a needle in and take the fluid off the cyst. And then I had to go back to see him, Trev … Dr Symonds, for the results of the tests on the fluid.

'When I went back, he made a special appointment for me one evening, after work, and he told me the tests were normal. I was so relieved. I began to tell him, not exactly how I felt, personally you know, just how grateful I was for all the help he'd given us, how much I admired him. Maybe it was my fault, maybe I said too much …

'Anyway, then he said he wanted to look at my breast again, to make sure it was OK, and I could just sit there in the chair and take off my bra, not to worry about getting up on the couch. Which – well, naturally, I did what he said, he was the doctor, and everything … So I was just sitting there, topless, and then he began, not just to look at my breasts like a doctor does, but to stroke them, and to touch my nipples. And then I realised … how excited he was … and he asked me if I would … go all the way with him … said he found me … *a knockout* is what he said … and he said that he thought maybe I felt something for him …' Her voice trailed off.

'And?' Jane prompted, hoping she didn't sound too interested in salacious detail.

Samantha sat up sharply.

'Well, naturally I said no. I … I put my clothes back on as quickly as I could, and I ran out the door.'

'But I couldn't possibly tell Brian, he wouldn't understand.

He's always been the jealous sort, he'd think I'd encouraged it, which I don't think I did at all … But I couldn't see him … Trev … I mean Dr Symonds again, you see; I couldn't go to him again and take Kianna. And no way could I go for a Pap smear. But if I started going to someone else Brian would wonder why, and I didn't know what I'd say … So I just put it all off, kept away from doctors altogether, until I really had to bring her.'

Jane took shelter behind her professional manner, brisk but soothing.

'Well, for the Pap smear, you can see my practice nurse, that's easy. Meanwhile we must sort out Kianna's problems straight away. I'll make an appointment with Dr Skeggs for as soon as I can. The booster shots we can work out later. And yes, what you have told me is confidential – between us.'

For the rest of that day, though, Samantha's story kept coming back to Jane. For one thing, she simply could not tell Lyndall – she was her closest friend in the town but she was also Trevor's wife

Lying in bed that night, Jane looked at her husband, and decided to broach the subject with him. A black man living in a largely white society, George was an astute judge of character. She'd agreed to keep Samantha's secret, but there was no need to mention any names.

'What would you say,' she began, 'to a patient who tells you their GP suggested they have sex?'

George had folded his arms behind his head, looked up

at the ceiling, and smiled. 'What would I say?' he asked. 'A local GP?'

'Yes,' replied Jane cautiously.

'Well, I'd say, since it's almost certainly a male, that it's not Paddy McBean or John Donaldson, and unlikely to be Mervyn Chang, but it could be Trevor Symonds.'

'George! That's not what I meant at all! Umm … how did you know that?'

'So I'm right? Don't worry, I won't breathe a word. He's divorced, or almost, which is a perfectly normal thing to be when you're a philandering bastard. There've been … a few incidents. I did, for example, see him a few years ago in the hospital car park late at night, with a woman not his wife – in fact, that rather nice Sandra, the secretary who used to work in his practice – dropping her off to pick up her own car, and I did think, aha, that's a curious event. And I might say,' he grinned, caressing his wife's breast beneath her nightdress, 'in my case I really *was* working late. Why don't you put that book down now …'

'But George,' Jane persisted, 'what should I advise her? Should she complain to the Medical Board?'

'Certainly, if it's true it's deplorable. Nurses and secretaries, which seem to be his usual targets so far as I know, are one thing; they're adults. I neither approve nor disapprove. But patients are different, the doctor–patient relationship makes them much more vulnerable, quite apart from the fact that it's forbidden by the Medical Board, and by medical ethics from way back. But – did he just make an advance, and get rebuffed? He didn't actually have sex with her?'

'No. Well, so she says.'

'Well, it would be her word against his, wouldn't it? She'd be very exposed. People would find out. And despite the rumours and the drinking, Trevor's still quite well-respected around here. There'd still be colleagues who would testify on his behalf. When did this happen?'

'I think about nine months ago.'

'And she didn't complain then? Even less likely to be believed now. I'd do nothing.'

'But George, he may be trying it on with other women too. He shouldn't be allowed to just get away with it. And maybe he needs help. We're all being told to help our colleagues. In fact we're really supposed to report stuff like this now. But no way could I do that. He drinks a lot, I know. Why does he behave like that?'

'Honey, I'm surprised you're even asking. That's just the way some men are, you know that. He was probably like that long before he met Lyndall. Some men just think with their dicks; having a medical degree or a family doesn't change that. If he's making a regular thing of it with patients, eventually he'll be caught. Probably turned in to the Board by a woman he breaks up with. You know what our ethics tutor told us in med school back in Montreal? Don't have sex with your patients, guys! But he added – if you do, don't stop, it's the disgruntled ones who'll turn you in.'

'Oh George. But jokes aside, should I do something? There's supposed to be this mandatory reporting now …'

'Sweetheart, I don't think you can do anything, except just be sympathetic to this woman. And be a decent doctor for her. Which I know you'll do.' His fingers stroked his wife more urgently, her nipples hardened in response, and she forgot all about Trevor Symonds for the moment.

In the following days, however, Jane turned the problem over in her mind. Trevor might try this on other women, on women who were more vulnerable than Samantha, who had probably compromised her child's health as a direct result of Trevor's behaviour. Jane decided that she must encourage Samantha to make a formal complaint. Maybe Brian, her husband, wouldn't need to be told about it.

Joe Skeggs telephoned Jane. Kianna's shunt had become disconnected. He'd been able to fix it fairly easily. The little girl had needed only a few days in hospital. Now that the pressure was off Kianna's optic nerves, there would be no further deterioration in her sight. But that would not fix the damage already done. She would always have some impaired vision and would need glasses.

Shit, had been Jane's first thought. If Trevor had left Samantha alone, she'd have taken Kianna back months ago. He'd have looked at her, found out about it, done something … he was still a competent practitioner. There was all the more reason, in her mind, to press ahead with a complaint.

She saw Kianna for a follow-up visit four weeks later.

The little girl was bursting with energy, running around the consulting room and down to the toy room. It was clear that the shunt blockage had been making her very unwell before. But her mother looked drawn and anxious.

'I caused it all, didn't I? I should have brought her in earlier,' Samantha suggested.

'Oh, Samantha, we can't really say that, we don't know how long the shunt was blocked. You mustn't blame yourself. We'll just have to do the best we can with the sight she has left,' Jane reassured her. 'But, I did want to talk to you, you know, about what you told me, last time.'

'You didn't tell anyone, did you?' Samantha asked.

Jane skirted the question. 'I think you should do something about this, Samantha. For the sake of other women, maybe not as strong as you, that he might make suggestions to … If you made a complaint to the Medical Board, your name wouldn't be published anywhere, everything would be completely confidential. And I'm sure, if Brian did have to know, he would understand why you were doing it.'

Samantha flushed a deep red, twisted her rings, looked at the floor. 'It's more difficult … there's more to it than I told you.' There was a long silence.

Then she said: 'You see, I did have sex with him, that time, when he asked me, in the surgery, and other times …'

'Oh,' said Jane feebly.

'I … I said to you, that I did think he was … more mature, more sophisticated than, than Brian, and I was flattered, I suppose, that he was interested in me, that he liked me. Or at least,' she added with obvious ill-feeling, 'I thought he did. I never thought someone like him, a doctor, would notice someone like me … I knew he was married. But he told me he didn't have sex with his wife any more. I know that can happen. And Brian and me … well, it's always been rather flat, our sex life, especially since we had Kianna. We tend to blame each other for her problems, and that affects … everything else. So, you see, that would all come out if I made a complaint, wouldn't it?'

Jane took a deep breath, and then said slowly: 'Yes, it might. It would certainly make it worse for him, but even just making suggestions, as he did initially, as you said he did initially, would be bad enough for the Medical Board. The fact that you were … willing … wouldn't affect that. It's one thing that's strictly forbidden, for us, for doctors. And for you, yes, I can see, obviously you were not intending to tell Brian?'

'No, and I could never mention it, and say, he just made a pass at me, and look Brian in the eye, and not have him know.'

'No,' agreed Jane. And added gently, 'It's not still going on, I take it?'

'No,' Samantha gave a bitter smile. 'If it was, there wouldn't have been any problem for me, would there? I could have just taken Kianna to see him … even had a Pap smear! But he broke it off. After a few weeks. I always went to the surgery. As the last patient in the evening. He would always write something on my notes and bulk-bill me.' Jane's eyes widened at this novel use of Medicare funds. 'Then, suddenly, he just said, he was very sorry, we couldn't go on, although he would still be our GP and everything. And he said he thought I was mature enough to understand.

'But I was devastated … and I couldn't talk to anybody. And for months I just couldn't go to another doctor. Now, I feel, yes, that I would like to dob him in, I'm really angry at how he used me, the bastard. I'd even thought … it might lead somewhere … that I might leave Brian.'

Jane thought of George's lecturer's advice: it's when you stop that the trouble begins, hell hath no fury, etcetera, but she still felt that even though Samantha *had* been willing, even if she'd thrown herself at his feet, Trevor had a clear professional duty to resist temptation.

Samantha said again, 'I can't complain because I can't risk Brian finding out.'

Jane spent days going over the problem in her mind. Should she go and talk to Trevor herself? She could no longer stand the man, now that she'd heard Samantha's story. Quite apart from what had happened to Lyndall, she would be betraying Samantha's confidences. Even if she didn't mention any names, he'd obviously know who she meant. Of course he'd deny everything. It might make him more prudent towards patients in the future but she couldn't even be sure of that. Should she sound out the Medical Defence Union, the Doctor's Health Advisory Service? To do anything properly, there'd have to be a written complaint, she'd have to make it and thus betray her own patient's confidence.

Jane had still not resolved the issue when, three weeks later, she received a letter from Samantha. The family was moving to Melbourne. Samantha asked to be referred to a GP there.

Jane replied immediately with the name of a colleague she'd trained with, prudently choosing a woman. This solved some of the immediate problems, she thought. But long-term, it only made matters worse. It did nothing to change Trevor Symonds' behaviour, or, to take a more charitable view, to get him help.

'Well,' George had said, when Jane confronted him again with the problem, 'I guess some of us, say, me and Tim from the Medical Staff Council in the hospital, and maybe someone senior, like Arthur Mellish, could just have a word with him. Tell him there have been rumours, that we'd be concerned if they were true. Remind him about mandatory reporting.'

'That would be good. It should be just a male thing, I think,' Jane responded. 'But is Mellish the best person to ask? After Nimal?'

George had got himself onto the selection committee for the new hospital surgeons and managed to push through Nimal Jayasinghe's application for a post.

'Oh he's got over it now that Nimal's taken on Arthur's weekends on-call. And Trevor has some respect for Mellish; he's been in town a long time.'

So it had come about that at 2 pm on a Friday afternoon in September of 2010, George, Tim and Arthur Mellish had gathered in Tim's office for the appointment with Trevor Symonds, who had not been told the purpose of the discussion.

'Old Arthur was very uncomfortable about it all,' George later told his wife. 'I guess it's a generational thing. Just mentioning the "s" word seemed too much for him. Sex with patients – he was red in the face, didn't want to even think about it! I can't imagine he and Winifred get up to much these days. She's a pretty straight-laced old biddy. Probably wears corsets.'

Jane laughed and punched his arm.

In truth, the three of them had sat there waiting for half an hour. The office was above the Emergency Department. They heard an ambulance come in, its siren going. Nobody took any notice. Tim took out his mobile and called Trevor's number but was just switched over to voicemail. Damn the man! They all had much better things to do than have cautionary talks with Trevor Symonds.

After forty minutes they gave it away.

'I'll write him a letter,' George said. 'Tell him we've a serious matter reported to the Medical Staff Council that has to be discussed. And make another appointment. Thanks for coming along, both of you.'

Cairns, 2 March 2011

Early on Wednesday morning, following the visit to Paradise Close, all three detectives met in Drew's office to discuss progress. The previous afternoon, warrants had been issued for the search of both Janvier properties – the Earlville house and the Portsmith office – and the search had gone on late into the night.

'There's nothing there,' said Troy Barwen, who with scenes-of-crime officers had spent a large part of the afternoon at Portsmith. 'At least, no legit cleaning business working away like you'd think there'd be. Just a sign. Kwality Kleening. The place looks as though no-one's been there for weeks. Needs cleaning, really. About five hundred flyers for pizza and gym membership clogging up the letterbox but interestingly no business mail.

'It's one of those industrial estate places, and Janvier's unit is at one end. Next door is empty. Two doors down is a panelbeater, takes up two units. The bloke there says he sees Janvier occasionally. Never the wife. They say hello, that's about all. He sees him come in at odd times during the day but no visible business ever conducted there. And I mean no business. It's not like people are rolling up there for something other than cleaning, or that he's stashing something there. The panelbeating bloke used to own Janvier's unit, sold it to him about twelve years ago – for cash, which is interesting – and says he's always been a bit of a mystery. He couldn't remember the last time he saw Janvier, but he reckoned it was after Christmas but before Yasi.'

Troy showed them numerous photos of Janvier's unit. There was a small front office area with a sink, looking dusty and neglected as Troy had said. There were a few brooms and buckets and cleaning products, none showing signs of recent use. Behind the office was a toilet and a storeroom.

'There were a few empty files in the office,' Troy said, 'and some receipt booklets. Unused. And some letterheads that looked like they'd been set up by Janvier himself. But there was no computer or printer.'

Across the back wall of the store was a cupboard containing piles of newspaper. 'Old copies of the *Cairns Post* and the Brisbane *Courier-Mail* going back for years, in no particular order,' Troy said. Beside that stood a rack of steel shelves, empty apart from a few more newspapers. The store was clean and the piles of newspaper tidy. There seemed nothing else to find.

Outside, photos showed the unit was at the very end of the row. To its left, beyond the empty unit, was the panel-beating workshop, which spilt out onto the courtyard in front. The main entrance to the whole complex was further down, beyond several more units – a cabinet-maker, an ironmonger, an importer of office furniture. Troy had spoken with everyone in these units. They all knew Michel

Janvier by sight and had passed the time of day with him but otherwise had no contact.

Beside the unit was a stormwater canal with a bridge across to a side street that led in turn onto the main Portsmith road. The allocated parking spot for Janvier's building was on the canal side of the unit. Drew studied the photos carefully.

'It looks like Janvier could park on the other side of the canal and cross the bridge and get to his place and hardly be seen by the panelbeaters,' he said.

'Yep,' said Troy, 'he could. If he had some reason to do that. The other thing that's interesting,' Troy added, 'is that the only prints here match many of those in the Earlville house. We're presuming for the moment that these are Michel Janvier's. But there's no evidence of anybody else ever having been in that office. None at all.'

Cass swallowed the last of her first double shot of the day and said: 'I checked with ASIC and the tax office and drew a complete blank.' Kwality Kleening of Portsmith was not a registered company name. It appeared to have no bank accounts. There was no record of it making any money, filing a tax return or having any employees at any time in the last ten years.

At the Earlville house, valid Australian passports for both Janviers had been found in a desk drawer. They were now on Drew's desk. There were also out-of-date European passports identifying the couple as French citizens. Cass studied the passport photos of both Janviers but especially Odile.

'Still hard to say it's her,' she remarked. 'But having seen the body there's nothing in these that would make me feel it's definitely someone else. And it certainly looks like these two are missing from home.'

Cass had ascertained from Immigration that there was no record of a Michel Janvier leaving Australia on any other passport in the past four weeks. So wherever the man might be, he had not legitimately left Australia.

At Earlville the search had turned up bank statements showing regular sums paid into the couple's account from France. Around 3000€, appeared to have gone into their joint account each month for as far back as the records went.

'That's about $4000 – a nice little earner,' Cass said. 'But is it enough to pay for all those clothes? Those shoes with the pricey red soles? And whatever else the woman who wore them wanted? Everything we saw in that bedroom? I don't think so.'

Apparently there was no mortgage on the house; certainly no payments could be identified. Credit card statements were scanty, mostly for electricity and other utilities. Otherwise the Janviers seemed to use cash, which they drew regularly from ATMs.

The neighbours in Paradise Close reported that no visitors ever came to the house, apart from one young man about a year ago. Mrs Berry had remembered him turning up, but nothing about his appearance or that of his car. There'd been an argument and the man drove off quickly soon after.

A cabinet marked 'Medical records' had proved interesting. Leah Rookwood had said that the dead woman had been in good health up until close to the time she died. Whereas Odile Janvier appeared to spend a great deal of time visiting doctors. In the past year alone she'd made three or four visits each week to a variety of general practitioners and assorted specialists. She'd undergone ultrasounds of various types, blood tests, X-rays and sundry other investigations. Medicare forms and bills were meticulously filed in chronological order.

'Do all these doctors know about each other, do you think?' Cass asked. 'Is there some kind of central coding bureau in Medicare that flags this kind of thing?'

'I don't know,' said Drew. 'For prescription drugs, yes there is. But for other things, X-rays and doctors visits, maybe not.'

The bathroom cabinet had revealed only the kind of items one might expect in a suburban household – aspirin, paracetamol, some hormone preparation for her, some stronger analgesics for joint pain and some out-of-date antibiotics. No scheduled prescription drugs, no oxycodone, no benzodiazepines.

More important, as far as the identification of the body in the mortuary was concerned, were bills from a Cairns dentist, Dr Wilfred Lam, although the last visit had been four years ago. In the Earlville bathroom were toothbrushes and hairbrushes containing hairs so DNA testing could establish whether the body in the rainforest had been an inhabitant of the house, but using the dental records would be quicker and cheaper.

'Diamond,' Drew said, 'I'm sending you to see that dentist, as soon as his surgery opens.'

One curious thing was the amount of photographic and video recording equipment in the house. There were several standard cameras and video recorders, but also two tiny cameras of the kind used in police surveillance work that immediately caught Leslie's attention. One was a Playmobil Spy Camera, and the other a Mini Spy digital micro camera, just seven centimetres long. Both could be used to produce videos. Drew had looked on the Internet, and found that both were available for around fifty dollars. So far, however, no films, cassettes or CDs that might have been produced from the equipment had been found in the house.

Equally remarkable was the absence of laptops or computers in the house and shed. And Troy had found no computer in the office. Were laptops also missing, along with Michel Janvier?

There also seemed to be no family photos or letters. The Janviers read magazines in English and French but apparently few books. There were moderate amounts of food and wine. There was a phone directory but no address book – as Leslie said, people use their phones now for such things. Odile's mobile had not been found although the number had been obtained from Telstra. Cass had tried calling but got an 'off or out of range' message. She'd also called Michel's mobile, with the same result. Both phones showed very few calls except to the other. Records showed her phone was last used on 28 January to call her husband; his last call was to her, on 29 January.

The backyard shed had proved to contain Michel Janvier's personal gym. It was lined with timber, was air-conditioned and well equipped. An exercise bike, a treadmill, some weights – all looked well used. On the walls were many photos of Janvier, taken over a number of years. Clearly the man was a fitness fanatic. He had dressed himself carefully for these, and styled his dark hair. He was a short, solid fellow with sculpted arms and thighs, which he displayed from all angles to the camera. As a younger man he had worn his hair slicked down, with a side part, together with a well-trimmed beard and moustache, but more recent shots showed him clean-shaven and with a Caesar cut. All these photos appeared to have been taken inside the shed. Given that the neighbours reported an absence of visitors, Drew pointed out, they had to have been taken by his wife or by Janvier himself.

But there was absolutely no clue in the house as to what had happened to him. His wife's red Honda was in the garage but his own white Mitsubishi Outlander 2005 four-wheel drive was not. There was no evidence of anyone at all having been in the house for several weeks. The use-by dates on food and milk were all for early February.

Leslie had ordered a nationwide search for the Mitsubishi, with no positive sightings yet. The rainforest around where the body had been found was still being meticulously combed. So far no item pertaining to the Janviers had turned up, apart from her second red-soled shoe under a bush near the road.

Finally, what was truly striking was the vast wardrobe belonging to the (presumed) late Mrs Janvier. Two policewomen were at that moment fully occupied in searching and cataloguing this. So far they had notched up 39 skirts, 131 shirts and blouses and 86 pairs of shoes, which they estimated to have cost more than a hundred thousand dollars. None of these items had yielded any clues.

There was also the matter of the Hermès scarves. Eleven of these had been scattered around the bedroom. 'Like someone was in a frenzy,' Cass said of the scene. 'Counting the four on the body, that makes fifteen of these things. And one more at least in the wardrobe. All pretty much the same except different colours. That's 10,000 bucks' worth.'

'Think what else you could do with that money!' Troy moaned.

Drew had ordered that all the scarves be numbered, packed and sent to the lab for examination. 'There could be blood or other body fluids on them,' he said. 'It would seem those scarves are important to someone.'

Scientific staff had also collected fingerprints in the house but had so far only identified two different sets, neither of them in the Australian databases. One set matched the prints found in the Portsmith office. The others were in the house and the Honda, but not the office. The French police had been contacted to see if they had matches for either set.

'That should be back later today,' Drew said.

At 9 am Cass called the surgery of the dentist, Wilfred Lam.

'Dr Lam's surgery, Leanne speaking, how can I help you?'

'Leanne this is Detective Cass Diamond from Cairns CIB. I'd like to drop in to see Dr Lam to talk about identifying a person of interest to us, from his dental records. We believe Dr Lam has treated this person in the past.'

There was a moment's silence, then Leanne regained her wits. 'Um … can I have the name of the patient?'

'I'm afraid that's something I can share only with Dr Lam. Because of the nature of the matter, as you'll understand, that information is strictly confidential. This is quite important. We'd like to see Dr Lam as soon as we can.'

'Just a moment. I'll have to talk to him. Can I call you back?'

'No,' said Cass firmly. 'I'll hang on.'

Minutes passed as she endured a recurrent cycle of several bars of 'Greensleeves'. Finally Leanne's voice broke through and Cass was told the dentist could see her in half an hour.

Dr Lam was a small elfin man with large rimless glasses and excellent teeth. He was nervous and excited as he ushered Cass into his office, scarcely looking at her badge, explaining in a rush that he'd never had to produce records before like this although he'd learnt about it in dental school in Adelaide. Hell, she thought, he's going to be really upset to find he's lost a lovely patient like Odile Janvier, with her expensive ceramic teeth. And in suspicious circumstances.

But she was not prepared for the extent of his reaction.

'What I have to tell you is in the strictest confidence, Dr Lam. We wish to identify a body that's been found. We believe it may be that of a Mrs Odile Janvier who you treated as recently as 2007.'

For some moments all the colour drained from the dentist's face. Then he turned deep purple. He stood up, sat down, then stood up again. He seemed to be struggling to speak, but no words came out. Alarmed, Cass wondered if he was about to have some kind of seizure. She looked about the room – was there oxygen somewhere if it was needed? Finally, in a squeak that sounded as though he'd been inhaling helium, he asked: 'Odile Janvier … is dead?'

'We believe this may be the case. We have not yet formally identified the woman we believe to be her. If you have dental records we would like a signed copy of them so our pathologist can make a comparison. I'm sorry to be the bearer of bad news. Obviously this is quite distressing for you.'

'Oh, oh,' the dentist squeaked. 'No, it's just … a shock … such an … elegant lady, to think of her … dead … so sad.'

But it struck Cass that sadness was not the main element of Dr Lam's reaction. One might even say there was a hint of relief in his voice.

'It's four years since I treated her,' he said, recovering somewhat.

Is that right? thought Cass. *And do you remember exactly how long it is since you treated every one of your patients?*

'I'll get her file,' he said, 'and make you a copy.' Cass noticed that he was trembling as he left the room. Well, this was all very interesting. She studied her surroundings, which bore little resemblance to the caravans of the school dentists she'd seen as a child. Those guys had been astounded that an Aboriginal kid could have such good teeth. Because I never ate sweets, she thought. My Mum might have some bad habits but she taught me to eat good food. No sugar, no sweets when I was growing up. Even now she didn't eat them. A soundless television on the ceiling displayed a cooking show. There were some forgettable pastel prints on the walls and the air was sharp with the peppermint scent of the pale green mouthwash that stood by the dental chair.

Dr Lam took some time but eventually returned with a manila folder. He was still trembling but his voice had returned to its normal pitch. Behind him Cass could see Leanne, her eyes wide with amazement. Dr Lam firmly closed the door.

'Here are diagrams and X-rays from 2007,' he said, holding out a number of photocopies. 'I did eight implants for her altogether and four other crowns.'

'So she hadn't seen you since then?' Cass asked.

This innocent question produced a further spasm of alarm in Dr Lam and more helium squeaking.

'No, no, no.' He shook his head. Then, with difficulty, he said: 'I think perhaps she changed her dentist. Maybe she has a new dentist now.'

'There was some problem? She didn't pay her bill? Something like that?'

With a further effort he managed to say again: 'No, no, no.' And then: 'She always pay. Always. She … is a very good person.'

Deciding that she would get little further information from the discombobulated dentist, and that she risked having to perform CPR if she stayed much longer, Cass thanked him, picked up the documents, and made for the door. She would go immediately to Leah Rookwood's office. And then she would report her strange dental encounter to Drew.

Passing Leanne's desk, she nodded. Leanne jumped up, followed her to the door, and came out with her. She looked meaningly at Cass, put a finger to her lips, and hissed: 'There's something funny about that woman. He told me not to send her reminders for her check-ups.' She lowered her voice even more. 'I think he's afraid of her.' Then she quickly slipped back inside the surgery door.

Cass walked slowly to her car, thinking this over. She decided she would come back to ask Wilfred Lam a few more questions. Later this afternoon, once she was sure the dead woman really was Odile Janvier.

Later that morning Tim Ingram was standing in the antenatal clinic, holding an ultrasound probe over the swollen belly of a young woman with twins. The senior registrar, Dr Susanna Ortega, was beside him. She had called him in because she was concerned about the growth of the second twin. Tim was just about to measure the blood flow in the baby's umbilical cord when his mobile rang. Propping the phone against his shoulder as he handed the probe to Susie, he smiled at the patient, and moved outside the consulting room, registering as he did so the precise tones of Inspector Leslie Fernando in his ear.

'Dr Ingram? We have met, a few years ago now.'

'Yes Inspector, I remember.'

'I hope I'm not disturbing you?'

'Not at all. What can I do for you?'

'I understand you were unlucky enough to be the discoverer of this body on Sunday, up near Kuranda.'

'Yes,' Tim said. 'We were coming back from a weekend in Yungaburra.'

'As you know, we'll need a statement from you. Shouldn't take long. But I wondered, also, if you might have time for a quick chat?'

'Um … yes … when would that be?'

'Well, at your convenience … but perhaps, is today possible?'

'Late afternoon? I have an operating list … say five o'clock?'

'Yes. Thank you, Doctor. Much appreciated.'

Somewhat perturbed, Tim returned to his patient. 'Yes,' he said to Susanna, as he studied the screen of the ultrasound machine, 'reduced Dopplers, down from last week.'

He looked at the mother of the twins. 'Jenny, you know the second one's growing much more slowly than the first. We told you last week that we might need to get them out early.'

She nodded.

'I think early is going to mean tomorrow. They'll both be fine, they're big enough, although the little one at least will need to be in special care. Maybe for a week or so.'

Susanna smiled at Jenny. 'I'll let you get dressed,' she said, 'then I'll explain everything to you about what will happen.'

'Thanks,' said Tim, and made his way back to his consulting room. Susie was a first-class doctor, he thought. Finishing her specialist training later in life, that couldn't be easy. Though it wasn't that late; she was still a good-looking woman. He wondered if Henry had asked her out yet. Since their conversation in the tearoom he'd noticed how flustered Henry became whenever Susie was around. Something she must have noticed for herself. Come to think of it, she was certainly looking well today. And – had she done something new to her hair?

Tim's thoughts swung back to his conversation with Leslie Fernando. Why exactly did the Inspector want to see him? A statement could easily be taken by one of the detectives Tim had met on Sunday night up in the rainforest. Tim's part in the drama, as Leslie had said, had been minor.

He recalled that first time he'd met Leslie. More than three years ago now. In the Emergency Department of the hospital, where Tim had been called by the ED registrar.

'There's a girl here you need to see,' the registrar had said on the phone. 'Bad vaginal injury. Rape case. We're getting the social workers and the sexual assault team, but she needs some gynae attention straight away ... could you come down?'

Tim had felt it again. That sharp pain high in the stomach. He usually managed to avoid rape cases, which were handled by his female colleagues. However, if there were major injuries admitted on his shift, he'd have to deal with them.

He'd been in the Birth Suite when he'd taken the call. He made his way down the stairs to ED, still in his surgical blues. By the nursing desk were the registrar, a policewoman and a senior detective.

'Dr Ingram?' the detective asked. 'I'm Leslie Fernando. Thanks for coming down so quickly. We understand this young woman's quite badly injured and will need some surgery. But we're hoping to get a report of the injuries as soon as you're able.'

'Yes,' said Tim. 'I'll see her right away. But if she's going to theatre, which sounds likely, I won't have a report until we've finished there. Probably tomorrow.'

'That's fine.' Leslie Fernando handed him his card. 'Please call me when you can.'

The girl was Chinese. She was in her early twenties, and despite the grit, tears and blood smudging her high cheekbones, exquisitely beautiful. She lay absolutely still, staring at the wall. Her sister, also very distressed, sat stroking her shoulder beneath the sheets.

'She speaks English,' said the sister. 'She understands you, but just now she does not want to speak. You must speak to me.'

The history was brief. The girl had been at the bus stop at the university soon after six o'clock, when the library closed. She was studying English there. After a long wait for a university bus that did not arrive, she had started to walk towards the highway, with the idea of getting a suburban bus into town. By then it was getting dark. On an isolated part of the road she'd been dragged into a car by two 'Australian' men and taken to swampland behind the beaches north of Smithfield, where she'd been raped by both men. There had also been injuries inflicted with a beer bottle. Her attackers had thrown her into the scrub and driven off. She'd crawled first onto the dirt road leading from the swamp, and then all the way to the main road, where eventually a motorist had found her. She was, the Emergency nurse said, bleeding quite heavily.

Her sister, taking charge of the situation, spoke rapidly to her in Chinese. With a slight inclination of her head toward Tim, she agreed to be examined. Tim had already been told she had numerous lacerations and bruises on her arms and legs, but no fractures.

He was appalled by her injuries. One long vaginal tear at the front led upwards toward the bladder, another at the back toward the bowel. They would need careful exploration and suturing under general anaesthetic in theatre. Quietly, Tim explained what needed to be done: some samples taken, the girl's clothes bagged for later forensic examination, then she must be taken to theatre. When did she last eat? Later, arrangements would be made for support and counselling, and finally, for the police to interview her.

Outside the cubicle, there was sudden shouting, raised Asian voices, 'No, no, let me see her, I must see her, let me in …' The girl sat bolt upright and spoke rapidly in Chinese to her sister.

'It's her boyfriend, her fiancé,' said the sister to Tim. 'Of course she cannot see him. Not now. Not ever. She is too ashamed.'

'Oh no, not never,' Tim replied. 'She will need lots of support, and love, but just now she must go to the operating theatre.'

'No. Because of our culture, she will feel too much shame. She cannot see him, she cannot be married now.'

Tim felt out of his depth. He said: 'The staff will be asking him to wait anyway, while they get her ready for theatre.'

He stepped out of the cubicle. He was badly in need of some fresh air. He saw the boyfriend being shepherded into the supervisor's office, clearly distressed, weeping and angry, struggling in the hold of two friends.

He crossed the ED waiting room where the TV screen beamed an American hospital drama over the waiting public slumped on plastic chairs. At the door, the ED registrar joined him, shaking his head.

'Shocking injuries … difficult to repair, I imagine?'

'Physically, it should be all right, though the bladder may be a problem. Psychologically and emotionally … maybe not. How could you ever be counselled into accepting that?

'Yeah, you're right. And you know what, I think we've got one of the blokes who did it in here too.'

'What?'

'Yeah, the cops came in with the ambulance. The story is, he and his mate stole a car at Smithfield then dragged her into it. They were high as kites on something. After they threw her out, they crashed the car on the Yorkey's Knob road. The other bloke managed to run off but this one hit the dashboard and fractured his femur. The orthopods are looking after him. I put him in the single room down the corridor. Nancarrow's his name. There's another cop guarding him. I told the cop, don't worry mate, he's not going anywhere with that leg.'

'Well … I'm going outside for a minute, for a breather.'

Tim stepped out into the cool night air. A police car with Leslie Fernando and the woman constable in it was just pulling away from the kerb. By the Emergency entrance the pale flowers of a frangipani tree glowed in the darkness. Tim stood in the shadow of the tree and the perfume wafted around him. There was that pain again. Behind him he heard the fiancé and his friends emerge, speaking heatedly. Though part of the conversation was in Chinese, Tim understood instinctively.

'Man, you'll have to wait to see her, like the nurse said. She's got to be stitched up. You know she just didn't want to see you now. She'll get over that.'

'I'll kill him, kill him!'

'Yeah, this is Australia, man, just cool it, you're not killing anybody. The cops will find him, take him to court. We know how you feel but just cool it now.'

The three crossed to the parking lot, climbed into a late-model Mazda, sat and lit cigarettes.

Tim stood in the darkness, reflecting. Cops, courts, social workers, counsellors … was that going to be good enough? He thought again, of Chris. Of their last days in Port Moresby, soon after they'd been married. It was seven years ago now, and still they thought of it every day. Tim stood a while longer, thinking, before turning back into the hospital and making his way to the operating theatre and the girl.

Now, as he worked his way through the morning's clinic, three years on, Tim's mind kept turning back to the events of that night. He'd written the report the police had requested, and had personally taken it to Sheridan Street, where he'd met briefly with a young detective constable who'd taken a routine statement. Tim confirmed that he'd first seen the girl in Emergency, had treated her in the operating theatre, and was still caring for her now in the hospital ward.

Then the constable had said: 'Doctor, Detective Fernando, who you met the other night, wants me to ask you one more question. Did you at any time during that night meet Kaine Nancarrow?'

Tim had frowned. 'Who?'

'Nancarrow. That's the man charged with the girl's assault. Well, one of them. He was in the Emergency Department as well that night.'

'I believe he was brought up to the operating theatre after we had finished our case. But no, I didn't see him there, or in Emergency, or at any other time.'

'You didn't speak to him?'

'No, I had nothing to do with him at all. The orthopaedic surgeons were looking after him, not me.'

'OK, thanks, Doctor. That's all. We really appreciate your help. Shouldn't have to bother you again.'

Tim had made a brief appearance in court. He was asked again, by the defence, whether he had seen Nancarrow that night. He had replied, truthfully, that he had not. Nancarrow and his mate were convicted of rape and grievous bodily harm and sentenced to eight years. Not long enough, in Tim's opinion.

He had not seen Leslie Fernando for years, or thought much about that case. Now he'd had a personal call from the Inspector, who seemed to remember him quite well, and who wanted to talk about the woman in the rainforest. Was he just planning to ask him about the events of last Sunday? Or was he also going to bring up that night in the Emergency Department, three years ago?

Cairns, 2 March 2011

Cass dropped off Odile Janvier's dental records to Leah Rookwood. Then she drove to the post office in Bungalow. A post-office box key and tag had been found in the Earlville house. The key fitted easily into box 113C, but there was little of interest inside. *Paris Match* and French *Vogue*, circulars, bills for electricity and mobile phones. No personal mail. Looking at the postmarks and dates, Cass confirmed the mail hadn't been collected for at least three weeks.

Back at the station, she got herself another coffee and took a moment to look at her phone. There was a text from Jordon: *gran called, bella had her puppies she said do u want one???* She texted back *not possible* and had just sat down at her desk when her phone rang. It was Leah.

'The woman is definitely Odile Janvier,' she told Cass.

'Right,' Cass replied, at the same time noting an incoming message on her mobile. 'Now we can let the sons know, and then we can go public. Hopefully we'll get some tips.' She opened the message – no text, just a photo of a very small, very new and very cute dog that was clearly at least half border collie. She texted again *not possible sorry*i, turned off the mobile and was soon on her office phone calling interstate.

Hobart Police would contact Damian. The prison

manager in Wellington would talk to Dominic.

An hour later, Cass took a call from Damian Janvier in Hobart.

'I've just heard about my mother,' he said quite calmly. 'And that my father is missing. I've spoken to my boss and he's giving me time off so I can come up north. I'll be there on Friday evening. Is that soon enough? Is there anything I should do before then?'

'Are you in touch with your brother?' asked Cass.

Damian hesitated a moment then said: 'Well, you probably know this anyway – he's in jail. In New South Wales. We only have contact when he can call me and only for a few minutes. We talked last week. I should go and visit him on my way up to Cairns.'

'Yes,' said Cass. 'I think that's a good idea. Do that, and then come in and see us on Saturday morning. It looks like we'll be working through the weekend on this.'

Once Odile Janvier's identity had been made public, information began to trickle in. Late afternoon, Drew held a meeting to gather everything they knew so far. Leslie sat in on this.

'Michel Janvier first,' Drew said. 'The man is missing and probably has been away from home since at least 29 January. But he has not touched any of his known bank accounts, nor apparently has he left Australia. Troy, tell us what you know about his record.'

Troy had been making inquiries through Interpol. Janvier

had first come to Australia in 1975, when he was twenty. There were charges of fraud against him in France.

'He ran away from them, all the way to Western Queensland. The charges were later withdrawn by the complainant. So there's not much detail on the records about what happened. Anyway, he stayed here three years and got citizenship. Then he returned to France. Worked there for a while. Then – this is more interesting – he gets a conviction in 1981 for attempted blackmail involving a relative. Suspended sentence. A year later he marries and comes back to Australia and has apparently lived here ever since. No further convictions in Australia or elsewhere that I can find. The family in France is well-off and seems well respected. They live in a place called St André, his hometown.

'We've got his tax records from the Earlville house,' said Drew. 'Last tax return was in 1995 when he claimed an income of $20,000 from part-time work as a cleaner. After that he seems to have dropped under their radar. Nevertheless, as we know, around $4000 a month is going into his bank account from a Paris bank.

'Odile Janvier has a tax file number but she is only recorded as having worked as a receptionist for a few weeks in 1995. Otherwise she's never paid tax. When she was employed she worked for Hewitt Constructions.'

Leslie looked up. 'She worked for Jim Hewitt?' he asked.

'Well, for the company,' Drew replied.

'Interesting,' Leslie remarked. 'I wonder if Jim knew her?

Anyway, go on about the husband. Michel.'

'He owns his supposed business premises outright,' Drew went on. 'Pays his council rates on the Earlville house and the Portsmith unit in cash. Unusual, eh? Conducts no visible business. Seems to have no employees or business associates and certainly none who have missed him. Has two sons who seem to have had nothing to do with him or their mother for a considerable amount of time.'

'He lives an apparently quiet life in suburban Cairns with his wife, respected by his neighbours,' Cass put in. 'Insofar as they know anything at all about him, which they admit they don't, really.'

'Looks like he spends a lot of time body building,' Drew commented. 'Has no known friends and apparently no business associates. He does seem to have some interest in bushwalking and that may hold a clue. He has maps of the Davies Creek area and bushwalking gear, but he has maps also of every bushwalking area in Far North Queensland.

'Despite being a fitness freak,' he added, 'Michel Janvier is a heavy smoker. There's an overwhelming smell of tobacco in that shed. Not weed, just tobacco. Lots of discarded butts in wastepaper baskets and ashtrays. Smokes Philip Morris. There are cartons of them at the back of the shed.

'We know a lot of cigarette butts were found in the mud close to the road, near where the body was found. Disintegrated but identifiable. Probably at least ten butts. We're waiting on the analysis to see if they could be Philip

Morris. There was another one behind the fig tree – between it and the road. Maybe Janvier waited a while behind the tree and then longer at the road after tying up his wife. If it was Janvier ... Or maybe he was arguing with her in the car before he killed her. If he killed her.'

Detective Barwen had been given the task of sorting through the small collection of pornvideos also found in the shed. He rolled his spaniel eyes.

'Nothing too way-out,' he said. 'Some Lolita porn. Completely hairless waxed dolls, hopefully in their twenties but made up and with pigtails like thirteen-year-olds. Tiny tits like strawberries. All of it heterosexual. Pretty ordinary stuff; what you'd expect in Earlville. Nothing weird.'

'There were handcuffs and a couple of whips in the main bedroom, the woman's bedroom,' said Drew. 'But this stuff is everywhere these days, like Troy said. There's a dozen adult shops in Cairns that would sell it to you. I don't know that it's got much significance.'

'So not many leads in any of this,' said Leslie. 'But this man, who may or may not have killed his wife, and who may or may not have been killed himself, has totally vanished, together with a white four-wheel drive. Apart from the cigarette butts, which may or may not be his, there's no trace of him in the area around where his wife was found, or of his car. An alert for the car went out yesterday but so far it hasn't been picked up.'

Cass had spoken to the prison director in Wellington. Dominic had been there for the last year, they said. No doubt about that.

'Definitely there since Christmas. He's actually a model prisoner. Studying and working. So we can rule out Dominic as being involved in whatever has happened.'

'But I don't think we can rule out an associate,' Drew pointed out. 'He might have organised a mate to do it. Bearing in mind, for example, that with both parents dead the two sons would inherit the two properties. Probably two-fifty or three hundred thousand bucks for Earlville, and maybe a hundred for Portsmith. Dominic himself with a perfect alibi. Damian probably with a good one as well, since he lives in Tassie.'

'Yeah, Damian is getting together an account of himself for the week before Yasi,' Cass said. 'He told me that he hasn't been out of the state since last September, when he went to see his brother and holidayed in Sydney with his girlfriend. He works Wednesdays to Sundays in the restaurant in Hobart, except in January he also worked Tuesdays because they were short-staffed. His girlfriend does the same. They live together and usually go to her family out of Hobart on their days off. He'll probably have good confirmation of all of that from several people.'

'And if he has,' said Drew, 'while he might have had time to fly to Cairns and back from Hobart, pausing long enough to take his mother up to Davies Creek and tie her up, and be given an alibi by the girlfriend, could he have also disposed of his father and the car? Hard to believe. Or at least he'd have needed an accomplice. I gather he didn't seem too distressed by his mother's passing, when you spoke to him, Cass?'

'No, he didn't,' she answered. 'But he didn't sound indifferent either. And we know he'd left home years ago. On the phone he sounded, um, intelligent, straightforward. A nice guy who's had some not very good news. We can see for ourselves on Saturday. Although from what Dr Symonds said in her report, Dominic might have wanted his mother dead, Damian seems to have just decided to get on with his life.'

There'd been several calls from members of the general public who'd known Odile or Michel Janvier at one time or another. But none shed any light on what might have happened to them.

Michel had been a member of a gym in central Cairns until four years ago.

'The manager's a guy called Brett,' said Drew. 'He called in and we talked. I know Brett, went to school with him, he's been manager there for years. He remembered Janvier well. Said he was a fanatic. Spent several hours a day on solo work. Never talked to any of the other regulars much. He quit after an argument with Brett because he was in the habit of going outside for a smoke and standing close to the club's door. Others complained and Brett asked him – politely he says – to move away from the front of the gym while smoking. Not good for the image, clients don't want to be breathing in smoke when they are coming and going, etcetera, etcetera. Janvier became very het-up, quite aggressive, threatened violence but as soon as the police were mentioned he shut up, left and never went back. I got the impression that Brett wasn't too unhappy with that. But he hasn't seen him since and he doesn't know anyone else who might have.'

Bob Willis, who managed a cattle station to the west of Cairns, was pretty sure he had worked with Janvier in 1977 when he was in his early twenties. 'But he called himself Mick January then,' he'd told Barwen. 'What I remember is that there was something not quite right about his story. He was supposed to have a scholarship from the French government or something to study in Australia but then he'd decided he wanted to stay and live in the outback. He was quite good with his hands – we worked together building a house on the property – and he told me he'd picked up some building skills in Cairns. Then one day the local cop from Normanton turned up about something quite minor, an unregistered vehicle or whatever, and Mick just shot through. Blokes evading the law, the tax department, wives and girlfriends, is just run-of-the mill out there. I hadn't given Mick another thought until I saw his photo on the telly and it hit me – that's the bloke I knew.'

A French teacher from Baptist College had told Barwen that she'd known the couple briefly.

'They participated in some activities many years ago, barbecues for our French national day, things like that, but they didn't really socialise much.

'She's not a teacher. I don't believe she even finished

secondary school in France. She had a small job speaking French to students at Baptist, before I was working here. She was asked to leave. I don't know why. Maybe because of their children. Expelled from two private schools, including Baptist, at least the older one was. For drugs. He'd been suspended from the high school for the same thing. I hear he went to jail. It doesn't surprise me.'

Tom Stewart from the Friends of the Bush walking club had spoken to Leslie. 'Michel Janvier was in the group years ago,' he said. 'Sort of – he wasn't very communicative. A solitary character who never really fitted in. We're a pretty convivial group as you know, so we found him hard-going on a four or five hour walk. Once he went up Bartle Frere alone, to stay the night. Took a tent. A guy rope snapped and broke his finger and he had to walk back out alone next day, having the spent the night in a lot of pain, I imagine. We told him he should follow the rules – walking with others, letting people know where he was going. He didn't seem to appreciate the advice. We saw him less and less although I did see him a few times out walking with his sons. On Glacier Rock once. That would be twelve years ago at least. I never met his wife.'

'So he might well have known the way into the rainforest road at Davies Creek,' Drew now said.

'And so might his sons,' Cass put in. Leslie nodded.

Amy, the manager of Louise's Hair Salon, told Cass she was shocked to hear what had happened. She'd known Mrs

Janvier. 'I've done her for the past three years,' she said. 'She seemed like a very nice person. Talked about her garden, about fashion. She seemed to know who's who in Paris fashion, like she went there often, knew people there.'

'Did she actually say she went to Paris at any time? To France?'

Amy thought for a moment. 'Well,' she said, 'you know how it is. You talk to clients to pass the time. About everything and nothing. I don't think she did ever say she'd been there in the time I was doing her hair. She had colour every two weeks and a treatment. Eyebrow wax and shaping every week. And facials. She uses a lot of makeup, always the best. At least – she did – Clarins, Chanel, Lancôme. And she has such beautiful clothes. I never saw her in the same outfit twice. So different from most women in Cairns. You got the feeling that getting dressed each day was a big performance. I got the impression that she had a lot of friends and a hectic social life. She was always wanting her hair to look exactly right, like for some special occasion – she'd often come in twice during the week for a shampoo and blow-dry and style. But no, I don't recall her going away for any length of time.

'We were really surprised when she didn't turn up for her appointments earlier in the month. She never gave us a phone number so we couldn't text her. It's awful to think she couldn't come because she was *dead*.'

'It's weird,' Cass now said to her colleagues, 'that she seemed to spend so much time on her appearance yet had no friends, no visitors to the house, no-one apparently wondering where she was when she went missing four weeks ago, apart from her hairdresser.'

'Have you contacted the psych yet?' Leslie asked her. 'Dr Symonds?'

'I called the consulting rooms,' said Cass. 'They're over in Lake Street. There's a recorded message saying that she's away till next Monday and if there's a medical emergency to contact the hospital. But I'll try to track down her mobile number and see if I can get hold of her that way.'

'Yes,' said Leslie, 'it would be good to get her impression of the family dynamics, even if it's from some years ago. Especially what she thinks about the older son's attitude to his mother.'

Leslie's phone rang.

'Di at switch, Inspector. I have Dr Tim Ingram here for his appointment with you.'

'Please send him up.' Leslie looked at Drew.

'I don't want to interfere with the way things are going,' he said, 'but I'd just like a few words with Ingram. Having met him on that other case.'

'That's fine, Sir.'

Cass returned to her desk with the intention of tracking down Lyndall Symonds. She would try the hospital, see if she could get a mobile number. She noticed three messages on her mobile, all from Jordon. Three more photos of the dog. Which was very cute. But in a North Cairns two-bedroom unit? Well it was ground-floor and had a tiny garden. But no … She texted back *yes nice dog but still not poss mum*. As she turned to call the hospital, she glanced at the police intranet, to see that an hour earlier a white Audi A5 registered in the name of Wilfred Lam had been driven at high speed off a cliff on the Port Douglas road. Right now police divers were extracting a single body from the wreckage.

Tim was happy to accept the Inspector's offer of tea. It had been a long afternoon in theatre. Now he sat in a comfortable chair, with a splendid view of the Inlet and the mountains toward Yarrabah.

'You knew that forest road, I take it,' Leslie began. 'You'd been on it before?'

'Yes, I had. I know it's private land, water catchment. But it's a beautiful drive and goes right through to Lake Morris and the dam. We've done it a few times.'

'And it was you who decided to go on the road on Sunday?'

Tim hesitated a moment. There was a deliberation in Leslie Fernando's voice that hadn't been there before. And he could see his hesitation had not escaped the Inspector's notice.

'No,' he said finally. 'It was my wife's idea. I thought the road might be blocked by fallen trees. I didn't really think about the bridge.'

'Hmm. So how did you come to find the body? I

understand it was quite well concealed behind trees.'

'It was the smell, Inspector. A particular type of putrefaction. I knew it from a case I was involved in once, in Moresby. It's unforgettable.'

Ah, that piece of the jigsaw fits after all, thought Leslie. 'And your wife?' he asked. 'Did she see the body?'

'No. I had a pretty good idea of what I might find so I told her to wait on the road.'

'I see. Just one other question. The creek. It was flowing quite fast?'

'It was. A bit more than a metre deep, I'd say. I tested the bridge. Thought it was OK. We were very lucky.'

'So if someone had fallen into that creek, or somehow ended up there, they would have been swept downstream?'

'When we were there? Yes, I think they could have been. And just after the cyclone, the water would have been completely over the bridge, the current would have been stronger then. Ah, do you think that's what happened? To another person? Someone connected to the woman? Her killer?'

'At the moment we're still pursuing several lines of inquiry. And of course searching the area very thoroughly; you may have seen that on the news. We really don't know yet what's happened. But we intend to find out. Thanks again for your time.'

Tim made his way out of the Inspector's office. He decided to take the stairs at the side of the building, which gave a good view over the mountains to the south of the city, right down to Walsh's Pyramid. On the first landing, as the sun was sinking behind the mountains, he stopped to take in the view. And to think, again. About that night in ED. The Chinese girl. And about Chris and what happened. Their last days in Port Moresby.

It was ten years ago now, and still they thought of it every day.

Port Moresby, September 2001

Tim was in the leprosy ward of the Moresby hospital when his phone rang. He always did a round there in the mornings.

He'd been looking at Ubi Warenga's foot; the plaster had just been cut off and to the great delight of Ubi's wantoks, maggots had been found wriggling in the wound. There were screams of laughter as hard brown feet squashed the maggots onto the cement floor. Tim had been appalled the first time he'd seen them; he was fresh from the antiseptic wards of Australia then. Pretty soon he realised maggots do their job well. Apart from a little slough, the wounds were clean.

He had walked out into the Papuan sunlight to answer the phone.

'Tim!' Chris spoke slowly, grasping at the words. 'Please just come home now. Don't ask. Just come.'

Oh God, he thought, she's having another miscarriage.

'Just hold on there love, I'm coming now.'

Damn, damn, he thought, as he reversed the car out into the highway, narrowly missing a small girl with a cooking pot on her head. I should never have brought her here.

But she'd wanted to come. They'd spoken enthusiastically about it at home before he'd signed the contract. They'd studied Pidgin language books and read about the Kokoda Track. 'I'm fed up,' he'd told her, 'of eternally filling in forms and putting in drips. This isn't why I went to medical school. I want to go somewhere I can really use my medicine, feel that I'm doing some good.'

Chris had understood. She was eager to come. She wouldn't be able to work, as ex-pat nurses couldn't get work permits, so they'd hoped to start a family. But after two miscarriages, she was six weeks pregnant again, and she was anxious and depressed.

He swung off the highway and down the track leading to their townhouse. On the left was one of the country's oldest squatter settlements, the huts of rusting iron camouflaged with dripping bougainvillea, papaw and mango trees. Chris sometimes took the children food.

She was sitting upright on the bed, white-faced, hair dishevelled, nightdress torn, lip bleeding.

'Darling … my God, what's happened?'

'I've been raped. He came from the bathroom.'

He got her into the car and back to the hospital. A private room was found. An Indian colleague, a gentle elderly man, examined her and confirmed the assault. So far the pregnancy was unaffected. But she wept into Tim's shoulder.

'Oh God, I feel so dirty, to have had him touch me there … the baby, everything that was ours … he's just destroyed …'

Later, Tim held her hand as Sergeant Arua made laborious notes. Chris had torn a piece of blue and white checked cloth from the man's shirt as she'd struggled. She thought she'd seen him before, maybe in the squatter settlement. He was certainly a Highlander, not much taller than herself, but squat and solid. Barefoot and armed with a knife that tapered to a fine point, which he'd held at her throat with one hand while the other kneaded her breast. No, she hadn't answered the door to him, today or any other day.

It seemed to Sergeant Arua that the man had watched the house, noting Tim's regular departure time; knew Chris was alone. This was the third case of rape in the area this month, said the sergeant.

'We'll leave, go home,' Tim told her, when the Papuan policeman had respectfully departed. 'Straight away, within a week – there's no need for you ever to go back to the house.'

'But your contract, and your patients … there's no-one else to do the work.'

'That doesn't matter.'

Toward evening, Sergeant Arua rang from the police station. The suspect had been arrested, could Tim please come down. When he arrived, the sergeant was smiling widely.

'Doc, he was still wearing the same shirt with the piece missing. Chimbu – from the settlement. Bad, bad people. Come with me, I'll take you down to the cells.'

The sergeant stood up, and Tim realised with a rush that he was about to see the man who had raped Chris. The tight feeling he'd had in his stomach since morning suddenly expanded into nausea. He followed the sergeant down a concrete corridor that stank of urine and lysol.

In a small windowless room he saw a terrified Highlander, with matted hair and a ring-pull from a San Mig can in each earlobe. So terrified he'd pissed all over his shorts. Terrified because he was being held by two constables. Blood trickled from a graze at the corner of his mouth.

The sergeant chuckled. 'Right doc, five minutes. My boys will hold him for you. Just don't break any bones.'

It took Tim a moment to understand. Then the nausea swept over him again. Christ, payback. The sergeant expected Tim to beat the man. Of course, Bomana Prison was a joke: three meals a day, cigarettes, wantoks in other cells, no punishment at all. But he hadn't foreseen this.

The constables clearly expected it of him. Looking at Tim, towering above the prisoner, they didn't see an idealistic young doctor who'd come from Australia to help the people of Papua. They saw a white man whose wife had been raped and who surely expected revenge. And the prisoner, he expected it too.

Is this what Chris would want? She'd been concerned about the squatters' hovels, the sickness of the children. But how did she feel after this morning?

Tim hit him first on the chin. The man winced, but didn't cry out. The nausea grew worse, then suddenly was replaced by hot rage. 'You bastard, black bastard!' Tim shouted. He hit him again, on the head, in the chest, tearing checked shreds from his shirt. He was dimly aware of a cut over one eye and blood running from his dark nostrils. Then, blindly striking out again, he felt himself held by one of the constables.

'Doctor – enough, enough … we don't want too many marks, his wantoks are outside …'

Dazed, Tim let himself be led by a constable back to the car park. In the dimness, he glimpsed white flowers of a frangipani tree. The air was fragrant with their perfume. He fumbled for his keys, climbed into the car. Then, as the policeman left, he leant out and vomited, again and again, beneath the clear Papuan night.

That Moresby experience was on his mind the night the Chinese girl came to Emergency. When, under another frangipani tree, he watched Detective Fernando and the policewoman drive away. He'd been thinking about his life here in Cairns. How it had all worked out in the end. He was in his final year of specialist training. He and Chris were the parents of two healthy girls. She was nursing three days a week, and he had every prospect of a good consultant post here next year; Henry had assured him of this. Moresby was the past, wasn't it?

Tim turned back into the hospital that night. He made his way to the operating theatre. He'd done his very best, professionally, for the Chinese girl.

But first, he crossed to the parking lot, put his head through the window of the Mazda, and spoke quietly to the Chinese boys.

Sydney, 2 March 2011

Henry threw the stick as far as he could across the park. The dog raced after it.

'Come on, boy!' he called, and the labrador obligingly bounded back, dropping the stick at his feet. 'Good boy, Fred,' he said, patting the dog's head.

They'd done this now at least fifteen times. Henry didn't know much about dogs but he felt he'd fulfilled Emma's instructions about a good workout for Fred, who otherwise spent most of his day in the small back garden of his daughter's North Sydney townhouse.

He clipped the lead onto Fred's collar. Perhaps they'd manage a couple of circuits of the oval before going home.

He'd not only promised Emma dog-walking, he'd also promised dinner. She was a lawyer in the Attorney-General's office, and tonight she had a late meeting. This morning, grabbing her laptop and pecking him affectionately on the cheek, she'd asked, 'What about your risotto, Dad?'

He had only a few recipes but the asparagus and lemon risotto was well rehearsed. He'd spent the early afternoon shopping, making the stock for the risotto and preparing a marinade for two barramundi fillets now in Emma's fridge. It was good to be able to cook for two sometimes.

Which brought him back, immediately, to Dr Susanna Ortega. Not that she'd been very far from his mind at any waking moment since he'd been in Sydney. Well, at any time at all in the past four weeks.

He'd mulled over the advice Tim had given him. Thought about what he should do. Then, in the end, it had all happened very fast.

There'd been several difficult theatre cases that Dr Ortega had managed very well on her own. Henry planned to find her alone for a moment and compliment her on these. That would be a start. In his mind he practised this conversation. But somehow it took more than three weeks to get to the point. Well, the cyclone had taken up a lot of time. Then the previous Thursday, he'd almost stuffed it up completely. Seeing her alone in Recovery, writing up the notes after a challenging caesar, he slipped alongside her. She looked up, surprised.

'I just wanted to say how well you handled that,' he began. She flushed with pleasure at her boss's praise. 'Thank you,' she said.

'I was thinking, perhaps, a little celebration? We've all worked so hard these last couple of weeks, since Yasi.'

'You mean, something for all the registrars? Drinks somewhere?'

'No no,' said Henry hastily. 'I was thinking, er, of, just yourself. And me. Dinner, er, actually. Somewhere. I hear there's a nice place at Trinity Beach. L'Unico.'

After a moment's hesitation she said yes, she'd love to come, but she reminded him that he was starting two weeks' leave that weekend. And she was on call for the weekend. Henry was about to back away, cowed, when she said:

'But tonight is possible ...'

So before he'd had time to worry about it they had a reservation at L'Unico and he was picking her up, in the Peugeot he'd bought in Cairns but hardly ever had occasion to drive, since he lived practically next door to the hospital, and they'd sat beside the sea and talked non-stop, first of all about the weather, the cyclone and all that had happened with it, then about work, about rainforest walks, about visiting the northern beaches, and then as they moved onto their second glass of merlot (like him she preferred red, and she knew a lot about Chilean wines) about divorce, and how difficult it was, and the loneliness that followed. And then dessert was finished and he was driving her home, wondering what was to come, and whether he should have self-prescribed himself some Cialis, just in case; after all, it had been four years. Four bloody years ... because of that woman and her tricks. The injustice of it.

But at her gate she leaned over in the front seat of the car and kissed him quickly, but hard, on the cheek, then said: 'Henry I've really enjoyed the evening and I'd love to get to know you better. But it's going to have to wait until you get back from leave.'

Then she was out of the car and waving, and the last thing he remembered seeing was her hair, which had been demurely piled on her head at dinner, falling down over her shoulders as she swung the gate behind her. The memory of it now brought a rush of blood to his loins; he felt he probably wouldn't need the Cialis after all.

He had planned to spend his leave in Sydney, with Emma and friends from his many years in practice there. Yet all he could think of now was Susie's laugh, and her hair falling to her shoulders as she swung the gate shut.

How could he possibly tell her? he'd asked Tim that Sunday night before Yasi hit. They'd been sitting in Henry's office going through the perinatal charts. It had turned out to be quite easy to talk to his younger colleague. He'd told Tim there'd been a misunderstanding, that he'd been compromised. And in the end, he told him about the money.

Tim had given good advice, at least in regard to Susanna. In regard to the money issue, what he'd suggested sounded just too dangerous.

'Just be upfront about it,' he'd said immediately, of Susanna. 'Stuff happens. You've been married and divorced, so has she. Obviously there have been other things in your life. In hers too, I'm sure. Write her a letter, a nice letter, if you feel you've got to get it off your chest.

'But,' he'd added, 'I'd keep it brief.'

It was a plan, and Henry had already composed several brief letters in his head, and discarded them all. Now, as he walked the oval at the end of Fred's lead, words began to form more clearly in his brain.

A short description of the unfortunate events. Of his misunderstanding of the woman's purpose. Of his subsequent compromise. Of the involvement of money. Of his inability to change the situation. Of his hope that this would not mar the prospects of a possible relationship. *Mar*, he liked that word.

It was past six o'clock.

'Home, Fred,' he said. The animal trotted obediently beside him along the well-manicured street that led to Emma's house. A series of young men, all in Henry's view quite inadequate for his daughter, had passed through her life in the previous few years, but at present she seemed perfectly happy with Fred's sole company. She'd made it very clear some time ago to her obstetrician father that she had no interest in children, and that he should nurture no expectations in this direction.

He let Fred out into the garden and, in keeping with Emma's instructions, measured out the scientifically-balanced dry food that suburban canines apparently required these days. He then returned to the kitchen, washed his hands thoroughly, donned an apron, and found a deep frying pan. He poured himself a good measure of Scotch to assist with the cooking of the risotto. He flicked the television on so he could watch the evening news when it began.

The rice turned golden in the bottom of the pan. He chopped asparagus and garlic, sliced lemons. It was important to do things slowly with this risotto. He added the bubbling stock one spoon at a time. Occasionally he looked up at the television.

Egypt was in ferment, but Obama was being reticent about support for the protesters. He took a sip of the Glenfiddich Emma had given him. She was a thoughtful girl. The frypan sizzled. There was more trouble in Pakistan.

But Henry was really thinking about his letter. 'Not mar the prospects.' That was a good phrase. 'Compromised.' Yes, he'd been compromised by that woman.

So it took him a moment, when he heard the name 'Inspector Leslie Fernando' on the news, to realise that it was familiar, and to look up and see the camera pan over the Inlet and across Cairns to the Sheridan Street police headquarters, where a poised young blonde woman was interviewing the inspector.

Who had just announced that Odile Janvier was dead.

Paris, 2 March 2011

Lyndall Symonds wheeled her cabin baggage along Terminal 2E at Charles de Gaulle towards Gate 91 and the flight for Singapore. She pulled her mobile from her handbag. She would turn it off while she thought of it. To her surprise it began to ring.

That morning, she and Bernard had got up late. He had no classes to teach until the afternoon. They'd ambled into the village for coffee and croissants then walked back to his cottage, through oak woods still crisp with frost. Later, he'd driven her the ten kilometres into Clermont-Ferrand, and he'd held her tenderly in his arms, making her promise all over again that she would come back soon, before she boarded a high-speed train for Paris. She was still inhaling that odour that was his alone, that she had remembered from so long ago. The smell of arousal, she thought now, remembering how, coming in from the frozen woods that day, he had warmed her hands in front of the stove, and then led her back into the bedroom. She hoped the sensation would stay with her as far as Australia.

He had called her already when she had reached the Gare du Nord and was changing trains for the airport. She hadn't expected another call.

'Hello?' Her voice echoed through a satellite, *hello, hello*. So, not Bernard. This must be from home.

'Oh hello! Dr Symonds? Lyndall Symonds?' It was a woman's voice, crisp, authoritative.

'Speaking.'

'Dr Symonds, this is Detective Cass Diamond from Cairns CIB.'

Lyndall's first thought was that something terrible had happened to one of her children but the woman, no doubt understanding this, quickly went on: 'I'm ringing about a professional matter, not a personal one. I'm sorry to trouble you, especially as it sounds as though you're out of the country.'

'Well, I'm on my way back. I'm at the airport in Paris.'

'Paris!' said Cass. This case was getting more French by the minute. 'I see. Well, um, we were hoping to speak to you about a relative of a former patient of yours who appears to be missing. We don't want to know anything confidential – we're just hoping you might be able to help us locate the missing person.'

Lyndall tried to grasp what this was all about while observing that the line to board her flight was getting shorter with every passing second.

'Can you tell me the name of this person?' she asked.

'Dominic Janvier,' replied Cass. 'We understand that you've treated him in the past.'

'Dominic? I haven't seen Dominic for quite some time. Umm … I really only saw him – as you may be aware – when he was in the Children's Court. But Dominic must be in his mid-twenties by now. I have seen Michel more recently.'

'Michel Janvier? You've seen him recently? How recently? In France?' The detective's voice bounced sharply off the satellite.

'Oh, no, about six months ago, in Cairns,' replied Lyndall, and heard the woman at the other end of the line give a small sigh. *Hmm*, thought Lyndall, *what has Michel been up to now?*

'Yes, six months I think,' she said again. 'He is also my patient. Fairly intermittently, but I have been seeing him for some time. Years. Can you give me some idea what this is about?'

'Obviously in France you won't have heard the news,' said Cass. 'Michel's wife Odile has been found dead.'

Lyndall felt her throat contract. 'Odile Janvier is dead? How? She was killed? Murdered?'

'We're still looking for the answers to those questions,' replied Cass, noting how quickly the doctor had moved to the possibility of murder. 'Which is why I'm calling you. Did you know Odile Janvier? Was she also a patient of yours?'

'Odile? No, never,' said Lyndall, thinking to herself *and thank God for that.* 'No, I've never even met Odile, but I've seen her around Cairns a few times. I know what she looks like. Well, looked like … I certainly know a great deal about her but most of the information I have would be quite old, and also confidential, from her son and her husband. Can I ask what happened to her? Is Michel involved? Where is he?' *Has he been arrested?* she wanted to ask. Obviously something major had happened, though it seemed somehow nosy to ask that outright.

'That's just what we don't know,' said the voice from Australia. 'He's the missing person. He seems to have been missing since the time she died, about three or four weeks ago now. Her body was found in the rainforest outside Kuranda. All the information we have is being broadcast on Australian news sites, if you're able to access the internet.'

'So … she was murdered?' Lyndall asked again. It would not surprise her.

'The body was not … well preserved. We're waiting for the results of further tests. But she had been tied up.'

Lyndall thought for a moment then said: 'Tied up? Not I suppose with a Hermès scarf?'

'What?' Cass was startled. 'You've heard that?'

'No, no. I've been in France for the past six weeks. I've been in a small village in the south, not in Paris, and I've only been in touch with my kids from time to time. So I didn't know any of this. I only asked about the scarf because she wore them, and Michel liked them. So she was strangled? And Michel's disappeared?'

'No, Odile Janvier was not strangled, that I can say, although she was tied up. And yes, he has disappeared, along with his Mitsubishi four-wheel drive. It seems he hasn't left the country, and he hasn't withdrawn any money from his bank accounts.'

'It sounds as though he might be dead too,' said Lyndall, and she was immediately aware that this might sound a little heartless.

'Yes,' said Cass, 'we have come to that conclusion ourselves.'

'And Dominic,' asked Lyndall, 'isn't he in jail somewhere? Or is he out now? And his brother?' She tried to remember what Michel had told her at his last consultation.

'Yes,' said Cass, 'Dominic is in Wellington in New South Wales. He has a rock-solid alibi. His brother is also accounted for – he lives and works in Tasmania. Neither of them seem to have much time for their parents, particularly their mother.'

'No,' said Lyndall, 'that doesn't surprise me. Odile Janvier was a very destructive mother to those boys. If Dominic's turned out badly it's entirely her fault.'

'Madame! Madame!' Lyndall heard a call. She looked up – the final boarding call was flashing, the last passengers were disappearing through the gate, and an irate Air France attendant was indicating that she should join them. Toot sweet.

'Listen, Detective,' said Lyndall, 'I'd better get on this plane or they're going to start offloading my baggage. I'll be back in Cairns on Friday morning, flying in from Singapore. I'll call you then.

'I don't know what I can tell you that might help you,' she continued hurriedly. 'I have no idea where Michel is now or what has happened to Odile. But I do know certain things about the Janviers which would not be confidential and that I can tell you when I'm back in Cairns. And one thing I can say: I think it's very unlikely that Michel murdered his wife.'

With that she said goodbye and hurried towards the boarding gate. God, she needed a drink after that. Toot sweet.

Cairns, 3 March 2011

On Thursday morning, Drew called another meeting to discuss the Janvier case. Cass explained she'd found Lyndall Symonds in Paris on her way back home.

'She's had Michel Janvier as a patient,' she said, 'as well as his son. But she hasn't seen him for about six months and doesn't know where he might be now. One thing she was definite about. She thought Michel was unlikely to have killed his wife. Because of his mental state, I gathered. And she's his psych.'

'Well,' said Drew, 'we all know that most murderers are related to the victim, and most often a partner. I've known more than a few cases where someone who'd never been violent felt provoked to commit a homicide. And this Janvier seems to have a few unusual traits to his character. Never say never, is what I think.'

'Well she'll be back in Cairns tomorrow morning,' Cass said. 'We can hear more then.'

Detectives Barwen and Borgese plus a team of scenes-of-crime officers had spent Tuesday afternoon cataloguing the personal possessions of the Janviers at the Earlville house. This hadn't made them any wiser, either as to the fate of Odile or the whereabouts of Michel.

Cass raised the subject of Wilfred Lam. 'Alive and well yesterday morning,' she said, 'but died instantly when his car plunged into the sea in the afternoon. So whether he could have told us any more we shall never know. I want to go back and talk to his receptionist.'

'OK,' Drew said. 'Before that, go down to the Traffic Branch and talk to the forensic guys in Crash Investigation, see what they think happened. Troy, you and I can keep going through the Earlville material.'

Cass took the two flights of stairs down to talk to the traffic officers dealing with the Lam case. On the way she checked her mobile, finding a text from her son: *can i please borrow car tonite? party at Gordonvale J*. She rapidly texted back, conscious of where she was going that very moment: *only if ur sleeping over no driving back at nite mum.*

'We'd set up a speed trap just north of Ellis Beach,' Constable Dawson told her. 'I was behind a palm tree on a section of straight road, with the camera, and Dan was in the car about 600 metres away. I clocked this new white Audi doing over eighty in the sixty zone. So Dan flashed his lights for him to stop but he just sped up and went straight on. Dan gave chase but, you know that road, Detective, it winds along the coast, only two lanes, carries a lot of traffic. Too likely to kill some innocent driver coming the other way. Plus there's only one way out, just south of Mossman, so Dan got on the radio to the Mossman station for them to pick him up at the other end.

'But then Dan gets another call. White car gone over the cliff just past Wangetti. Y'know the spot where the hang-gliders jump off? Must have been doing more than 100 by then. Lost control, crossed to the other side, fortunately no oncoming traffic. Hit the barrier and rolled right over it. Cliff's seventy, eighty metres high there. Lot of rocks at the bottom. By the time we arrived the car was submerged but I reckon he died as soon as the car hit the bottom if not on the way down.

'Two divers got him out. Well, as much of him as they could.' The constable grimaced; clearly it had been an unpleasant task.

'His son identified him. Not easy for the lad. The son knew that you – well, not you personally, but that police – interviewed his dad yesterday morning. But he has no idea why. And I don't know either so I couldn't help him on that. But it did seem that the sight of a policeman shook Lam up.'

'So what are you thinking, Constable?' Cass asked.

'Well, the Crash Unit will be looking at it closer, but I don't know that it was an accident,' said Dawson emphatically. 'It's possible he planned to write himself off. Maybe it was a sudden decision. He sped up when he saw Dan. Maybe because he didn't want to be stopped and miss his chance. Maybe he really was trying to get away. There were tyre marks right across the other lane at the top of the hill. Maybe he saw there was nothing oncoming? Anyway he turned the wheel hard right and lost control. If he was planning it, he was probably aiming to go over the edge further on, where the crash barrier ends. But he was going so damn fast he did the job anyway.'

Cass finished the morning by typing up her findings so far. In the afternoon she took a car from the pool and made her way to Wilfred Lam's surgery. A tearful Leanne was behind the reception desk.

'I'm really sorry to be coming back under these circumstances,' Cass said, 'but I do have to ask you a few questions.'

Leanne nodded. 'I know, it's not your fault,' she said between sobs. 'It's all something to do with that woman isn't it? She was murdered. I saw it on telly last night. He killed himself because he'd killed her?'

'Hang on,' said Cass. 'What makes you think he killed himself? He was involved in a traffic accident.'

Leanne shook her head. 'I don't think it was an accident,' she said. 'He left me a note saying where his Will was kept. In his lawyer's office in Brisbane.'

'Ah,' said Cass. 'I'll need to see that note. How long after I left here did he leave?'

'He cancelled all his patients for yesterday straight away,' replied Leanne. 'Even the ones in the waiting room. Told me to tell them he wasn't well. It was the truth: he was shaking all over. He sent Rhonda home, that's the nurse. She was as confused as I was. I had to stay to deal with all the appointments. Then he shut himself in his office for about an hour. I was busy on the phone for most of that time. I had no idea what was going on. Then he got up and just left, without another word.

'I closed up about three o'clock. Then last night I saw that they'd identified the woman who was murdered and it was Mrs Janvier. I was in shock at that. I couldn't sleep. This morning really early his son called me to say that his dad had passed away. On the morning news they had pictures of the car. It was horrible. I only found the note this morning. That's when I realised he meant to do it.'

She held out the note for Cass. It was not more than a few words, written by hand, and clearly that hand had been trembling. But it was simply the Brisbane address of his solicitor. It was not a suicide note.

'Did he kill Mrs Janvier?' asked Leanne. 'I just can't imagine he could do such a thing.'

'We don't know yet what happened,' Cass said gently. 'I'm going to take that note and I'm giving you a receipt for it. I must ask you not to touch anything here. In fact I'd advise you to go home and take it quietly for the rest of the day. If the media contacts you I'd recommend that you don't speak to them, but that's up to you. We'll need to conduct a search here, probably later today, but first we'll speak to the family.'

At five o'clock, Cass went back to her apartment on McLeod Street, and changed into her running gear. She badly needed a break from this case. In the kitchen it was clear that Jordon had come in and gone out again. Two-thirds of a chocolate cake and half a loaf of bread had been dispatched. Also a litre of milk and most of the bananas. That was fine. She took a precooked lasagne and an apple pie out of the freezer and put them beside the sink to thaw for dinner. On second thoughts, she added another frozen chocolate cake in case Jordon brought friends back here before the party. Thank God for Sara Lee.

At the back of her mind was a plan to train up for the Sydney half marathon. Leslie was also a runner and he'd told her that 'anyone could do it if they put their mind to it.' It was a matter, he said, of dividing it into do-able bits. Like any job. This was the kind of approach Cass understood. This was how she'd got herself through TAFE when Jordon was just three and Richie was dead. It was how she'd got through university when Jordon was in primary school and she'd been living on a student allowance. (But stop kidding yourself, she thought, you loved uni. Auntie Nell had been right. *You've got the brains for it; you'll find you like it. I never had that chance*, was what she'd said.) It was also how she'd got through the breakup with Rufus and then her police training, and balancing her work with being around for Jordon and keeping him out of teenage trouble. And it was how she'd worked her way to a black belt in tae kwon do.

Divide everything into do-able bits, and then just do each bit in order.

She could run five kilometres easily, she did that several times a week, although so far this week she'd missed out, working overtime on the Janvier case. She'd push herself to eight kilometres today and see how it went. Then aim for ten, working up to fifteen and finally twenty-one. And then? Might she one day attempt a marathon? Start at the beginning, girl, she told herself.

This evening she would run to the Esplanade, then along it. She had often done that, and come back the same way. That was about five kilometres. But today she would go further, along the water, past the convention centre and out along the Portsmith road. Quite near where Michel Janvier's unit must be. That entire area was light industrial. Probably not too many people about now but she felt quite safe going along there. It would not be fully dark for another hour or so. She'd noted that the Portsmith road had a wide verge up until a right turn led back towards the area of Janvier's unit. She could run past the unit and have a look. Running all the way there from the end of the Esplanade, and all the way back, and then home by her usual route should be about eight kilometres. She clipped her mobile onto the waistband of her running shorts together with her water bottle. Jordon might call. She plugged in her iPod and selected Florence and the Machine. With 'Rabbit Heart' streaming into her ears, she set off.

It was still very humid but there was no rain this March evening and a breeze off the water made running a delight. There were children playing on the sand that the council periodically dumped on the mangrove flats to create a beach. Families gathered around barbecues. There were other runners, some serious, some less so. There were couples ambling hand in hand, teenagers on skateboards and mums with strollers. A few black and white ibis wandered across the grass, and out on the water a flock of pelicans rode a gentle swell.

Cass ran at a steady pace. At the end of the Esplanade she passed an impromptu folk and roots band. Tourists were splashing in the shallow pool.

She ran on past the Hilton hotel and along the boardwalk, then back to the footpath beside the convention centre. There was less traffic here, and fewer people were about, although once she reached the end of Sheridan Street and the connecting link to the main Portsmith road there were plenty of commuters in cars heading towards the southern suburbs. Wanting to avoid them, she crossed at the traffic lights and turned into the industrial area. The only traffic here was workers heading home.

She ran on for another few hundred metres, starting to feel the distance a bit now. Her running clothes were soaked in sweat. She slowed and took a few sips from her water bottle then picked up her pace again, matching her stride to the song in her ears, 'Dog Days Are Over'. She was not tired.

She would run all the way to the bridge over the stormwater canal and past Michel Janvier's unit then return.

From behind she heard a car and she moved to the side of the road. It slowed to pass her. A Subaru WRX, jet blue, brand new by the look of it. Tinted windows. With two quite big guys inside. Instinctively the detective in her noted the rego number, and the woman in her looked around – there was no-one else in sight. The car turned right about 100 metres ahead. Probably a security detail checking a factory, she thought. Snazzy car, though. By the time she also took the right-hand turn the car had vanished. Cass ran on – further down this road was the stormwater canal, and by turning right again she'd come back out on the main Portsmith road and could begin her homeward journey.

She was panting by the time she arrived beside the canal next to Janvier's unit. She pulled up short. In the parking spot next to the unit was the blue Subaru. The two men were nowhere to be seen. All her training told her that something was up.

There was a scrawny poinciana tree sprouting beside the canal. She took cover behind this and dialled police headquarters. There was no obvious evidence of anything being amiss here, let alone criminal, but it would be no harm if a squad car checked it out. And she herself would pop across there just as soon as she'd given Di the information.

A car was on its way, Di said.

Cass looked across at Janvier's unit. There was something odd about it. Yes, that was it, there was a small barred window in the side wall. But according to the photos Barwen had showed her there had been no interior window, either in the office or the store. And the building seemed much longer than she'd imagined from the photos – as if there was a room behind the store. But there was no door through there from the office.

So there must be a back room entered from the narrow passage between the units and the warehouse behind it. Maybe a space that didn't belong to Janvier. A wooden gate leading into this passage swung half-open. The passage itself was dark from the shadow of the warehouse. That might be where the Subaru men had gone. Of course they might be innocently checking out some other property in the complex, and if so, the duty cops would just leave them to it.

Cass stepped from behind the tree and silently crossed the bridge. She passed the Subaru and inched around the corner of the building. Cautiously she swung open the gate. And realised – too late – that the men were indeed behind the building. Both were dressed in black. They were in the act of cutting the bolts on a steel door leading into the back of Janvier's unit. They saw her as she saw them, and they acted at once.

The bigger one – nearly two metres tall and about 100 kilos – was holding part of the lock in his hand and came straight towards her with the clear intention of smashing it into her face. The other one, smaller but not much, and solid, swung around and prepared to help his mate.

Cass had several thoughts at once. The squad car was probably several minutes away. There was probably no-one else here in the complex. These guys were serious and they could seriously hurt her. If she told them she was a detective they probably wouldn't believe her, or even care. She could run, but they might have guns. They did have a car, so they could chase her. She could be dead before the squad car arrived.

She needed to take some action. Immediately.

Tae kwon do was technically non-contact but a black-belt holder was expected to have a few tricks up the sleeve of her neatly pressed uniform. As the first guy advanced on her wielding a sharp piece of lock she stepped aside, then performed a double knife-hand strike on his throat, twisting her hand to enhance the technique. The effect was dramatic – he fell to one side, dropped his weapon, and began to vomit. There was no time to lose though: the other guy was lurching towards her. Keeping her arm straight, she closed her fist tight with her thumb around it and brought the first two knuckles into his nose, feeling a deeply satisfying crunch. For good measure she brought her knee hard up into his groin. He screamed and doubled up with pain, staggering away. Sensing that he might come back at her, she grabbed his arm and twisted it behind his back.

'Police!' she got out between clenched teeth. After a few deep breaths she continued: 'Detective Diamond. Don't try anything more, either of you. There's a squad car on its way and they've got your car number. Breaking in, attempted entry, attempted assault of a police officer … you're gonna have a lot of explaining to do, fellas.' She was relieved to hear at that moment the sound of a police siren and a few seconds later the squad car appeared. She dragged the smaller guy towards the gate so the two officers could see her.

'Over here!' she called to the constable getting out of the car. 'I've got them ready for you.' He broke into a run, but she waved at them to stop.

'I caught them cutting the lock, breaking and entering,' she said, when the constables reached her. 'They both tried to attack me. I was forced to defend myself.'

'You took on these two guys?'

The first constable seized hold of the man with the bleeding nose and held him at arm's length. 'Looks like you might have broken something, mate,' he said. 'We'll take you to ED first. Then charge you.' The man said nothing, he was too busy wiping the blood from his face on his sleeve. The vomiter, still on the ground, just growled sadly.

'You're working overtime,' the second constable said to Cass. 'What is this place?' He turned around to look at the building. 'Some kind of warehouse?'

He made as if to enter the building but Cass stopped him.

'I'm not sure what it is,' she said, 'but there's something here that interested these guys, and it's probably going to interest us. Can you give Di at switch a call, see who they can send down. Let Inspector Fernando know, if Drew's not there. He might still be in his office.'

'Jeez,' said the man with the nosebleed, 'we ain't done nothing. We just work for Ji—'

'Shut up!' said the vomiter suddenly. 'Don't say nothing! We don't work for anybody!'

'All right,' said the constable calmly, 'you don't need to say anything apart from who you are. I've some tissues in the car for that nose, and some handcuffs. And when our back-up arrives, we'll take you boys off.'

Leslie arrived within ten minutes, to Cass's great relief. She was feeling pooped after all this excitement. But there was still the question of what was in the building. Soon Troy and Drew arrived, Drew technically off duty, and two scenes-of-crime officers. That was good. If there was something – or someone – in there, they could get to work at once. As the squad car team led the two men away in handcuffs, Cass explained the story briefly to the others.

'They've made our job easy,' said Drew, after the technicians had inspected the door. 'Interesting. It's flush with the wall, that door, and painted the same charming shade of grey so it's quite hard to see even where it is. No signs, no number, no information about what's here. Yet there's a letterbox in that door.'

A wide slit for mail had been cut in the upper third of the door. Leslie pushed the door open, and they went in. It was now nearly dark outside, and there was practically no light coming through the tiny barred window that Cass had noticed. One of the officers flashed on his torch, found a light switch and the room lit up.

The side wall abutting the vacant unit next door was completely covered by a huge video screen. There was a high-quality DVD player on a stand nearby. A laptop was also connected to the viewing equipment. A leather couch was drawn up at a comfortable viewing distance. Against the other three walls were rows of metal shelves, neatly labelled with names and dates. There were Lever Arch files on one shelf, and more stacks of newspapers. There was also a pile of newer shelves, waiting to be put up.

In the far wall, between the rows of shelves, backing onto Janvier's storeroom, was a door. Yet there had been no door visible in the back of his storeroom.

And just inside the entrance was a scattering of buff envelopes. Clearly these had been pushed through the mail slit, and had accumulated over some time.

All were addressed to 'The Controller'.

Paris—Singapore, 2 March 2011

Lyndall settled herself in Business Class as the plane levelled out high above eastern France. She accepted a second glass of an excellent chablis. Flying Business between Paris and Singapore made up for the harsh necessity of the budget airline from Singapore to Cairns, which was the most direct option.

Her thoughts turned, as they did so often now, to Bernard. She was delighted that she'd plucked up the courage to call his mother's number, eighteen months ago now. You're being ridiculous, she'd told herself, you were just a passing fling. He's probably even forgotten your name. He will have moved on, with many more women. Very likely married, maybe has children. And was his mother even still alive and living there?

After two rings the phone had been answered by Madame Maupan, who was in full command of her faculties, had no problem understanding Lyndall's halting French, and told her to wait a moment, her son was visiting and she would call him in from the garden. Within thirty seconds Lyndall was connected to Bernard who not only proclaimed himself delighted to hear from her, but seemed to intuitively understand her situation. When was she coming to France? he asked.

Lyndall had not even considered such a thing till then but suddenly it seemed perfectly reasonable. Her house was for sale. She had emptied it of furniture. She'd bought a new apartment in the centre of Cairns so that she could simply lock up and go whenever she wanted. She had leave due from the hospital and could easily find cover for her private practice for three weeks. Before she knew where she was, she had committed herself to going to France in a fortnight. For three weeks. She had never before set foot in Europe. The United States, Bali and Fiji had been the extent of her overseas travels, and always with Trevor.

In the two weeks before that first visit, as she rushed around renewing her passport, booking flights, arranging her practice, there were flurried email exchanges with Bernard, and then, as they discovered more about each other, increasingly lengthy phone calls.

He had indeed married. He had also divorced, apparently fairly amicably, four years earlier. His ex-wife had custody of their eight-year-old daughter, whom he saw on a regular basis. There had been a number of women since the divorce, including one who'd lasted two years, but she too had moved on. And although there had been someone else recently, that was all done with too.

Lyndall, who was forty-two and had only the same unfaithful husband to report on that she'd had at the time of their Australian liaison, had no illusions about any of this. Bernard was thirty-eight and his emailed photos showed him in the prime of his middle years, still with all his hair and as trim around the middle as he'd been at twenty-six. But she was going to France and if things worked out when she got there, well, she would enjoy it while it was on offer, and accept it philosophically when it ended. And if it didn't work out, well, she was still going to see France.

She'd learnt that Bernard taught music at a lycée in Clermont-Ferrand, as well as having private pupils and playing in a chamber music group. His mother was living in her own apartment in the centre of the city, but, although spry, she was increasingly dependent on him, which was why he'd stayed in his home town, a charming and sophisticated place, Lyndall found, when she eventually had a chance to explore it.

She had expected to book herself into a hotel in Clermont-Ferrand, to stay for a few days, and then travel on her own a bit around France. But Bernard announced that he would come to Paris to meet her, make all necessary arrangements, and show her the French capital when she recovered from her jetlag.

And there he had been, at Charles de Gaulle airport, with a bouquet of lilies and a booking for two rooms in a small and beautiful hotel close to the Palais Royal, with a statue of Molière right outside. A hotel where it quickly turned out that Lyndall's jetlag was not as bad as had been predicted, and only one room was needed, in which a good deal of champagne was available. It was a full twenty-four hours before they re-emerged onto the streets of the city, and Lyndall felt twenty-three again.

Since then she'd been to France four times. Over the eighteen months the relationship had deepened and her French had improved, but she still wondered how long-term it would be. His mother's need for him meant that Bernard could not contemplate coming to Australia, although they'd managed some wonderful weekends in different parts of France. So far it had been very much up to Lyndall to make the long journey between the two countries. And of course she had no idea what he might be doing when she was not there. For the moment though, she was happy just to enjoy things as they were.

She put down her glass and took out her laptop. She must think about what she would say to that detective when she got back to Cairns. She had not given a single thought to Dominic Janvier for years, and very few to Michel outside of working hours. Opening the computer, she created a new folder labelled 'Janvier'. Then she made a new file which she called 'Dominic'. She thought about this for a moment. She then opened another new file, called 'Michel', and began to type into it. She would make notes now, she thought, so that she had it all in order when she arrived home, undoubtedly jet-lagged. If the police were treating Odile's death as a murder they would want information sooner rather than later. She'd need to think about what information she could give them, and what was confidential.

Michel Janvier. Lyndall had first met him at the end of 2000, when he came with Dominic for consultations. It didn't surprise her that it was Dominic's father, not his mother, who brought him along. Odile had been an appalling parent. At the beginning, Michel seemed self-absorbed. It was only after she'd had several meetings with his son that Michel asked if he could see her himself. She'd been reluctant but he'd said he needed help and would see her privately. It was true, he did need help. And he still does, thought Lyndall, if he's still alive, but he was never ready to accept the kind of help he needed.

She'd quickly learnt that his French family was wealthy, in some kind of timber and construction business. There was also quite a lot of inherited family money. In a narrow sense, Michel was quite intelligent. He'd finished school but he failed his final exams, which didn't please his family, and which meant he didn't go to university. He did his national service and started working in the family firm when he was about nineteen. He was not particularly good at this and there was tension with his father.

What happened then? Lyndall cast her mind back to those first sessions with Michel. Ah yes … things went further downhill when it was discovered that he was siphoning money from the firm's accounts and also from the account of a long-time client and family friend. The client made a fuss, went to the local police, and Michel was charged with fraud. Michel had made no secret of this with Lyndall. One day he left home with nothing but his passport, and used some of the stolen money for a one-way ticket to Australia. This must have been in the late 1970s when immigration rules were more relaxed, Lyndall thought.

Michel made his way to outback Queensland and worked there doing various building jobs, she seemed to remember. Certainly he had obtained permanent Australian residence and then citizenship. Lyndall was no longer sure in what order things happened, but at some point his father appeared in Australia and found him. His mother had died, his father had somehow arranged to pay off the defrauded client and had the charges lifted, and he wanted Michel to come home. Michel agreed to do so only if his father gave him a regular allowance and a nominal role in the affairs of the company. Lyndall recalled that this caused a good deal of argument with the father, not surprisingly, but the result was that Michel did go back to France.

However it seems he hadn't changed. Somehow he met Odile – was that on a train somewhere? She couldn't remember the details. Anyway, he fell passionately in love with her. After the war her family had moved to where Michel's family lived. They moved because her grandfather was a prominent supporter of the pro-Nazi Vichy government during the war and after the war he went to prison for a long spell. It was quite a notorious case in France. As a result, Michel's family strongly disapproved of Odile's family and the marriage, which made Michel more determined to go ahead with it.

Most of this Lyndall had heard from Michel, over several

consultations. The man always tended to ramble so it was hard to know exactly what happened when. Some she had first heard from Dominic. Michel's version was different from Dominic's. Dominic had just told her the simple facts as he knew them. Michel, Lyndall thought now, painted his father as the devil incarnate, whereas he was probably just a pretty straightforward bourgeois Frenchman whose family had hated the Vichy government, and who had worked hard to expand a business he wanted to hand on to his only son.

It was Dominic who told her the details about his parents' marriage. He said Odile agreed to marry his father when she was on the rebound. She was engaged to be married to a young doctor. They had an engagement party which her cousin attended. Within days, the engagement with Odile was broken off and the doctor was engaged, and soon married, to the cousin. This in Dominic's opinion was the source of Odile's obsession with doctors.

Dominic also said that his father told his mother that if they were married he would take her to Australia where she would be the mistress of a large property, a cattle station out west, with a staff of servants at her disposition and the life of a lady. It was supposedly on the basis of this that she agreed to marry him. But although Michel had an allowance from his father it did not extend to anything like such a lifestyle. So he tried again to cook the books of the company, only this time for a larger sum, and was caught by his father before he could take the money, and Odile, out of France. This time, as Lyndall remembered it, the police were not called but Michel's father told him that he was to leave France and never darken his door again, etcetera. He would get a modest allowance, but he would also have to work to support his wife. His father arranged his affairs so that Michel would inherit virtually nothing.

Michel then took Odile to Australia, to Cairns where he'd spent some time. However, instead of being mistress of a grand domain, Odile found herself in a breezeblock bungalow that Michel himself was building, far from a bus route, in Smithfield. Very soon she also had two children.

When she first heard this aspect of the story Lyndall had felt some sympathy for Odile's position, although it was not all that different from the situation of many young women in Australia. Or for that matter in France. That sympathy evaporated when Lyndall discovered how she had treated those children. Odile Janvier was possibly the worst mother she had ever come across in all the years she had practiced psychiatry.

Lyndall put aside her laptop to accept an entrée of lobster mousse, and another glass of wine, thinking about what she could note down next. She meditated on her professional diagnosis regarding Michel. It was a complicated story. Michel was a walking collection of psychiatric disorders. It would be better to wait until she spoke to the detectives. Michel might be dead, in which case the details of his sexual obsessions would be irrelevant.

An Air France attendant was offering a choice of chicken or fish. Lyndall selected the trout with almonds. She saved her notes, closed the laptop and put it aside. Michel Janvier could wait. She gave herself up entirely to the pleasures of French cuisine and thoughts of Bernard.

Cairns, 3 March 2011

Leslie had planned an evening out that night with his wife. Dinner at the Taj Mahal and maybe a movie if there was something worth seeing. One look at Michel Janvier's secret hideaway told him that those plans were on hold and that he would have to reschedule with Claudine.

Drew and Troy were looking bemused but already Leslie was pretty sure of what they'd stumbled on, although the how and why of it had yet to be discovered.

'This looks like cash,' Troy surveyed the bulky envelopes. 'Lots of it.'

'Yes,' Leslie said. 'As soon as we have prints we can look at some of this. I think what we've got here is a nice little earner for a Frenchman. Something that even I know the French for. *Chantage*. Singing. Somehow Michel Janvier's got people singing.'

He thought a moment and then added: 'Or is it both the Janviers?'

Cass's face cleared. 'Blackmail,' she translated for her colleagues. She looked more closely at the shelves. Each one was labelled with a single name and on each was a Lever Arch file and several CDs or DVDs with hand-written labels.

'Crikey!' she said. 'Look at these names! That one I don't know, but look: Dr Wilfred Lam!'

'Yep,' said Drew. 'I'm looking. Reads like a *Who's Who* for Far North Queensland.'

'Men,' said Cass slowly.

Troy looked at her. 'Men?'

'They're all men. All men's names. This is something to do with porn?'

'We'll have to see,' said Leslie. 'First, what's in the envelopes? And then what's in those videos? Meanwhile, let's have a look at that door.'

They studied the door between the hidden room and the front office. Prints had already been taken from the handle. Drew tried to turn it but it was fixed. Then he noticed a button on the wall. He pressed it and the door slid to the left. Immediately behind was the back of the cupboard in Janvier's storeroom. As Drew watched, a concealed mechanism slowly moved the cupboard to the left until he could step directly into the storeroom. Not only had the cupboard moved sideways, the shelves which concealed the mechanism when the door was closed had moved forward, so that the cupboard fitted against the wall behind the shelves. But why had Janvier, presumably, done this?

The scenes-of-crime officers were working quickly. Drew was handed one of the envelopes and a Stanley knife.

'Hold that by its edges, Detective, and open it with the knife.'

Drew slit the top of the A4 envelope. Inside were twenty used $50 notes. He looked at the pile of envelopes on the floor and whistled.

'This must be Janvier's collection for the past four weeks,' he said. 'If each of these contains a thousand bucks that's about $5000 in cash here. More than $60,000 a year, if it's the ongoing arrangement I'm beginning to suspect it is. Even if there's less it's a lot of cash. Enough to keep Madame in her extensive wardrobe.'

He looked carefully around the room.

'The explanation must be on the videos,' he said. 'And it's probably not a pretty one. Rather than run any of them through Janvier's state-of-the-art movie player here I want all of this bagged and labelled and taken to headquarters. Every last piece, with a description of where it was found. We're going to have to work right through the next few days I'm afraid. But given we've got a body, a missing man and a probably-related suicide we have no option.

'Cass,' he turned to her, 'you've done well. But you're going to have to do more. Take one of the cars and go home and get changed and eat, then come back here. There's several hours' work in this.' Looking down, Cass realised that she was still in her running clothes.

'Right,' she said, accepting the keys. She was glad she'd be involved. Having met Dr Lam, and given his abrupt departure from the world, she was particularly interested in what the file might have on him. She stepped outside. There were police cars parked out in Janvier's parking space as well as on the other side of the bridge. There were also numerous police working in the room behind her, but for the moment she was alone in the lane at the back of the building.

Her attention was caught by a movement to her left, further along the complex, beyond the panelbeaters' unit. It was dark and it took a moment to focus on the spot. Then she realised there was a man there. The moment he saw that he'd been seen, he turned and ran, down the complex and away from the canal.

'Not again!' she thought. 'Stop! Police!' she shouted and gave one loud thump on the closed door behind her to attract Drew's attention before starting out after the man. He'd reached the end of the units, where a security light had come on, and she could see that he was probably in his fifties. Then he turned the corner and disappeared. She was twenty years younger and conveniently dressed for active pursuit. She reached the corner in seconds and saw him heading for a car parked on the roadside.

'Stop! Police!' she shouted again and, redoubling her efforts, came up beside him. This time there was no need for karate chops. She simply swung her fist to within six inches of his nose and shouted *Ki-Yupp!* with a fervour her tae kwon do instructor would have been proud of. The man stopped still, dropped his car keys and doubled up in pain, whimpering like a puppy.

Thundering behind Cass came two officers plus Drew – all in all an alarming sight, she thought. Two uniformed policemen, a six-foot-tall ex-basketballer and a black woman in running gear suddenly appear out of nowhere, chasing a guy probably only intent on a little break-and-entry on a Thursday night. The man stopped whimpering but was still bent over, catching his breath. Plainly he didn't get enough regular exercise.

Coming along behind the others at a more leisurely pace was Leslie. As he arrived the man began to recover and stood up straight. Leslie stepped back in astonishment.

'Dr Jolley!' he said. 'What on earth are you doing here?'

Paris—Singapore, 3 March 2011

Lyndall finished her orange tart and accepted a small glass of Cointreau to follow. She'd found it easy to adopt certain French customs. She pressed the buttons that turned her seat into a luxurious bed, and stretched out. She planned to sleep for at least eight hours.

When she awoke, it was to the aroma of breakfast and they were three hours from Singapore. With breakfast behind her, and a wash and tidy up, she found herself with two hours to go. She would look back at her notes on Michel Janvier.

She opened her laptop and thought for a while. Why should she not tell the woman detective with the jewel of a name about the scarves? If Odile's body had been found with a Hermès scarf tied to it then an explanation of that peculiarity of her husband's was going to be needed anyway.

It seemed to have begun as a simple attachment for something that Odile often wore. Although, thought Lyndall, for a woman in her early twenties in the 1980s it was a singular choice. Lyndall had never felt any inclination to own a Hermès scarf, but she was sure they were expensive. They seemed to be an emblem of a certain type of lifestyle – establishment, horses, dogs, chateaux, apartments in fashionable parts of Paris (or houses in fashionable parts of Sydney or Melbourne, for that matter.) They also seemed more suited to women of the age that Odile was now. Or had been. *Hell*, thought Lyndall, *I do need to remember that the woman is dead. Possibly in horrible circumstances.*

A Hermès scarf was also an unusual fashion item in tropical Queensland. Yet, over the past ten or so years, on the few occasions when Lyndall had seen the person she had realised must be Odile Janvier, she had indeed been wearing a Hermès scarf. Usually with a smart suit and high heels. Those were the things that made her stand out, sitting on her own in a coffee shop in Cairns Central, with every other woman in the place including Lyndall dressed in cargo pants or shorts and T-shirts. She was also perfectly groomed and heavily made-up. Michel had told Lyndall that his wife spent hours each morning getting dressed and doing her makeup. This, in order to go nowhere more exciting than Myer and Gloria Jean's, and visit the hairdresser and beauty parlour, and for the occasional private Pilates session, which was how Michel described the fleshing out of his wife's day.

Lyndall added her notes on the significance of the Hermès scarf to the bottom of her short account of Michel Janvier. It was really only to get her own thoughts straight, anyway. She could choose what she wanted to tell the police when she got back to Cairns. When she knew a bit more about what had happened, and whether Michel himself had been found. She pushed the Air France headphones into her ears and spent the last hour before Singapore half-asleep, with Mozart flowing softly into her head. If she felt up to it en route to Cairns she would make some notes about Dominic.

Cairns, 4 March 2011

On Thursday night, Drew and his team, plus an increasing number of technical staff, worked through. They had bagged and taken to Sheridan Street all the computer equipment, files and envelopes in Janvier's hideaway. On Friday morning, Leslie called a team meeting together with all the tech staff, in their lab, for an interim report. Everyone was red-eyed with fatigue.

'You know most people use passwords that are dead easy,' Gino, one of the technical staff, had told Cass the night before. 'You got any suggestions for this guy?'

'Hmm … what about trying "Hermès"?' she suggested.

Ten seconds later Gino gave a cry: 'Eureka! Brilliant, Detective!'

'Proves your point, I guess,' answered Cass. 'But also tells us that Michel Janvier was pretty interested in Hermès scarves. Which is what the psych told us.'

Gino now told the team: 'Even without the password we were able to open all the folders and download the files. Which we've put one by one on separate USB sticks for you all. And matched them to the emails. Already we know there's some damn hot stuff on the videos. Not pretty. I'm glad it's you people who are going to have to watch all this and not me.'

'How big are the files?'

'There are videos – thirty, forty minutes long – and short clips. Then there are emails. The guy's had about forty or fifty email addresses over the past few years. He's deleted most of the emails in the "Sent" boxes but we can go in the back and retrieve these. That's what Mark's doing right now.' He indicated his colleague in the corner.

'What's on this laptop seems to be a duplicate of what's on Gino's,' Mark said. 'We've got a long way to go through all this. But we're starting to see a pattern.'

Drew had inserted one of the USB sticks into a spare computer in the corner. The others pulled up chairs as the first of Michel Janvier's creations began to roll.

Dr Wilfred Lam's name appeared on the screen. Then there was footage of Dr Lam's surgery, taken from across the building's car park. To dispel any doubt, the camera lingered on the sign: *Dr Wilfred Lam BDS. Dental Surgeon. Cosmetic Dentistry.* The time of the filming was noted, 5.30 pm, 14 June 2006. The filming was slightly shaky but the images were clear. After a moment Cass saw Leanne, the receptionist, come out of the building, soon followed by another woman in a white uniform, presumably Lam's dental nurse, Rhonda.

There were a few moments of inactivity in the car park, then the women drove away in separate cars.

Next, the back view of another woman appeared on the screen, walking towards the steps leading up to the surgery. She could be seen only from behind but her dark hair was sleeked back and held in place with a band. She wore high heels, fishnet stockings and a suit. Around her neck was tied a scarf. No, Cass corrected herself. Not tied. Draped.

Odile Janvier.

She disappeared up the steps and into the building.

Now the camera seemed to change. There was footage of – what? Blurred images that cleared and then a door opened and a figure swam into view. Wilfred Lam. He came closer and Cass realised that the camera must have been in, or attached to, Odile Janvier's handbag. It was recording continuously as she moved towards the dentist. He disappeared for a moment, then reappeared, in focus, walking ahead of Odile into the room where Cass had interviewed him. Odile hesitated a moment; maybe she was shutting the door. Then she must have set the bag down on a chair beside her. There was now an excellent view of Wilfred Lam and a partial view of Odile talking across his desk to him. There was no sound, but she appeared animated and smiling. He too was smiling, he shook his head a little as though she had complimented him in some way that he appreciated but didn't want to seem too flattered by. This went on for some minutes.

Then there was a sudden flurry of activity.

'Jesus Christ!' said Drew. 'Did you see what I saw?'

He pressed stop and rewind, and went back to where Odile was still talking. Then, yes, they had all seen what Drew had seen. Now they saw it again.

She casually undraped her scarf, and then in an instant was on his side of the desk, where she tied his hand to the back of his chair in one swift movement, then flung her leg over his lap, straddling him, and began to kiss him hard on the mouth. His free hand flailed in the air but he did not resist, in fact it quickly came to rest on her right leg, tracing a path upwards under her skirt and revealing the garter holding up her stocking. He tugged frantically at this and after a moment she removed her mouth from his and stood up, hitching up her skirt. She unzipped his fly, then bent down. The camera could take in only a partial view but there was no doubt from Wilfred Lam's delighted expression what was happening.

'Jesus,' said Drew. 'Giving your dentist a blow job – that's a new take on oral sex!'

'Maybe she just wanted to show him how good his dental work was,' said Gino.

The sequence continued for what they later learned was 70 seconds but seemed much longer. Cass really did not enjoy this kind of stuff although she knew the Internet was awash with home videos of porn. She could see that her male colleagues, although joking and somewhat aroused, were also pretty pissed off. They were all wondering – what was done with this material? Was it the source of the cash-stuffed envelopes? Had it been used to blackmail Wilfred Lam? The answer seemed unavoidable.

The segment came to an end and the screen went blank.

But soon there was a second, different date but the same initial sequence: departure of Leanne and Rhonda and arrival of Odile Janvier. This time Wilfred Lam was prepared. He sat grinning in his chair and put out his arm to be tied to his chair with the scarf. He was obviously willing to have his trousers removed. The rear view of Odile showed her hitching her skirt to her waist to reveal sheer black stockings and suspenders but an absence of other underwear. She straddled the dentist, clenched her buttocks and began to move rhythmically on top of him. Drew pressed Escape.

'Hell,' he said. 'I think I'm getting the idea. This involves her even more than Michel. Bits and pieces are starting to fit together.

'We have the many visits she makes to doctors. And, I suppose, dentists. She picks likely victims. Finds out their office hours, when they're likely to be alone. No doubt has softened them up a bit beforehand.

'Those scenes across the car park – that must be Michel holding the camera. But she also takes a camera in with her. Probably one of the little Nikons that we've found in the house. They look quite a lot like a mobile phone. She could just have it lying on the top of her bag. The victim wouldn't suspect a thing – just look at how Lam behaved. I'm bloody glad there was no sound, even though it might have given us even more evidence.'

'Yeah, the sound of him jerking off I can certainly do without,' said Troy.

'Then at some point, once they've got a few sequences, they show the guy a copy.'

'Yeah,' said Mark from his corner. 'They send an email, from an untraceable address. Hotmail. Gmail. Yahoo. I'm gathering them all here. But it's the same instructions for them all. Cash, in plain envelopes. He gives them a number – a sort of reference number – so he knows who it's from. They have to put the envelope through the back door of the Portsmith unit, marked with that number, at a time he gives them. And from what you people collected last night it looks like that happens every month.

'And if they don't do it – you can imagine the consequences. That guy Lam – there are two threats. One is they'll tell the Dental Board. I guess it must be illegal to have sex with your patients if you're a dentist. Like doctors. The other is that they'll tell his wife.'

'I saw a French film once,' said Mark. 'With English subtitles. *Madame Bovary*. About a woman in France, married, who had sex in a coach pulled by a horse, riding around the town. Not with her husband, you understand. Other guys. Then tried to get money out of them. Seems like we've got the Madame Bovary of Earlville here.'

'In defence of Flaubert, who wrote the book the film was based on,' said Leslie, 'I'd have to point out that Madame Bovary liked sex. I'm not sure Madame Janvier does, from what I've seen. Which is enough for me, although I suppose I'm going to have to see a lot more before we're finished with this case. She's very practised. But lust? I don't think so.'

'In the emails, the guy always signs the same way,' Gino said. 'Just to show who's boss. He calls himself "The Controller". And that's on the front of all the envelopes.'

'Looking at that film,' Leslie said, 'I'd say she was as much the controller as he was.'

The Controller. That was the name Henry had given Leslie the previous evening. Now Leslie outlined Henry's tale of woe to Cass, Drew and Troy.

Outside the Portsmith unit he'd taken Henry gently by the arm. 'Henry,' he'd said, 'I was surprised to see you here. There's no suggestion that you're breaking the law, is there Detective?' He looked questioningly at Cass, who was trying to take in this new development.

'No Sir,' she said. 'Ah, I just caught sight of this gentleman when I stepped out the door. He turned and disappeared, and I called to him to stop. Which he has done …' She looked at Henry. 'I'm sorry. I didn't realise …'

'Yes,' said Leslie, 'Dr Jolley and I have met socially. He works in the hospital.' The man nodded but did not speak. He still seemed to be suppressing sobs, but whether they were of fear, anxiety or relief Cass wasn't sure.

'Henry,' said Leslie, 'can I invite you up to my office? It's five minutes away and I have my car. I'm certainly not detaining you. But you might like the opportunity to calm down a bit.'

Still speechless, Henry had nodded and followed Leslie towards the police cars.

'Detective Borgese,' said Leslie over his shoulder, 'can you make sure all that stuff is bagged and brought to the lab as soon as possible? I'll see you there.'

In the office, he called for a tray of tea. Then he opened a cupboard, found a bottle of single malt Glenlivet, and poured a generous glass for Henry.

'I'd join you but it looks like we'll be working long into the night,' he said. Henry nodded gratefully and took a gulp.

Leslie continued: 'I'm happy to have a conversation with you off the record. Obviously there are some things that need to be explained. Several things,' he added, remembering his conversation with Henry at the Christmas party. Had Henry in fact been referring to himself? Was the 'misunderstanding' he'd described the prelude to blackmail?

'But anything that you don't want to tell me you needn't, and anything that looks like it might be … compromising for you, I'll stop you.

'I must tell you that we are investigating the death – which the papers are calling murder, although we haven't said that ourselves – of a woman called Odile Janvier. Her husband is also missing. We'd very much like to find him and talk to him. That is, of course, if he's alive. He had an office, of sorts, very close to where we met you. We had only just begun to investigate there when Detective Diamond ran after you. So I have no knowledge at all of why you were there, but I'd have to say that I don't think it's coincidence.'

Henry took another swallow of his whisky. God, it was a good drop. Then he managed to say: 'Yes. I know Odile Janvier. Or, I knew her.' For a few moments he looked down at his hands. 'I'm sorry I ever met her,' he continued. 'But she came to me as a patient.'

'Ah,' said Leslie sympathetically. 'When was this?'

'Very soon after I came up here,' answered Henry. 'About four years ago.'

He sat silent for a moment then looked up at Leslie. 'It's not a nice story,' he said. 'She came as a private patient. She had a minor problem. I recommended some surgery, day surgery, which she had. I later realised that she hadn't really needed the surgery at all, it had been a ploy to see me, and trap me. She seemed to have an obsession with doctors, gynaecologists especially. She told me once that she was supposed to marry one. I don't know what happened, but certainly he had a lucky escape. At the beginning, I thought she was quite an attractive woman, quite vivacious, and well, French, you know.

'About two weeks after the surgery she called my receptionist very late one Friday afternoon and said she had a problem and needed to see me. Jo, my nurse, said that the rooms were closing and she should go to ED but she was very persistent. Finally Jo told me and I agreed to wait back and see her, without Jo, who wanted to go home. She eventually arrived after about half an hour, looking very dressed up and not at all in pain, but still complaining of a problem.

'I don't normally examine a female patient without another woman close by if not actually in the room but I didn't have any choice and I was not, for God's sake, expecting any difficulties. I told her to go into the examination room and take off enough clothes for me to examine her.

'A few minutes later I went in, expecting to see her covered up with the sheet. In fact she was stark naked apart from black stockings and one of those scarves that she wore. They have a very particular design.'

'A Hermès scarf,' said Leslie. Henry nodded.

'Before I could size up the situation and work out what to say to her she had jumped up and – look, I know this sounds ridiculous, but there was a chair next to the examination couch and she pushed me into it and tied my arm to the chair with the scarf and then started … to undress me.'

Henry buried his head in his hands and Leslie tactfully poured himself some more tea. He would have much preferred a glass of Glenlivet himself at this point. When Henry still did not speak he asked: 'So – did this then develop into something between the two of you?'

'Yes. Yes. I'm afraid it did. Well, I'm divorced, it had been quite some time … and she was very persuasive. So even though she was a patient I allowed it to happen. Well, more than that. I met her several times in a motel.'

'She arranged those meetings? Or you did?'

'She found the place. Well, frankly, I think she already knew it, and that was how she set me up. I'm sure I wasn't the first. But someone else is involved. The person who … can I have another drop of this? It's quite a long story.'

Leslie poured a generous measure and Henry continued: 'We met several times and I have to say I was an active participant. I asked her to come to my flat. I knew she was married but I was quite attracted to her. But she wouldn't go anywhere except the motel. She booked the room and I paid in cash. But I didn't pay her; she wasn't a prostitute. No, she was much worse than that.

'I met her, I guess six or seven times over several months, and we spent maybe half an hour together each time. We, er, didn't talk very much. I really knew very little about her. Then she called me one day and said she couldn't see me any more. I was … disappointed, asked why, said if she changed her mind to ring me. She hung up.

'A week later a letter came to my rooms. Marked "personal". Inside was a USB stick and an anonymous typed note directing me to look at what was on it, but on my personal computer, not on a government one. I found this message quite unsettling and I wasn't sure what to do. In fact I did nothing. I put the letter in a locked drawer at the bottom of my desk. I thought about it during the week but I couldn't think what it was about and I was anxious that it might damage the laptop. I thought it might be pornography but I never thought of it coming from her.

'A week after that I got another letter, much the same, but much more threatening. With another USB stick. The letter said I had "disobeyed" the previous instructions and I must immediately open the file on the USB or I'd be sorry.

'I thought about coming to the police but I felt uneasy about what might be on the file, although I still didn't think of Odile Janvier.'

'Did you talk to anyone about this?' asked Leslie.

'Mmm, no,' answered Henry, but there was a moment's hesitation.

'Go on,' said Leslie.

'Well, later that evening when I was on my own I put the stick into my laptop and opened the folder on it.

'It contained videos of every one of my encounters with Odile, in graphic detail. She must have had a camera all set up in the motel room before I arrived. But I'm sure someone else was involved, maybe her husband? With the videos came threats from this person – "The Controller". He would tell the Medical Board that I'd had an affair with a patient and she would complain that she'd been "violated". The only way I could avoid this was to pay. And pay. He wanted a thousand dollars a month. In cash. I was given instructions about putting the money – well, you probably know where. In the back door. I was given very specific times and told that if I missed them the pictures would be sent to the Medical Board and the local paper and my career would be over.

'I had to produce the first payment within a week of getting the demand. I was in a terrible state. I decided I would do it that week to buy myself time, and then think about what to do. The following week, I received another letter, a warning that I shouldn't think of reporting the demand to anyone or of not making the payments.

'The more I thought about it the less I could come up with a solution. The fact that it seemed to me to be consensual sex wouldn't make any difference to the Medical Board. She was definitely a patient, I'd operated on her, there were hospital notes. I knew her well enough by then to realise she could spin quite a story if she wanted to. I would be deregistered. My family would be horrified, all my colleagues would be appalled. Obviously these people know that … knew that.

'Another thing about it was that she'd given my secretary a post-office box address. I never knew where she lived. And she always called me; I never had a mobile number. So this had been planned a long time before the first … incident.

'So I've just paid. Every month I've tried to find a solution and every month I've just paid. It's got worse for me because I've now got a … well, what I hope is a relationship, with someone else. Another doctor. And I don't know that I could ever tell her about this.'

'You might be surprised,' remarked Leslie. 'I think when it comes to blackmail most people side with the victim. What you're telling me is not a nice story, but I don't think you come out of it too badly. Um, so can I ask you when you last saw Odile Janvier?'

'Saw her?' Suddenly Henry looked up as he realised the implications of the question. 'Leslie, I never saw her again once she broke it off. Not like that and not as a patient. I've seen her once, at some distance, in Myer and I immediately left the store. And Leslie,' his face grew haggard, 'I didn't kill her, if that's what you're thinking.'

'No,' said Leslie, 'I'm not suggesting you killed her. Apart from anything else, if you had it's unlikely you'd have been where we found you this evening. What took you down there?'

'I saw the TV news yesterday evening; found out that she was dead. I was in Sydney, staying with my daughter. I decided I should come back here and I took this morning's flight. My daughter was quite perplexed, I couldn't tell her why I was suddenly changing my plans. But I was worried there might be more tapes of me. Well, I'm sure there are. I didn't really have any plan apart from seeing if I could get in there and maybe take the tapes. I put some tools in the car, silly of me really, but I didn't have any definite plan to break in. Whenever I've been there before I've always just made the drop then left straight away, as they told me to.'

'Did you ever think that the Controller could be Odile Janvier herself? That she might be doing it all?'

'No, I didn't.' He seemed surprised by that idea. 'The letters – they seem to imply another person. A man, I've always thought.'

'You have them still?

'They're locked up in my rooms. With the USB sticks. I was always hoping that some day I'd get some justice in all this.'

'That time may have come. But we are going to ask you to make a statement. Although we've only just started to go through the material we've found in Janvier's office, from what I've seen and what you've told me I'm pretty sure we will find film of you. And it would be part of the evidence in any court case. Blackmail's an ugly business, I'm afraid.'

Leslie stood up and added: 'Well, that's quite a lot for one night. I suggest that I get one of my men to drop you home, and that you give him your car keys so we can bring your car back to you. I think you might be approaching the limit to drive yourself. And then maybe tomorrow we can arrange to talk to you formally, get a statement, about your relationship with the Janvier woman.'

Leslie called Sergeant Garth and arranged Henry's transport home. He shook his hand in farewell. But as he watched him retreat down the corridor he wondered about Dr Henry Jolley. Was he telling all he knew, about Odile Janvier and his presence at Portsmith? He'd noted Henry's hesitation when asked if he'd told anyone else about the blackmail. Who might he have spoken to? Had he, for example, ever discussed the problem of Odile Janvier with his colleague Dr Ingram?

And what kind of alibi did he have from 28 to 31 January, the days during which her death had most likely occurred?

Far North Queensland, 4 March 2011

Mid-morning, Friday. Two traffic police were cruising along the highway near Innisfail, south of Cairns, listening to local radio. 'If You're Gone' by Matchbox 20 was playing.

In front of them was a dirty white Mitsubishi Outlander with NSW plates, going just a bit above the speed limit. It slowed when the driver saw the police car but otherwise proceeded normally. Something sparked deep in the brain of the officer in the passenger seat. A white Mitsubishi. He couldn't quite remember what it was but he decided to run a check on this one. Then he saw that the rego number was partly hidden by mud. Well, that could happen on dirt roads; there was quite a lot of mud on the vehicle itself. Was the middle number 53 or 58? Or even 33?

He started to run through all three numbers in the database, muttering to himself. As he was doing so, the Mitsubishi pulled left suddenly onto a side road, and picked up speed. The police car continued along the highway.

'So 53 is a white Honda. 58 is a grey Honda, must be from the same factory batch. 33 is a Volkswagen … what the fuck?'

'Mitch,' he said to his partner, 'something funny here. Let's go after them.'

A row of semis was coming towards them, followed by a motorbike, so there was a pause until Mitch could turn the car, and then they were stuck for a few moments behind the semis before they got back to the turn-off.

'A white Mitsubishi Outlander, Dave,' Mitch said. 'That woman who was found in the forest near Kuranda …'

'Yep. That's it! Fuck! I hope we haven't lost them.'

Mitch put the accelerator to the floor and followed the road towards Silkwood. It was mixed countryside, small farms of bananas, some fields of sugarcane, some original rainforest. Each time they passed a house or a sidetrack Mitch slowed and they peered in, looking for the tracks of the Mitsubishi. Dave called up another car, which would take a while to arrive but would come into the area from the north. Between them they could cover the whole district. Meanwhile, Dave had learned that the NSW car with 53 in its rego, the white Honda, was reported stolen six months previously.

Forty minutes later Mitch noticed new tyre tracks in a dirt road leading deep into the bush, close to the base of Mt Cullumbullum.

'That looks like it could be him,' Dave agreed. Mitch nosed the car in and began to follow the tracks. These went on for several kilometres. There were a couple of small acreages to either side that petered out into low rainforest and scrub. Deep ruts in the mud made progress slow. Nobody was about.

'The track's getting worse,' said Mitch. 'And I don't have room to turn here.'

'OK. I'll call up the others.'

'Shit!' The car had ground to a halt and its wheels were spinning. 'Now we're bogged!'

Dave jumped out and pushed while Mitch tried again but the car didn't budge, forwards or backwards.

'Ken!' Dave was on the radio to the other car. 'We're bogged in the mud on this track, about six k's from the main road.'

'Oh mate! Well, we won't follow you in. Keep trying yourselves, but we'll also get a four-wheel drive out there to you to pull you out. There's no other way out of there; that track ends about three kilometres further on, halfway up a mountain. So if the Mitsubishi has gone in there it can't go much further. And it can't leave without you knowing.

'By the way,' added Ken, 'that track leads to Danno Murphy's place, y'know.'

Danno was well known to Innisfail Police. He had several minor convictions for growing and dealing cannabis. He was a congenial character, often seen in the town's pubs, and up till this point not known to be associated with the theft of motor vehicles or the murder of associates.

'The woman in the rainforest,' Mitch said to Dave. 'Most probably involved with drugs too. Like the other one. Buscati. He was found not far away. Probably it's all linked. But Danno? I wouldn't have thought so.'

'Me neither,' said Dave. 'It's getting as bad as Melbourne up here. No loyalty among crims anymore!' He grinned. 'Well, we're stuck here a while.'

'Yeah, but if we wait long enough they'll come and pull us out.'

It was hot in the direct sun. Dave put the aircon up a notch and turned the radio on to Cold Chisel, 'The things I love in you'.

'I love these old songs,' Mitch said happily, humming along. Half an hour passed peacefully.

Mitch had just begun to snore gently when Dave noticed a flash of colour in the forest to their left. Someone wearing a red baseball cap. And then the glint of metal.

'Mitch!' he hissed. 'There's someone in the bush there watching us! I think with a gun!'

Mitch woke up just in time to catch a glimpse of movement himself. He killed the radio, threw open the driver's door and flung himself out onto the safety of the side of the track. Dave followed him, and moved cautiously to the front of the car while Mitch went to the back. They both peered out at the forest. Someone was moving quietly through the trees and scrub about forty metres away, at an angle to the track, towards a point where the forest gave way to grass.

Both men drew their guns and watched carefully. There was a slight ruffling of bushes as the figure progressed. Mitch moved quietly towards the front of the car with Dave and they both half-stood, ready for action.

When the bush about two metres from the road began fluttering, Dave called out: 'Police! We've got you covered! Come out with your hands up! Don't try anything funny!'

For a moment the movement stopped. Then a very haughty female cassowary stepped onto the track and, without even inclining her splendid blue and scarlet neck towards them, crossed into the scrub on the other side. The sheen of her body feathers was gun-metal grey.

'Shit!' Mitch exclaimed. 'We nearly killed a protected species!'

They both roared with laughter as they climbed back into the car, off their guard so much that the white Mitsubishi, reappearing from further up the track was almost upon them before they saw it, or its driver saw them. At the same moment they heard the rumble of a four-wheel drive behind them and the police LandCruiser swung into view, Ken at the wheel. He jumped out and surveyed the scene with some bemusement. What was so damn funny?

'Danno Murphy!' Ken addressed the driver of the Mitsubishi. 'I see you've got a new car!'

Danno nodded slowly. 'Yeah. Belongs to a mate. It came up from Sydney. He's planning to register it in Queensland next week.'

'And do you have any idea of the whereabouts of a Michel Janvier?'

'Who? Never heard of him.'

Ken walked carefully around the Mitsubishi, apparently appreciating its many qualities. With the toe of his boot he kicked the mud from the numberplate.

'Interesting!' he said. 'That's the exact same rego as a New South Wales car that went missing about six months ago. But that was a Honda and this is a Mitsubishi.'

Danno said nothing but he grimaced and swallowed hard. Ken opened the back door of the car. It appeared empty but the earthy smell of dried marijuana hung heavily about it.

Ken opened the bonnet and checked the engine and chassis number. He took a notebook from his pocket, consulted a page, nodded and smiled. He looked straight at Murphy.

'You realise this car is wanted in connection with the murder of a woman in Cairns?'

Murphy was genuinely shocked. 'Shit no! I just borrowed it off me mate from Mareeba. He said he found it in the bush up there or something.'

'He ... found ... it ... in ... the ... bush. How likely is that? This excellent vehicle?'

'No, seriously, that's what he said. He was out doing a bit of bushwalking somewhere up there in the rainforest with a couple of his mates, when they come across this car, pulled off the road, looks like it's been there a couple of days. Nobody in it. Nobody around anywhere. So they push off but when they come back a couple of days later, it's still there. So he figures it's abandoned. Starts it up easy, drives into Kuranda. Said he made some inquiries and couldn't find who owned it so he thought he'd mind it until the owner turned up. Honest. I don't know anything about any murdered woman.'

'Well, Danno, you're going to come with us. Just as soon as we pull these officers out of the mud. That splendid set of wheels you're driving is the property of a person of interest to Cairns detectives in connection with the probable murder of another person. So this afternoon you're going to be helping the police with their inquiries. As they say.'

Cairns, 4 March 2011

Once they'd watched the exploits of Odile Janvier and Wilfred Lam, Drew set the team members to work. Each had a computer, and a collection of USB sticks containing the emails to be matched up with the videos. Cass quickly found that it was one of the most unenjoyable tasks she'd ever been landed with in her whole time in the force and, listening to the exclamations of her colleagues in nearby cubicles, she gathered that they were not too happy either.

Around eleven Drew took the call from Innisfail. A white Mitsubishi Outlander had been located with false NSW numberplates. There was a pause and then his Innisfail informant spoke again.

'Umm … the bad news Detective is that the car following the Mitsubishi has got bogged in mud. The good news is that a LandCruiser is on its way to pull it out and that the bogged car now blocks the track so that there is no way the Mitsubishi can leave. The road ends in rainforest about three kilometres further on. So there's nowhere else that Michel Janvier, if it's him, can go.'

'Well, maybe not,' said Drew, 'but he's an experienced bushie. He could just take off into the rainforest. I'm coming down myself to talk to him. If it's him.'

Turning to his team he outlined the situation.

'I'll take Sergeant Garth and go down there now,' he said.

'And leave us with this shit!' moaned Barwen. 'I want to go back to traffic branch.'

'Yeah,' said Drew. 'I know. It's gross. I've just watched five straight episodes of oral sex. What am I going to tell my wife when she asks me how was my day?'

Cass sighed and picked up another USB stick. This featured a well-known local orthopaedic surgeon. She was glad when her mobile rang.

'Detective Diamond? This is Lyndall Symonds. I'm back in Cairns.'

'Oh hello. Thanks so much for calling. You must be very tired.'

'I'm awake enough to talk if that would still be of some use to you. But maybe there have been other developments?'

'Well, yes, there have, but I'd really like to hear what you have to say.'

It was arranged that Lyndall would come into Sheridan Street straight away.

'Sorry fellas,' Cass said smugly. 'I have to interview an important witness.'

Cass met Lyndall in the foyer, and was immediately warmed by her ready smile and relaxed manner.

'I thought we might get some coffee and take it up to my office. You might need it after your travels!'

'Thanks, I'd love a coffee. Umm ... you do have espresso?'

Cass laughed. 'We do. We wouldn't work here without it.'

Back in the office, Lyndall sat across the desk from Cass.

'You've been on holiday in France?' Cass asked.

'Well – kind of. I've, er, met someone there who I've been to see.'

'Right. I take it that person has nothing at all to do with any of the Janviers?'

'Nothing at all.'

Lyndall took out her notes. 'I spent some time on the plane getting my thoughts in order. It's been a while since I last saw Michel as a patient. I needed to refresh my memory. My actual patient notes are all in my rooms. Of course I can't let you have those or anything confidential in them without a subpoena, but I've noted down what I think I can tell you, given what you've told me so far. Is there any more news? Have you found Michel?'

'No, although we do have some new leads today.'

'Can you tell me any more about how and where, and when, Odile died?'

'When? Probably around 29 January, a few days before the cyclone. Where? Probably in the rainforest outside Kuranda. You know Davies Creek?'

Lyndall nodded.

'About five kilometres past the picnic ground. It's quite a remote spot. How? We're still not certain. She may have died from exposure. Or she may have been killed and left there.

Or possibly, though it seems less likely, killed somewhere else and taken there. She was certainly not strangled or shot, that much we have made public, so I can certainly tell you.'

Cass was planning to let Lyndall do as much talking as possible before she revealed any of the information they'd found in the Portsmith unit. She was keen to see what Lyndall knew about Janvier's very peculiar habits and tendencies. And if she was aware of what had been going on, had she felt compelled to keep quiet because it was confidential patient information?

Lyndall spread out her notes and began.

Cass listened closely, fleshing out what they already knew about the Janviers' earlier lives from the French police. She knew that Michel's father had sent him away, and had paid a modest amount ever since to keep him away. The father had remarried after the death of his first wife, and had adopted the three sons of his second wife, transferring most of his property to them.

'Can you tell me anything about his reasons for seeing you that's not confidential?' Cass asked. 'Anything that might help us find where he's gone and what he's done? The Hermès scarves, for example, what's the story there?'

Lyndall thought for a moment. Odile was dead. Some of the scarves were in the possession of the police. Clearly they already knew quite a bit about Michel. There was no reason not to give some explanation, she decided.

'You've done some psychology,' she asked Cass, 'in your police training?'

'Yes, and I've got a degree in criminology.'

'Oh!' Lyndall was impressed. 'Well, I'll tell you what I think could help with your investigations.

'Michel Janvier has a classic case of masochism. He's in what is, for him, an indissoluble relationship with his wife Odile who I think exhibits – although I have never met her – classic signs of sadism. But most couples in such situations, as you'll know, are role-players in a sexual script and they understand each other's parts. They know where to end the role-playing and the infliction of pain. They derive their pleasure, sexual and otherwise, from the "play" aspect of their roles. Michel would like the relationship to be like that. He's what's called a "bottom" personality and he would like Odile to be a proper "top". But while Odile certainly takes the dominating rôle she also really enjoys inflicting pain. Both physical and psychological pain. This tendency can't be controlled by Michel but nor can he leave her, something which her sons have been able to do.'

'And the scarves?' asked Cass. 'They have some role in this? In their sexual relationship?'

'Yes. Michel also has a sexual fetish that dominates his life, and his fetish object is the Hermès scarf. When he first came to see me eleven years ago he needed a Hermès scarf to be aroused but he was still capable of sex with his wife occasionally. He has since become impotent in any situation except when he is alone with a particular Hermès scarf. The scarf has a pattern of horses and chains.'

'Ah,' said Cass. 'That's what we found. Horses and chains.'

Lyndall absorbed that with interest before going on. 'Michel told me how Odile would taunt him by tying him up in her bedroom with several Hermès scarves, then spending a long time dressing and making herself up while he watched but couldn't move. Then she would take the favourite scarf away from Michel. This would make Michel frantic. Finally she would let him have the scarf but she immediately left the house. Michel hated all this but he couldn't do anything to stop it.'

'But,' said Cass, 'he was much stronger than her. There are photos of him in his gym, in the Earlville house. He was really into body building.'

'Yes,' Lyndall answered, 'he's physically stronger, but psychologically she'd completely got the upper hand. And he had no insight whatever into this.'

'So do you think he could have taken his wife out into the bush, tied her up with the scarves that matter so much to him, and left her there?'

'Well,' said Lyndall, 'I think it's very unlikely in the relationship as I have understood it. I think something else, something major, would have to have happened to bring about such a change. But the relationship's even more complicated than the fetishism and the sado-masochism.

'The sexual aspects of the relationship gradually spread so completely across their private and domestic lives that they formed a complete system of delusions about who they are.

Michel now believes that Odile was an important Parisian society hostess and that he is her servant or even her slave. Not having had Odile as a patient I cannot say for sure but she seems to share this delusion, in fact, almost certainly initiated the idea. What I know of her behaviour from Michel and Dominic, her appearance when I've seen her in public, and the amounts of money I understand she spends on clothes and makeup, all confirm a diagnosis in Odile of a psychotic delusion, a delusion now shared by her husband.

'There is a name for this in psychiatry, which funnily enough, is French. *Folie à deux*. Double madness.'

Cass considered all she'd heard for a few moments. Then she said: 'What about the children? Did this start when they were still at home? Or only once they'd left?'

'As far as Dominic's concerned,' answered Lyndall, 'it's not too much to say that Odile was always motivated to use him against Michel, maybe even before he was born. She found herself fairly much alone when they moved to Cairns. She could not go back to France without losing even more face than she already had when her engagement was broken off, and Michel could not go back there as long as he was accepting money from his father. She had no job skills, she had never had any kind of real training or work in her life. Damian was a complete accident; he was born a little more than a year after Dominic. Michel told me that she wanted an abortion but it couldn't be done in Queensland at that time. In fact she seems to have done less harm to Damian than she did to Dominic. Perhaps because from very early on Dominic tried to stand up for his little brother.

'Michel worked at a variety of jobs in Cairns and for a while it seems he was reasonably well adjusted. But he didn't make a lot of money, even with his father's allowance, and never enough to satisfy Odile's demands. Because she was always wanting new clothes and shoes and visits to hairdressers and so on. Even though they had very little social life. I think people in Cairns found her odd and aloof and she considered herself superior to them. She did learn English, mostly from watching television.'

'The clothes and shoes, they were perhaps part of her thinking she was a Paris celebrity?' asked Cass.

Lyndall nodded. 'Yes, I think that started out as a kind of justification for all the excesses, and gradually became a full-blown delusion.

'Also, as she gradually developed her dominant role in the sexual relationship, she extended this into their domestic arrangements. Quite soon Michel was doing all the cleaning and washing as well as the gardening, the shopping and the cooking. Over the past eleven years that I've known Michel it's been clear that he does all this and always with heavy criticism from her. He never gets it right, so he has to be punished, mostly by her tying him up. He has to plead with her for hours to be untied. Eventually she gives in and then he's allowed to be alone with the Hermès scarf. She also insists on him working out and staying at a certain weight.

She doesn't let him into the house until he's put in the time she prescribes in his gym.

'So to answer your question about the children – I think all this has developed gradually and become more and more bizarre over the past ten years since the boys left home. What was originally straight sado-masochism has become more and more delusional. When they were a family and the boys had to go to school and so on, outside reality intruded to some extent and there was at least a semblance of sanity in their daily life. Since it's been just them in the house they've retreated almost completely from the rest of the world. The result is the delusion that both of them hold – the *folie à deux* – that she is an important person in France and not an Earlville housewife, and he is her slave.'

Lyndall sat for a moment, biting her bottom lip. She needed to explain more clearly her interaction with the Janvier family.

'If I had known about the Janviers when the children were younger I would certainly have taken some action, probably informed social services. But I didn't meet even Dominic until he was in his early teens and by the time I realised how very odd the Janviers are – or were – the boys had both left. There didn't seem to be any physical danger to the boys or to anyone else and Michel would only see me occasionally, so I have confined my care to trying to give him some insight into his situation, with almost no success. What's recommended for treating *folie à deux* is separating the two subjects, and neither of them would agree to that.'

'How did they treat their children when they were still at home?' asked Cass.

'As the boys grew older Michel did become quite concerned about her treatment of Dominic. Often he'd come home and find Dominic tied to a chair or table because he'd been "bad". Michel would want to untie him and Odile would start screaming that it was up to her to control the boy, she was the one stuck with him all day. Michel seems to have retreated from all these encounters.

'When Dominic was about ten or eleven Odile found a part-time job – I'm not sure how that came about. She was working in the office of the Tropical Palms Hotel which was built by Jim Hewitt, who as you may know is a big developer and businessman in Cairns. She had a kind of receptionist job in Jim's office.

'Looking like she did, it was not surprising that she came to Jim's attention quite soon, and it wasn't long before she was having an affair with him. That was how Odile first learnt that people go to those cheap motels in Earlville for quick sex. Jim was a regular. But Odile, although she looked like a chic and sophisticated Frenchwoman, was really just a rather simple girl from the provinces, although a fairly nasty one. As the affair went on she became convinced that Jim was mad about her and would leave his wife for her. Her dream of being the wife of a rich and powerful man would come true. So when Michel found out about it she packed a bag and went and threw herself at Jim's feet. He was absolutely horrified; Jim had no intention of leaving his wife.

'Odile threatened to tell his wife about the affair. Jim apparently didn't feel too worried by this. No doubt his wife had seen it all before and decided to live with it, after all she was and is being maintained in the style to which Odile aspired. Nevertheless, Jim didn't really want a scene so he offered Odile some money – I've no idea how much – to finish the affair and stay quiet about it.

'Odile had nowhere to go but back home to Michel. She taunted him with the money, which she said was payment for her quitting the job, which of course she also did. He was very distraught about the whole thing, grovelled at her feet, and welcomed her back. She meanwhile began to realise that she could exert a particular kind of power over men, including her husband, and use it – this was both part of her basic personality, and part of her growing delusional state.

'The most distressing thing for Michel was that Jim took a fancy to one of Odile's scarves. He insisted that she wear it to her meetings with him, and in fact wear it throughout their encounters, while removing every other stitch of clothing. Michel at this time took that particular scarf from her and began to carry it with him. When I talked to Michel about why he thought he'd done this he said he felt that if he had it with him at all times then she wouldn't cheat again. At the same time he did realise this wasn't going to happen. He has a little insight into both his masochism and his fetishism, but no power, or indeed wish, to stop either of them.

'Not surprisingly, Odile didn't change either. I think she's had other affairs, but Michel has always been very circumspect about who they are and frankly I've never been very interested in Odile's life. Possibly some of them are doctors. As both Michel and Dominic told me, Odile is obsessed with doctors – well, she's obsessed with men whom she sees as powerful in our society. She feels she was owed a doctor, she should have been a doctor's wife in France, and instead she's married to a nobody who drifts from job to job in Australia. I've never really understood what work Michel does but he must be making some money if he's paying for Odile's wardrobe.'

'You've said that he used to be able to have sex normally – well, somewhat normally?'

'I think it's been many years since the Janviers had vanilla sex,' answered Lyndall. Then, seeing Cass's bemusement, she added: 'Vanilla sex is, well, a wide range of behaviours, but what I, you, well, at least, many people, would call normal sex. Not including bondage or S&M or D, etcetera, although many people do happily use elements of those within their normal sexual behaviours as I'm sure you understand.' Cass nodded and Lyndall flushed slightly as she recalled a few things she and Bernard had recently done together.

'We did find some soft porn in his shed at Earlville,' Cass said. 'The kind you can get in newsagents.'

'He probably wasn't much interested in it really,' Lyndall said. 'Probably just taking a look at what's available.'

'In regard to what you said about him not being capable of killing her,' Cass asked, 'could he be provoked by some behaviour of hers though? Like, if she had another affair?'

'Well in fact that's tended to excite him, the psychological pain she's inflicted. As I said I think she has had other affairs over the years.'

'But do – did – the Janviers live sort of normal lives in between all this?' Cass asked. 'Eat? Shop? Watch television? From what we've been able to gather they've lived for years in Cairns but with very little real contact with anyone else.'

'Yes, that doesn't surprise me. I think the Janviers had always lived quite isolated lives even when their children were younger, school-age, and they had to interact to some extent with the rest of the community. She grew up in a small town and never spent any time in Paris. Her family probably suffered some isolation too because of her grandfather's Nazi connections.

'One thing Michel did, which might have some relevance, is bushwalk. I'm sure he knew the area around Davies Creek very well. I think years ago when he first came to Cairns he had some connection with a bushwalking group. Then there was some falling-out with them, and he began to take solitary walks, long ones, several days. Up Bartle Frere – you know where that is? And the Pyramid?'

'Yes – that's the Pyramid right out the window there,' Cass said. 'And we've heard from the bushwalkers, although none of them had seen him recently.' She was a bit disconcerted to find that Michel Janvier, whom she found increasingly creepy, had climbed her personal mountain. But the information was interesting. There was bushwalking gear in the shed at Earlville, and in the room where Michel kept his clothes, she told Lyndall.

'I seem to remember that Michel took his sons bushwalking when they were younger,' said Lyndall. 'I think Dominic told me that. It was one of the few good things he told me about his childhood.'

'Their mother didn't go with them?'

'Absolutely not. Can you imagine Odile Janvier in walking gear – well, I guess you never saw her alive. Anyway, out in the bush I think the three of them got away from her for a while.

'How I would sum Michel up,' Lyndall continued, 'is initially as a rather reserved, solitary man who was dominated by his father, didn't succeed with the conventional things – school, business and so on. Made a disastrous marriage from which for various reasons he was unable to escape. Reacted by developing the masochistic side of his personality and his fetish and eventually became quite delusional and dependent in his relationship with his wife. Weird – but no more so than a lot of people I meet.'

She paused, then said: 'I did know Dominic quite well at the time I saw him for the Children's Court. And Dominic is surprisingly grounded, even if he's got an impressive criminal record.'

'Was Odile ever reported to DOCS? For tying up her son?' Cass felt sick in her stomach just thinking about this. She remembered Jordon at two and three, chubby and adorable. Temper tantrums, sure, he had those. But tying him up to punish him for them? She couldn't even imagine it.

'No, she was never reported to DOCS because Michel was the only adult who knew about it at the time.

'Dominic's reaction, as he grew up, was to spend as much time as he could away from home. He made friends and kept them but he also shoplifted to get things, mostly sweets when he was younger, to buy friendship. He was very good at it. He was never caught. Then as he grew older he began to use drugs. Use drugs, as in smoke cannabis, but also use them to gain friends. He was dealing, but he was informed on when he got on other people's patches.'

'He was kicked out of schools for drugs,' Cass said.

'He was, several times. Not surprising. Neither of his parents had much interest in what he did at school. He's quite bright and in a way quite self-disciplined. He's very computer-savvy and would spend a lot of time on PlayStation when I knew him. He had the money to buy what he wanted in the way of games. He'd often cut school and hang out in internet cafes, when he was fourteen and fifteen. Then when he was about fifteen he just stopped going to school. Stayed in Cairns until Damian could leave as well and then they just left home, left Cairns. Went to Sydney, I think. Eventually the law caught up with him. But Damian seems to have managed to escape that path. He never contacts – contacted – his mother but he did very rarely contact Michel. Michel told me he had gone back to TAFE and finished school, and then done something in hospitality. And then got a job, quite a good one.'

Cass nodded. 'Yes,' she said, 'we've been in touch with him. In fact we're expecting him to come in tomorrow. He lives outside of Hobart. But he's said he'll come up to deal with arrangements for his mother. Obviously Dominic can't come. And of course, the disappearance of their father is all over the news.'

'You've really no idea what's happened to Michel?'

'Well – there's a possibility his car's been found. Just this morning. That's where my boss has gone right now. We're not sure yet. Do you think Dominic could have arranged for someone to kill his parents?'

Lyndall considered this. 'What would be the point? Money? There'd be some, I suppose, but only if their house was sold. Revenge? Again possibly, but why now? I've always felt that Dominic waited until he and Damian were old enough to get shot of their parents, and then he just wanted the whole family thing behind him. I can't say that he wasn't involved in his mother's death, because I haven't laid eyes on him in years, but I think there would have to have been some development, some motive. Maybe if Damian needed money. But I'd be speculating.'

'Yes,' said Cass, 'we've been doing that here too.'

'Is it possible,' asked Lyndall, 'that there's someone else who knows about the scarves?'

'Well,' said Cass, 'yes. There is.' She liked this woman; she now must be frank with her. It was also likely to lead to more information about the Janviers. 'I'm sorry, I haven't been completely up-front with you so far. That's partly because there's a lot of information that we're trying to sort out the significance of. But it's also because I wanted to hear what you had to say about Michel Janvier from your own perspective.

'There is some evidence that Michel was at the site at some time.' Or, she thought to herself, someone who smoked his brand of cigarettes. It was about 60 per cent certain that the butts were Philip Morris, the lab had reported.

'But it also turns out we have other suspects. Lots of suspects. We're not even sure how many yet; we're still counting. All of them with good reason to feel negative about Odile Janvier and Hermès scarves.'

Lyndall gazed at Cass across the desk, trying to comprehend what she was being told.

'You have lots of suspects,' she repeated Cass's words. 'Men who might have killed Odile Janvier? Men who were involved with her? Lots?'

'It seems so. There's much we've yet to uncover. And of course quite a bit that I can't tell you. But as someone with an insight into Michel Janvier, and also it seems the dead woman herself, you may be able to help us get to the bottom of this.

'It seems that Odile, over a period of years – ten or more – enticed men into having sex with her. She then engaged in some kind of affair with each of them. Most she met in motels around the town. In those motels, and in other places, she secretly filmed what went on between them, possibly with the help of her husband. All these men were chosen carefully. Many of them are doctors. Odile Janvier had been their patient; she contrived reasons to go to them. Others are businessmen in the town. All these men were blackmailed. They were shown copies of what had been filmed and threatened with exposure if they didn't pay. They are relatively wealthy and all had a lot to lose. They didn't know who was threatening them and they were quite afraid of Odile herself. So they paid. And paid. None of them felt able to come to the police – well, in a town this size it would have been hard to keep a lid on the story.'

For several minutes Lyndall sat looking at Cass, taking in what she'd just heard. Blackmail. It certainly fitted with the early part of the Janvier story. So she just hadn't picked up on what Michel – or was it mostly Odile? – had graduated to. It certainly explained why Michel seemed never to have a job yet was able to maintain his wife in style. And – doctors? Which doctors? Specialists? GPs? My God – she thought, could one have been Trevor? But she couldn't bring herself to ask Cass that.

'So,' she asked finally, 'you think that among these men might be one who decided to kill her?'

'Well it's definitely something we are working through. There is a time frame in which the death most likely occurred, according to the pathologist, and we'll be asking each of those men to account for where they were in that time. Plus other investigations, obviously.'

Well, thought Lyndall, whatever else has happened, *Trevor* didn't kill her. Dominic might have a good alibi but Trevor had a better one.

'The Hermès scarves,' she asked Cass, 'she used those when she was with these other men?'

'In all the videos that we've seen so far, yes she did. And I can tell you that none of us, none of the guys, is enjoying having to sit through this stuff. We're taking it in shifts so that it's not too sickening. How film censors get through their days I don't know. I've had to see some weird stuff in my time in the force but this is up there with the weirdest.'

'I think,' said Lyndall slowly, 'that although there's the money, there's probably another aspect to it. And that is that Michel was partly turned on, but more than that, *taunted*, by seeing this material. Involving his wife, who he wants to hurt him, having sex with other men using the scarf. That's a really cruel but clever thing to do. I think there's probably a combination of reasons that led to them doing this. For her, there's the power involved. She's obsessed with doctors, but she also hates them. Especially gynaecologists.' Suddenly there flashed across her mind the thought of *Henry*. Surely Henry couldn't be involved. No.

That wasn't possible. He was far too sensible and charming. Then she remembered Henry's expression when she'd told him she was worried that Trevor might have had sex with patients. So maybe he *was* involved? But she didn't want to ask Cass this either.

Lyndall said: 'So first she gets power over them with sex. I'm quite sure her main motive was power not sexual pleasure. And then she just dangles them along, extracting delightful sums of money. I'm quite sure, the more I think about it, that Odile dreamt this up. She had so much to gain from it. And she could use it to taunt Michel. Endlessly.'

'Yes,' said Cass. 'I'm beginning to understand it all now.'

Drew got back from Innisfail late on Friday afternoon.

'Needless to say,' he told his assembled team, 'I didn't find Michel Janvier down there. But I did find the Mitsubishi. It's definitely his vehicle. In the possession of a certain Danno Murphy.'

Danno had been happy to help with police inquiries, particularly if it meant steering himself away from a murder charge. He stuck to his story of borrowing the vehicle from a mate in Mareeba.

'And it may well be true,' said Drew. 'The mate is Bugsy.'

There were grunts of recognition from around the room. Bugsy and Sam Gecko were both well-known dealers who worked together on the Tablelands. Mostly with cannabis.

'There'd obviously been a lot of weed in the car very recently. Danno got noted by the traffic boys. He realised it and turned off the highway and went home as quick as he could. Probably to dump a stash which he was going to take up to Bugsy. All in a day's work. Why else would he have Bugsy's car? Innisfail are checking that out. Probably going to take a little trip as well, along that road beyond Danno's place into the forest. They can handle all that.

'Meanwhile I've got Mareeba looking for Bugsy. And Sam Gecko as well, the two of them hang out together. So far they haven't been located. But we'll be very interested to know just how Bugsy got that car.'

Cass filled Drew in on her interview with Lyndall Symonds.

'I think we might ask her to come in and meet Damian Janvier tomorrow too,' he said, when he'd heard Lyndall's version of Michel's history.

'I'll give her a call,' said Cass. 'She said she's happy to help us. And talking of doctors, there's a Dr Mellish wants to talk to the Inspector. Said he's got to speak to the boss. None of us would do. He's coming in at ten tomorrow morning. After Damian.'

'There's a USB stick with Mellish's name on sitting on the desk over there,' Troy told Drew. 'We decided to leave that one specially for the boss.'

Cairns, 5 March 2011

As Cass had predicted, Lyndall had been happy to be present for the interview with Damian Janvier. Hobart police had already sent through Damian's full account of his whereabouts for the last days of January, which they had verified. He was with his girlfriend Katie, at her parents' farm outside Hobart for the nights of Monday 24 January and Monday 31 January. Her parents said he was there. Every other night since New Year, he'd been at work in a restaurant whose owner had nothing but praise for him. His girlfriend vouched for him being with her but so did several friends who saw him throughout that time.

'There's no way,' said Cass, 'that he's slipped out of Tasmania, arrived secretly in Cairns using a ticket not bought on his credit card, hired a car not with his credit card or licence, kidnapped his mother, killed her, ditto his father, then returned to Hobart in time to cook dinner on Tuesday evening. Hobart have established this without a doubt.'

Damian proved to be an engaging young man with thick dark hair, carefully gelled and spiked, and a tattoo of a lizard over his left biceps. He arrived precisely at nine in Cass's office and sat down at the table where Lyndall and Drew were already seated.

'I'm sorry you've had to come up here in these circumstances …' began Cass, but Damian shook his head.

'Thanks,' he said, 'but it's a long time since I had anything to do with my parents. Especially my mother. She was … what can I say?' He spread out his hands. 'She was just so not like anyone else's mother I've ever met, I guess.' He looked across at Lyndall. 'Doctor Symonds, you must know. Dom told me he trusted you. I went to see him in Wellington yesterday. He remembers you.' Lyndall nodded at this.

'OK,' said Cass. 'Well, as you know, we did have to check where you were around the end of January. That was routine. You are positively not suspected of being directly involved in your mother's death. We don't know about your father. We don't know where he is. We don't think you do either. But you may have some knowledge or ideas that might help us find him, and get to the bottom of this. So I want to ask you now: have you had any contact at all with your father in the past six months and in particular since the last week of January? Have you seen him, spoken by phone, received emails or in any other way had any news of him?'

'No,' said Damian immediately. 'I haven't spoken to either of my parents for more than a year. I did come up here to try to talk to them at the end of the year before last. 2009. When Dom first went to Wellington. I thought my father might go to see him there. Not my mother. But she practically threw me out of the house before I could even suggest it.

'I only spent a few minutes there. Dad hardly said a word. He was always scared of her. But that time he seemed more so, terrified even. And they both seemed to have become really weird. Almost cut off from reality, from the rest of the world. Behind that wall that he must have built himself around the house. They seemed to hardly know who I was. Well, of course I'd made it that way. Dom and I left more than ten years ago now.'

'How is Dominic?' asked Lyndall. 'You saw him yesterday? You stay in touch with him?'

'Yeah, I stopped over in Sydney and went up to Wellington. He's doing OK. You know, he just might even be better now our mother's dead. He's in for four years, he's done two and he's had good behaviour reports. He's doing some courses in there, trying to make up for missing so much school. I want him to come to Tassie when he gets out. Get away from the drug scene. That's what I was telling him yesterday. My girlfriend, Katie, she knows my brother's inside, she's totally cool with it.'

'You spoke about your mother's death?' asked Lyndall.

'Yeah. I think he's really shocked by it. By the idea that someone must have taken her into the bush and killed her. Not because our mother is dead. But by the idea of her being murdered. Like, he's done a few things in his life that were not totally legal. Obviously. But this, it makes you think, well, what had she done to the person who did that to her? Because we know, me and Dom, that she could do bad things to people.'

'Who did she do bad things to?' asked Cass.

'More to Dom than me,' answered Damian. 'Dom used to stand up for me. He would get between us if she was trying to smack me. If she tied me up he would try to untie me.'

'She tied you up?' Cass asked.

'Yeah. That was one of her special punishments. When we were little. Once Dom was seven or eight, she couldn't do it to him any more. He was stronger than her by then. And he would stop her tying me too. But she also did bad things to our Dad. Like I said, he was scared of her. In a funny way. Kind of like a puppy. Always trying to please her and never succeeding and then being kind of happy when she told him off.

'I remember once when I was very small, maybe the earliest thing I remember, him coming home with some flowers for her. A bunch in silver paper. And she took them and threw them back at him and they scattered all over the floor. He got down and picked them up and I saw the expression on his face – like he was going to cry, yet somehow this was what he'd wanted. It's that look that always comes into my head when I think of him now.'

'So how did you deal with all this?' asked Lyndall.

'I was lucky,' said Damian. 'I had, still have, a really good mate here. Frankie. He lives in Smithfield. That's where I'm staying now. We used to live in Smithfield; Frankie lived down the road. I spent all the time I could in their house. Big Italian family. He had four sisters and a little brother, they're all grown up now. Their family was just light years from ours. A normal family. His mum was more like a mother to me than my real mum ever was. Silvia. She's great. She taught me to cook – that's where I first learnt. My mother never cooked – she made Dad do it. He had to do everything – cooking, washing, cleaning, and he could never do it good enough for her. She was always on at him about it. And I don't think she ever cared how much time I spent at Frankie's place.

'Plus I had Dom looking out for me as well, at school. The only reason I ended up in court' – here he looked across at Lyndall – 'was because I wanted to be with Dom. I don't do drugs. And the reasons Dom got into drugs were all to do with our mother. They made him happy, for a while, and he made money that he could use to buy things for other kids, so they would be friends with him. Simple as that.

'Yeah, I try to stay in touch with him. We stayed together when we were first in Sydney. I needed him; I was fifteen. I got different jobs. So did Dom, a bit, but, well, obviously you know, he was dealing. He could make a lot more doing that. Then I got into TAFE, and finished school, and did hospitality. I met other people, and moved into a sharehouse. One of the tenants was Katie. She's from Tassie, which is how I'm there. But I've been back twice to see Dom since he went to Wellington, as well as yesterday. And we talk on the phone when he's able to call. I can't call him.'

'Do you know if he's had any contact with your father since he's been in gaol?' Lyndall asked.

'I'm 100 per cent sure no,' said Damian. 'He was, um, not exactly pissed off at me, for trying to see them, but he just said, "Look, forget it, that's all in the past".'

'Obviously we are putting a lot of effort into looking for your father,' Drew said. 'Do you have any ideas at all about what might have happened? About where he might have gone? Anyone in Australia he might have contacted or who might be sheltering him? Anyone in France he might have spoken to?'

Damian was silent for a few minutes. Then he said: 'First, I have to get my head around the idea that maybe my father killed my mother. I've been thinking about it since I got the news. Because … how to explain? I don't hate my father. I feel sorry for him, if I feel anything at all. It's been so long since he was part of my life. But I didn't hate him when I was growing up. I just wanted him to be different. Sometimes he would take us for walks, in the bush, up on the Tablelands or in the range. He'd take me and Dom. And for a while it would seem we were, like, normal people. A normal family. The Janvier kids and their dad. Then we would go home and the dynamics would all change back again.

'And I don't think Dom hates him, not now at least. Maybe he did once. But I think he feels like me. And like I said, he's put it in the past.

'I can't really say that Dad didn't kill her, because I just don't know. He was always put down by her. But he adored her, he would kiss the ground she walked on. He bought her everything she wanted. Clothes and shoes and makeup, mostly. French perfume. You probably know that. You've seen their house. I wasn't there long that time I went but I saw it was full of her stuff, the same as the house where we lived in Smithfield. She was nuts about her appearance. Every day she dressed up like she was going to a wedding. And then she'd just hang around Cairns Central. Try on dresses and drink coffee. On her own.' He paused and considered for a moment.

'Friends? They never had any real friends in Cairns when we were growing up. Or anywhere else in Australia that I know of. Dad knew a few people who he'd worked with on a property out west, and a few he used to bushwalk with, but even before Dom and I left Cairns he'd stopped seeing them. But who he might have got to know in the last ten years I have no idea. He could have joined one of those cults, done all kinds of weird things and I just wouldn't know.

'I'm pretty sure he's not close to anyone in France anymore, though. I never knew what happened but basically his father pays him to stay away. My mother got ditched by some other guy and married Dad on the rebound. When they had fights we'd hear all about it. How she should have married this doctor but her cousin stole him from her. How that was supposed to be Dad's fault I never understood. But it was a big deal between them.

'The only thing I can suggest since he's missing and the car is missing is that he's gone bush. He's pretty good in the bush. He can shoot and fish and look after himself.'

'Shoot?' asked Drew quickly. 'He doesn't have a gun licence. We checked that.'

Damian raised his eyebrows. 'Well he certainly had a rifle and several guns when we were kids. He did his time in the French Army. National service. He learned how to use a gun. I would have thought he still had one. Or more than one. Licence or no licence. He used to shoot kangaroos. Rabbits. Ducks. He was a good shot.'

Damian thought for a moment then added: 'I think if you haven't found any guns it's because he will have made a secret hiding place. Probably in the backyard or the shed, if there's a shed there at Earlville. He did that in Smithfield, he mostly built that house himself and he made a lot of hiding places. He dug a hole in the backyard and covered it with a vegetable patch in a planter box, and he put the guns there. He thought Dom and I didn't know but we did. We were always too scared to dig it up and have a look. There was no way he wouldn't have known if we'd done it.'

'Right,' said Drew, mentally cursing himself for not having thought of this earlier, and making a note to get the Earlville house checked for guns as soon as they'd finished with Damian. The man who'd made the concealed door in Portsmith and probably set up the surveillance of Odile's trysts was obviously a master of the techniques of camouflage. Maybe he'd learnt something about those as well as about guns in his time in the French Army.

'So any ideas about where he might go? Would he stay in Queensland? Or the Northern Territory, maybe? New South Wales?'

'He's really only ever been in Queensland as far as I know,' said Damian. 'Even when he first came here. He was out near the Gulf, and on the Tablelands, and in Cairns. That's why they came back here. My mother had no idea what she was coming to. She thought they'd have some huge property. Staff to do all the work. He must have spun her a story in France. That was another thing she'd go on about.'

Lyndall nodded.

'How long are you staying in Cairns?' asked Drew.

'My boss gave me a week. I didn't know what I'd have to do here. I guess I'll have to arrange, I don't know, some kind of funeral. I don't know anything about how you do that.'

'That can all be done for you by a funeral company. Once her body's been released – and that may take some time. You should also get yourself a solicitor here. There's a list at the front desk, ask Di or Tracy there. Because you'll have to deal with your mother's estate if we don't find your father. And I have to say, as I'm sure you understand, we may not find him. And, well, he too may be dead. So perhaps try to prepare yourself for that.'

Damian nodded. 'One thing: do I have to go to the house?'

'The Earlville house? You don't have to go there. You don't want to?'

'No. I've only been there that once. That house, it's kind

of isolated from the street. From the rest of the world. What would happen to it, if my dad's not found?'

'I think it would become yours and Dominic's,' answered Cass, 'but I can imagine there would be a lot of legal paperwork and time involved. And of course we still have to find out what happened to your mother.'

'But,' put in Lyndall, 'there are people, services, who would clear the house out for you, if you couldn't do it yourselves. You don't have to worry about it.'

'It all seems unreal,' said Damian. 'Just finding out what's happened, and where my father is, is all I can manage at the moment.'

'Well thanks for coming in,' said Cass. 'We have your mobile number; we'll call you if we have any news. Or any other questions. And let us know when you're going back to Hobart.'

They shook hands and Damian left. When the door was closed Drew said to the two women: 'He seems as straight as a die.'

Lyndall nodded. 'And remarkably unharmed by his upbringing. There's one thing that struck me, though. And that's his feeling that his father wouldn't kill his mother. He talked about him almost worshipping her, kissing the ground and so on. I know you two were sceptical when I said the same thing, that I couldn't imagine him killing her. And you've met more killers than I have, though I've met a few. But it's something that Damian feels instinctively even after ten years away from them. I haven't seen Michel often but I have seen him professionally and fairly recently and that's also the gut feeling I get. So maybe there's another explanation.'

While Cass and Drew were talking with Damian, Leslie had been meeting with Arthur Mellish.

Leslie had met Mellish on several occasions over the years. When Leslie's daughter Lily was eight, Mellish had operated to remove her appendix. Inside her, rather than appendicitis, he'd found something very rare called a Meckel's diverticulum: a bit like an extra appendix, he'd explained. He'd removed this and her appendix at the same time, so that she didn't get appendicitis in the future. 'Par for the course,' he'd told Leslie and Claudine, following the surgery. To Lily he'd said she'd now be able to go to Antarctica; you had to have your appendix removed before you could work there. 'Ready for battle, young lady,' he'd said. Lily had liked that idea.

Leslie had found the doctor polite, but reserved. By their second meeting, when Mellish did some painful but necessary things to a hernia Leslie had developed, Leslie had realised this was entirely a matter of skin colour. Mellish had no idea how to talk to someone who wasn't white. Or at least, no idea that it was just the same as talking to someone who was the same pinky-grey shade of white as Mellish himself.

Having sat through the Mellish video the previous evening, Leslie had not been surprised to hear that the man had called. He was also not surprised when Mellish called again on Friday morning just as Leslie got into his office. At the other end of the line the doctor was not his usual bluff self.

'Ah, good morning, Inspector. I … ah … you know I've arranged to come and have a word with you? I'd, ah, rather explain in person what it's about. I'm a bit … on the ropes, so to speak.'

'I'm happy to see you, Doctor. Your appointment is for ten o'clock. You're OK to come down to my office, or shall I come to see you?'

'Oh definitely I'll come down to Sheridan Street. That is – there wouldn't be any of those reporter chappies hanging about there, for any reason, would there?'

'No no, anything for the press is done via our media unit. Just go to the front desk and tell Di or Tracy that I'm expecting you.'

'Thank you, Inspector. As it happens, it's been a bit of a knockout punch.'

Leslie crossed the room and picked up the file labelled *Dr Arthur Mellish* that Cass had prepared the previous day.

Recalling his consultations with Mellish, he wondered what were the odds, that in his opening sentences Mellish would describe Odile Janvier as having moved the goalposts …

But Mellish, when he arrived, continued with images from the ring. And for a while he came out of the corner swinging and stood toe-to-toe with Leslie. It seemed he was taking it on the chin.

'This unfortunate woman who was found in the rainforest. Mrs Janvier. Bit of a low blow for her family, what? I just wanted to tell you that she was a patient of mine.'

'Really? Are you able to tell me anything about her? As you probably know we are still investigating the case.'

'She came to see me several times – referred by Trevor Symonds, poor chap. With bellyaches. Very consistent story for gallbladder stones. Only problem was we couldn't see any stones on her ultrasound. But several times she came back with this same story. A lot of pain, just exactly where you'd expect it with gallbladder colic.

'She's a damn persuasive woman. Ah, I mean she was … an attractive woman, but a dark horse. She kept coming back to see me. Wanting her gallbladder out. Wouldn't take no for an answer. Finally I threw in the towel and took out the gallbladder. Precious little wrong with it.'

'It does seem,' said Leslie, 'that she had a fascination for doctors …' He looked across at Mellish, who slowly began to change colour.

Leslie continued: 'I have to tell you, Doctor, that since Wednesday evening my team has been going through a large amount of material found in premises belonging to the late Mrs Janvier's husband. We haven't yet been able to locate Mr Janvier himself. We don't know whether he is alive or dead. But we do know that over the past few years he has used, ah, compromising images of a number of Cairns doctors, and others, for the purpose of blackmail. Apparently very successfully.'

Mellish visibly deflated. Was he out for the count?

'Will my wife have to know about this?' he asked.

'Not necessarily,' answered Leslie. 'We do need to ask you some questions. We're still in the stage of documenting all the evidence we've taken possession of in the past few days. The good news is that you can stop putting fifty-dollar notes into plain envelopes. Wherever Mr Janvier is, he won't be collecting any more.'

'Her husband was The Controller?'

'He used that term with you? We think yes, or that both he and his wife were equally complicit. There doesn't seem to have been anyone else involved. And let me tell you, Doctor, our society despises blackmailers.'

'Well,' Mellish brightened up. He was beginning to take to Inspector Fernando. He liked the cut of his jib. Why, it was almost like talking to a white man.

'This is a new ball game all right,' he said. 'I can't say it's been easy, the past few years. But,' he hesitated, flushing again, 'are there, um, copies of …?'

'Yes. Copies of everything, I'm afraid. They had very good equipment and understood the technology to make sure the images were compelling for their victims. Well, you know that. But we will be keeping all this locked up. And I can also tell you, Doctor, there are some of your colleagues involved. She was very practised at what she did.'

'You mean – the scarf ...?'

'Yes – she always used one or more. And that was what was used in her killing. Or so we think.'

Mellish's head jerked back and his mouth opened as understanding slowly dawned upon him. For once he resorted to plain speech.

'You don't think ...? My God, man, I was blackmailed, but I didn't kill her!'

'No, no, I'm not suggesting that for a moment. I take it, though, you were in Cairns at the end of January?'

Mellish thought for a moment, then reached into his breast pocket and retrieved a College of Surgeons black leather diary. 'No, we were in Sydney. At least, I went there on the afternoon of 30 January. That was a Sunday. That's right, bit of a worry about the cyclone even then. Winifred was already down there, she'd been staying with her sister since the previous weekend, doing shows and whatnot, arty things, you know. And then we were supposed to be going to London, until we got wind of the cyclone really coming. So Winifred went on anyway, she's still there, with her mother, but I came back here on ...' he turned a page, '1 February, to help with the evacuation and whatever else was needed. Batten down the hatches. Clear the decks. Sat it out in a cyclone shelter in case anyone needed help. Bit of a sticky wicket for a while all right. We were bloody lucky.'

Leslie took a deep breath. 'So in that week before you went to Sydney you were working as usual?'

'Yes. Flat chat actually. Because I thought I'd be away more than two weeks, had a conference in London I was going to. Missed that. Didn't miss seeing my mother-in-law too much, though. Ha!' He passed the open diary to Leslie.

'Consultations and clinics all that week except Australia Day, and I was in and out of the hospital the whole 24 hours, a lot of sick patients. Is that ... do you think that was when she was killed?'

'We're not sure yet,' answered Leslie evenly. 'We're waiting on some more forensic evidence. Can I ask you when was the last time you saw Odile Janvier?'

'You mean, as a patient? I haven't seen her at all since the day – the evening when ...'

'I see,' said Leslie comfortingly. 'Can I ask, did she call and say she had a problem after her operation, and arrive late so that you'd be there alone?'

Mellish's features brightened. 'Yes – are you saying she's done the same thing to other chaps?'

Leslie nodded.

'By Jove,' said Mellish, 'how many? At a thousand dollars a month, she must have been raking it in. She had me by the short and curlies. Threatened to send – well, pictures, to Winifred. And the Medical Board. Um – will you be having to tell the Medical Board?'

'I understand,' answered Leslie, 'that a complaint to the Medical Board needs to be made by or on behalf of a particular patient. That doesn't seem to me a likely outcome.'

Mellish gave a sigh of relief.

'So,' asked Leslie, 'when was the last time you saw her, for any reason whatever?'

'Just as I told you. That night.'

'You didn't meet her again?'

'Good God no! She suggested meeting in a motel. Can you imagine it? I'd walk into a place like that in this town and there'd be someone at the desk whose appendix I've removed. Everyone knows me even if I don't always remember them. Besides – just horse sense, really. I won't say I don't know the lie of the land. Was in the Army Reserve, had a few big nights out. And once in Bangkok. That's years ago. But I knew with that filly, I could really come a cropper.'

Leslie glanced down at Mellish's diary. Against Saturday 29 January was a pencilled note: 'E Creek.'

'E Creek?' he asked Mellish. 'Is that the name of a patient?'

'No that's our farm, outside Kuranda. Emerald Creek. Let me see …' He leaned over and stared at the diary.

'Saturday. That's right, I went up there to check the house was closed up, because of the weather.'

'So you went up to Kuranda that day?' Leslie asked. 'What time?'

Mellish thought for a moment. 'Mid-afternoon,' he said firmly.

'You went alone?'

'Yes, my wife was in Sydney. As I said. I didn't stay long.'

'Did you see anyone else? Anyone who could confirm that you were there?'

Mellish looked intently at Leslie. The implications of his presence near the Davies Creek rainforest that day were sinking in. Suddenly he brightened.

'Yes. Tegan. The manager's daughter. They live next door. We have mangoes, macadamias and so on but only smallscale. Tegan's family manages it for us. She drove past and stopped for a moment. I think she talked about the cyclone coming.'

'Well,' said Leslie, 'I'll be asking you to talk to Detective Barwen. We'll have to get a complete record of where you were, you understand, what you were doing that week, and proof that you were in Sydney. We'll be asking quite a few people the same thing. But I think that at least you can stop worrying about paying the Controller now.'

Leslie's second interview of the day was with Tim Ingram. Tim was coming back to Sheridan Street to sign his typed statement.

Leslie had found himself thinking quite a lot about Tim since the start of this case. It was interesting that he was the one who'd found the body.

Leslie had never forgotten the rape case of a young Chinese student and the assault on Kaine Nancarrow. The

Chinese student had been treated by Dr Ingram. Leslie had always had a gut feeling that Tim Ingram knew more about the assault of Nancarrow than he'd let on.

Nancarrow had been brought into the hospital that night having rolled a stolen car on the Yorkey's Knob road. He'd fractured his femur so he hadn't been able to run away like his mate. However, they'd caught up with him and the two of them were now in Arthur Gorrie Correctional Centre in Brisbane.

In the hospital, though, in the Emergency Department, Nancarrow had nearly died. Not because of any lack of medical care but because while the constable on guard had gone to get a cup of tea, someone, never identified, had gone into the room and stabbed Nancarrow repeatedly. Someone who knew exactly where to find him.

Nancarrow had been doped with morphine and was able to describe his assailant only as a 'slitty-eyed bastard'. There was CCTV in the ED waiting room but none in the corridor of the ward where Nancarrow had been held. Leslie had no sympathy for Nancarrow but the incident had made the duty policeman look foolish and they'd never been able to solve the case. They could find no evidence to charge the most obvious suspect, the girl's fiancé.

When Tim was interviewed by Leslie's team he denied knowing anything about Nancarrow, but there had been something in the way events had unfolded that had suggested to Leslie that he'd anticipated how things might turn out.

Leslie could never quite put his finger on why he thought this. And for some inexplicable reason whenever Leslie thought about Tim Ingram he seemed to smell the scent of frangipani flowers.

Now Tim again sat in Leslie's office overlooking the Inlet.

There was no record in Michel Janvier's collection of Tim having been one of Odile's victims, and he was a generation younger than most of them. But that didn't mean she hadn't tried. There was another possibility too – that Henry had taken Tim into his confidence, despite his having told Leslie he'd told no-one. And then Tim might have decided to help Henry in some way. If Tim knew Henry was being blackmailed then he might even have helped him kill Odile and Michel.

It quickly became clear that Tim had never met Odile, professionally or otherwise, until he found her body.

'All my work is in public obstetrics,' he explained to Leslie. 'That woman was never in that category in the time I've been in the hospital. I'm certain the first time I ever saw her was in the rainforest.'

'The woman was obsessed with doctors,' Leslie explained. 'So we're asking all Cairns doctors where they were around 28 to 30 of January.'

Tim produced his phone and showed Leslie his rosters for the week before Yasi. He'd worked every day, up to sixteen hours a day, in the week leading up to the cyclone. And he and Henry had been called back into the hospital the minute it was safe after Yasi, when he'd worked every day up until the Saturday when he'd gone to the Tablelands with his wife. It seemed unlikely he could have fitted in a complicated double kidnapping and murder.

Leslie's eyes lingered a moment on the phone. Then he asked: '30 January – you had a meeting with Henry? Dr Jolley? That was on a Sunday?'

Tim looked puzzled for a moment, then his face cleared. 'Oh yes,' he said, 'we met in the hospital, to go through all the perinatal deaths for 2010. We had to prepare a report and we could never find time during the week. So we both went in after dinner that night. I remember it was just before Yasi so we had a lot to talk about as well as going through all the medical charts for the report.'

'So this was in your office? Or Dr Jolley's?'

'In Henry's. Next to the outpatient clinic.'

'I see. How long were you both there?'

Tim considered this for a moment, then said: 'Well, I must have arrived about 8.30 I think. Bedtime for my daughters is eight o'clock and I remember my wife and I put them to bed, and we were talking about the cyclone. Then I went to the hospital. Henry was already there.'

'And the meeting took, what, an hour or so?'

'Oh no, much longer. We went through a whole year's charts. I think I got home about midnight.'

'Did you talk about anything else?'

Tim eyed Leslie for a moment. What was the Inspector

getting at? 'We also discussed the cyclone,' he said finally. 'Whether Yasi was coming. How to prepare for it, with so many women scheduled to give birth. Henry was planning how we would cope.'

'Well,' said Leslie, nodding, 'you all did a fine job.' But going through his mind was the question, Did you also talk about Odile Janvier? He leaned forward.

'I take it,' he asked Tim, 'that you consider Henry Jolley a person of integrity?'

Tim looked directly at him, his head tilted a little to one side. 'Absolutely,' he said. 'I've worked with him as a consultant for four years now. In some quite tight situations, because we don't have a lot of back-up here, so far from Brisbane.'

There was no doubting Tim's sincerity. Leslie decided this was enough.

'Thank you very much indeed for coming in,' he said, standing up and offering his hand.

Leslie's final visitor of the day was Jim Hewitt. Jim was a Cairns identity well known to Leslie, a generous benefactor of police charities.

Jim had first come to North Queensland as an accountant for a mining company. After a while he bought the company. He'd branched out since then into apartment blocks and supermarkets, and everything he touched prospered. He ran his affairs as a family business with his sons.

Leslie was not surprised when he heard from reception that Jim had dropped in and asked to see him. Waiting for him to come up in the lift, he found the Glenlivet and a tumbler and placed these on his desk, together with a glass of water for himself.

'Jim! Good to see you!'

'Leslie, you too. How's the golf? Still playing Wednesdays?'

'Every week I'm in Cairns. You should try to get out and join us some time!'

At seventy, Jim was trim and fit. Clearly much was invested in private medicine, cosmetic dentistry and tanning salons but he's worked hard, thought Leslie, he's earned it.

'Look, Leslie,' Jim said, 'I'll come straight to the point. This woman Janvier who was killed up in the rainforest. I used to know her. She worked for me – though "work" is probably stretching it. Bloody useless. Good-looker though.'

'This was recently?'

'Lord no! Fifteen years ago. More, maybe.'

'And you had some involvement with her?' Leslie knew what Lyndall had told Cass about Hewitt and Odile.

'Well, yeah. Briefly, you know the kind of thing. Only she was difficult. Thought it was serious, that I was going to leave Natalie for her! Nuts! Turned up at the office with her bags! Next thing her husband and two little kids were there as well. The husband jabbering away in French.'

'So what happened?'

'Oh, I paid them off. Only thing to do. The husband was

threatening to shoot me and she was threatening to tell Nat. Nat and me, we've been through a few things, I would have survived, but I really didn't need any of it. I told them I'd give them five thousand bucks in cash, which I did, but they wouldn't get a cent more, and if I saw either of them again I'd come down here to Sheridan Street and report them for threatening me. And I said I had a lot of friends in high places. Which I do.'

'So this would be the reason that, ah,' Leslie consulted the notes on his desk, 'on the evening of 3 March, two persons known to work for Hewitt Constructions were arrested breaking and entering a property owned by Michel Janvier in Portsmith?'

'Yeah. Jesus, Leslie, your woman, the detective, really gave them the once-over.'

'They attempted to assault her. She's one of my best operators. They're lucky the charges are minor, Jim. They could have got serious assault. Or even grievous bodily harm.'

'Well they exceeded my instructions.'

'And what were those instructions?'

'Well, to make sure there was nothing compromising me or any of my family in Janvier's office.'

'And can I ask how you knew that was Janvier's office?' Leslie was intrigued. There had been nothing related to Jim Hewitt found among the videos or emails.

'OK. I'll tell you the lot. But … this is confidential, right?'

'Well, provided no crime's been committed. No further crime. I mean by you. You ended up paying her more?'

'Not me! My son. Aidan. You've met him.' Leslie remembered Aidan Hewitt. Nice lad, but not half as engaging as his father. Or as bright.

'Ah yes. Aidan.'

'Well. Seemed that Madame had Aidan in her claws as well. While she was still seeing me!'

'Ah. I see.'

'Yeah well I didn't see. Not at first. Then about two years after I'd paid off the Janviers Aidan comes to talk to me. Odile had given him the flick.

'"Good," I said, after I'd said a few other things about Odile two-timing me. Aidan was married then, to Shona. His first wife. Lovely girl. Would have been hell though if she'd found out.'

'And Aidan was paying Odile Janvier?'

'Yes. Because somehow they'd recorded – made a video – of Aidan and Odile at it. The husband must have been involved. Sick stuff really but they used it to threaten him. Said they'd send it to Shona. I think it was Odile who did it. He – Aidan – got sent an anonymous copy of the video with a letter. That had been about a year before he talked to me. In that time he'd paid about $6000 in cash to them.'

'And what happened then?'

'Well you see I knew where she lived, because she'd been employed by us. So I went to our lawyer, you know Curt

Bailey. And he wrote them a letter saying there would be no payments in future and if they so much as looked in our direction again we would go to the police and have charges of blackmail laid. And that put a stop to it.'

'So this was when, exactly?'

'This would have been about 1999.'

'So why would two of your employees be at Michel Janvier's back door in 2011, four days after his wife was found dead in highly unusual circumstances?'

'Because I didn't know … Shit! Leslie – you don't think I got someone to kill her?!' Jim was suddenly aghast.

'No, no. I'm just asking why you sent your blokes to Michel Janvier's unit.'

'Because we asked, at least Curt did, that they destroy all copies of the video. But of course we never knew if they did. There'd been no trouble from them since, but when I heard Odile was dead I thought this might come to light. And it could be embarrassing for Aidan. He's in Aspen, skiing. With the third wife. So I sent the guys down to have a look around. They stuffed up, though, badly.'

'How long has Aidan been away?'

'Um, he left the day before Australia Day. 25th. Comes back next week.'

'OK, Jim. Let me tell you that we have gone through everything we've found in Michel Janvier's set-up and there are no videos or photos of Aidan. There are many of other people though, and all with the same story.'

'Holy *shit*! Anyone I know?'

'Well I can't tell you that but I will say that we'll be very discreet. It's an unusual case, to say the least. And Jim, although I don't for a moment suspect you of involvement in Odile Janvier's death, we're going to have to get a full account of your whereabouts between 28 January and the start of Yasi.'

As Leslie talked to Jim Hewitt, Tim was slowly descending the stairs on the side of the police headquarters building. He stopped for a moment to watch as the last of the mountain mist was lifted away by the midday heat. He cast his mind back to the night the Chinese girl came to Emergency.

Standing outside the hospital that night, under the frangipani tree, watching Detective Fernando and the policewoman drive away, he'd remembered Moresby, and what had happened to Chris there. What had happened to both of them. What he'd done in the police cell.

He'd been thinking too about his life in Cairns. How it had all worked out in the end. He was in his final year of specialist training. He and Chris were the parents of two healthy girls. She was nursing three days a week, and he had every prospect of a good consultant post here next year; Henry had assured him of this. Moresby was in the past, wasn't it? He would do his very best professionally, for the Chinese girl. And she would have the benefits of the Australian justice system.

But was that enough?

Before Tim had turned back to the hospital that night and made his way to the operating theatre, he'd crossed the parking lot, put his head through the window of the Mazda, and spoken rapidly to the Chinese boys.

It had taken Tim nearly an hour that night in theatre to repair the girl's vaginal injuries, painstakingly matching up the pieces of torn and bruised tissue, inspecting the inside of the bladder, to make sure there was no damage there. While he worked, the surgical registrar stitched up lacerations on the girl's knees and a nasty cut on her right elbow. She'd clearly tried to shield her face from blows.

As Tim finished off, the theatre door swung abruptly open to admit the nursing supervisor.

'You boys going to be much longer?' she demanded briskly. 'Because we have an urgent case coming straight up from Emergency. It's the fractured femur – now he's got stab wounds to the lung, liver, the works … Seems the guard went for a cup of tea, and a young Asian boy burst in with a knife. Presumably a friend of this one,' she nodded at the girl on the operating table. 'Gone in a flash, too, before the cop could even get out of the tearoom. They have no idea how he knew the man was there … If you're right with this one, we'll move her up to Recovery quickly and clean up ready for a laparotomy.'

Tim was silent, but the surgical registrar, himself Asian-Australian, chuckled. 'And I bet the cops never find him again either,' he said. 'Nobody will know nothing.'

Still thinking about that night, Tim continued on down the stairs and made his way to his car. He'd need to get a move on, he'd be late picking up the girls from their swimming lesson.

Far North Queensland, 7 March 2011

The rest of the weekend was quiet. Detectives Diamond, Borgese and Barwen worked a shift each, typing up reports on the events of the week. Then, at nine on Sunday night, Troy Barwen took a call from Mareeba. Bugsy and Sam Gecko had reported to the station that evening. They'd declined to say where they'd spent the weekend, however they were very happy to show Mareeba police where they'd found the Mitsubishi Outlander.

'Detective,' the Mareeba officer told Troy, 'it sounds like it's about three kilometres further down that Davies Creek road beyond where the body was found. It'll be pitch black there now but if you want to come up in the morning we can meet you there. Whatever time you like. Well, some time after eight.'

At eight the next morning the team met in Drew's office. It was decided they would all three go to Davies Creek in a LandCruiser from the station pool.

There were squalls of rain interspersed with sunbursts as they made their way up the range, Cass turning to admire the view across to the ocean as they reached the lookout. Drew drove on past Kuranda to the Davies Creek turn-off. The 'secret' entrance to the rainforest road was now a wide-open track where dozens of police and search vehicles had passed. Mud slurped beneath the wheels of the LandCruiser as Drew navigated his way back onto the road inside water catchment land. There were still areas marked off by crime-scene tape where the most intense searching had taken place. The LandCruiser crawled across the broken wooden bridge, which had been shored up with planks.

Two men from Mareeba station were waiting about eight kilometres past Davies Creek picnic ground. With them were Bugsy and Sam Gecko, clearly not enjoying the experience. Bugsy and Sam were remarkably alike. Cass, who'd interviewed them in connection with the death of Wayne Buscati, wondered if they might be brothers. Small, nuggety men, prematurely middle-aged, both puffing on hand-rolled cigarettes which they stubbed out on the ground as the team arrived.

'Yeah,' said Bugsy. 'Like I said, we just found the car. Right in here. Behind the bushes. Couldn't see it from the road. About two or three weeks ago.'

He parted some scrubby eucalypts and they could see the rutted tracks where the Mitsubishi had been driven into the bush, and where it had been driven out.

'And what brought you to this neck of the woods?' asked Drew.

'Just doing a bit of bushwalking, like.'

'Hmm. So you took the car?'

'Nope. Not that day. Look, this is the honest truth. Come back again a couple of days later, it's still here. Leaves all over it. There was already a lot of mud on it. Like maybe it was here during Yasi.

'Still we didn't touch it. Came back another time, and thought, well, it's got to be abandoned. Asked around the pubs, nobody knew nothin' about it. So – started it up.'

'There were belongings in the car? Personal items?' Cass asked.

There was silence, then Bugsy said: 'We dumped everything in the council bins in Kuranda. All the documents.'

Sam Gecko added: 'OK. I'll tell you. There was needles in there. And glass that drugs had been in. Like someone had been shooting up. And panties. Women's panties.'

'What did you do with those?'

'Put them in the bins like Bugsy said.'

'How long ago was this?'

'I reckon two weeks.'

The bins would have gone to the Cairns waste-processing centre by now, Drew knew.

'What was the drug?' he asked.

There was a long silence. 'It was ketamine. Least, that's what it said on the label.'

'Interesting. How many glass ampoules were there?'

'Just two. Both empty.'

'You're quite sure there weren't more?'

'Yeah. It's the truth, Detective. I tried ketamine once. Saw all sorts of terrible things. Taipans coming at me, ghosts. Wouldn't touch the stuff again.'

'Anything else in the car?'

'Well. I guess you know. A spare set of keys. Danno had them.'

'That was handy! Saved you wiring the ignition!' Bugsy didn't rise to this.

'Honest, that's all I know. I never saw this car before that. I knew it was no-one from up here that had it. It was just sitting in the bush like I said. I don't know anything about the woman, Sam neither.'

'And the numberplates? You know anything about a white Honda that's missing, that had those plates?'

'Yeah, well, I did a swap with a mate. He's gone back down south.'

'So you reckon there might be a white Honda around with the Mitsubishi plates. Somewhere down south?'

'Well you said it, not me. But yeah, I reckon so.'

'There'll be some charges, Bugsy. You know that. You can go back to Mareeba for those. But anything else you remember, don't hesitate to let us know. It could be helpful for all of us.'

In the car on the way back Cass called Leah Rookwood.

'Ketamine, Leah,' she said. 'Would toxicology screen for ketamine in the samples they've got from Odile Janvier?'

'They can do that,' she answered. 'Ketamine? That's interesting!'

'Can you just remind me,' asked Cass, 'about ketamine's legal medical uses. I'm more familiar with the illegal ones.'

'A very useful drug,' said Leah promptly, 'for certain kinds of anaesthesia. It's very safe, because it doesn't depress breathing or blood pressure. It's used for minor surgery. It's also used in cases where there's serious trauma but a person can't be moved until something's done, like an amputation to get someone out of a vehicle or a collapsed building. The downside, the reason why it's not used a lot more in hospitals, is that it can produce quite dramatic hallucinations. People having out-of-body experiences, thinking they're God … that kind of thing. Which is why it's been popular with ravers, ecstasy-takers, who want big experiences and often mix it with cocaine. Sometimes doing that brings them my way.'

'It's something that would be easily accessible to doctors?' asked Cass.

'Yes. And dentists,' replied Leah. 'It's a standard, widely used drug.' Cass drew in her breath. *Wilfred Lam*, she wondered, *did he use ketamine*?

'Up here,' Leah continued, 'especially out in the bush, there'd be more doctors who'd use it in their practices, because they'd be more likely to do minor emergency surgery than doctors in the cities. It'd be common to have it in stock in the smaller hospitals outside Cairns, and in rural doctors' surgeries.'

'Is it in a special category? Can any doctor prescribe it? Surgeons? Gynaecologists?'

'Yes, any doctor can prescribe it, but there are only certain types of practice where doctors would prescribe it. Surgeons and gynaecologists, yes certainly, they could use it for anaesthesia. It's also used for various kinds of chronic pain and depression, in which case I think it's often taken orally, whereas for anaesthesia it's injected.'

'So it would be possible for a Cairns doctor or dentist to get a supply of ketamine, supposedly to use for his or her own patients? That they could then use in other situations?'

'Yes. You're thinking that a Cairns doctor got hold of some ketamine and then gave it to Odile Janvier illegally? But that would then involve a pharmacist, who would know that the doctor had ketamine. Although their possession of it would be technically legal they might be called upon to explain what exactly they wanted to use it for. And where.'

'Could it have been *prescribed* for her? I mean legitimately? If it's used for depression like you said?'

'Well, if she had been a hospital patient with *severe* depression or *severe* pain. That may have been the case; I don't know. I'm just a pathologist. It's the kind of drug you'd want to supervise quite closely. Not like prescribing Prozac. Does she have a GP? Was she seeing a psychiatrist? She seemed to me to be in quite good physical health prior to her death.'

'She seems to have consulted dozens of doctors. I can't tell you more than that at the moment. Though no psychs that we've come across yet. From what you've said though, Leah, it sounds like it could have been used to get her to that spot in the forest and tie her up?'

'Yeah, depending on the circumstances. If the tox testing's positive for ketamine that still won't tell us if she got it orally or by injection. Or both. But it would tell us that she got ketamine into her system some way in the few hours before she died. The fact that it wasn't fully metabolised would mean that she died fairly soon after she got the drug.

'But Cass,' she added, 'there's a fairly steady party trade in ketamine. It's very possible that she got it off the street, no? Maybe in the belief that it was something else?'

'Yeah, I'm just exploring the medical possibilities,' Cass said. 'Thanks for organising the toxicology, Leah, that's really helpful.'

Cairns, September–October 2010

Six months before the discovery of the body in the rainforest, Lyndall Symonds had been summoned urgently to the Emergency Department. Although she and Trevor had been divorced by then for several months, it was on his account that she was called.

Lyndall didn't know where Trevor had been when the world he knew had disappeared. All she was told was that he'd been brought into ED with the sirens blasting. She'd heard the ambulance from her consulting rooms in Lake Street, where she'd been thinking about a change of medication for a long-time patient with bipolar. As she'd written a prescription for droperidol and signed it, the paramedics were thumping Trevor's chest and giving him adrenaline and electric shocks, but there was no response. At the age of fifty-one Dr Trevor Symonds had succumbed to a fatal heart attack.

She was still listed as his next-of-kin. Despite the divorce, and all their years of emotional trauma, she had been shaken, setting foot behind the curtain, to see him laid out like that, cold and still, eyes closed forever, his face marked by patches of grey and purple as post-mortem lividity formed. They had been happy together, once.

Lyndall had quickly stepped outside the cubicle. She signed the papers that formally identified him, and walked out towards the sunlight of the Esplanade. She would call her children in a moment. And she would call Bernard as soon as it was morning in France.

There were two paramedics standing outside the ED as she passed. 'Heard you had a Billy Snedden,' one said to the other.

'Yeah, mate. Found in one of those motels out on the highway south. Died happy, though. The condom was full.' They both roared with laughter.

Nicola and David, Lyndall and Trevor's children, organised a small private funeral and a public notice asking those friends and patients of Dr Symonds who wished to mark his passing to contribute to the hospital's charitable foundation. She was glad it had been low-key.

'Mum, I know you're divorced and he could do what he wanted,' Nicola had said. 'But there's been a lot of talk and you didn't need to hear it.'

Jane O'Malley had been a great support to Lyndall when she'd first left Trevor, and she was again in the weeks after Trevor's death. They had lunch every Friday in the same place on the Esplanade, making room in the middle of busy patient schedules for it, and had a policy of never talking about work. Once Lyndall's divorce was proceeding and she was settled in her new apartment, Jane and her husband George, and other friends came often for drinks or dinner. Jane was totally enthusiastic about the reappearance of

Bernard in Lyndall's life. Envious, even.

One Sunday in October Jane had invited Lyndall for lunch. George was in Sydney for a conference. There would just be the two of them. 'Oh no, don't bother to cook, we'll go out,' said Lyndall.

'No, I need to be able to talk to you.'

At lunch, Jane opened a bottle of sauvignon blanc and poured them both a generous measure, as Lyndall watched, curious. What was this about?

'I've a tale to tell you,' Jane said, 'and I hope you'll understand why I didn't tell you before.'

She began to tell Lyndall the story of Kianna, and the consultations with Samantha. How Samantha had delayed taking her daughter back to Trevor Symonds and had eventually come to consult Jane instead.

Lyndall listened intently, the chicken salad in front of her sitting untouched. When Jane reached the point where Samantha had told her about Trevor's advances, Lyndall reached out and poured herself a second glass of wine.

'I'm sorry,' Jane said, 'I just couldn't tell you earlier what a patient had told me in confidence.'

Lyndall nodded. 'Of course not.'

'I spoke to George,' Jane went on, 'not mentioning any names. But he guessed at once who it was.' She continued to the point in the story where Samantha had moved to Melbourne and George had called the meeting with Tim and Arthur Mellish.

'George asked Trevor to come along to his office,' Jane said, 'at one o'clock on 16 September.'

'Oh,' said Lyndall faintly, recognising the date and time.

Jane nodded. 'Yes,' she said, 'all three of them were waiting there for Trevor. They heard an ambulance come in, but of course they were just above ED; they didn't think anything of it.'

George, Tim and Arthur Mellish were descending the stairs when they saw Nimal Jayasinghe emerging from ED.

'Oh Sirs!' he cried, when he saw them. 'Jolly bad news! Dr Symonds has sadly passed away. Brought in by ambulance. Probably an infarct. Very sudden.' He lowered his voice to a whisper and added: 'He was completely naked! In a motel in the middle of the day.'

'I had to stop myself giggling,' George had told Jane. 'Of course I felt sorry for the guy! What a way to go out. The opposite of panache. Hope it doesn't happen to me.'

'I punched him on the arm,' Jane said, before looking directly at Lyndall.

'I'm sorry I've had to tell you all this. But I did remember what you said to me, when I told you about your Pap report. From Samantha's account I'd have to say that it sounded like he might have been involved with patients before. No-one knows who he was with in that motel, as far as I know. But it just might come out that it was a patient.'

Lyndall nodded grimly.

'I've really hated knowing all this and not being able to

tell you,' said Jane. 'Now that he's dead it's all right. And Samantha's moved away, and you've never met her. So I felt that I could tell you, finally.'

Cairns, 8 March 2011

At midday on Tuesday Leslie called a meeting of the whole team for a rundown on everything they knew so far. Equipped with coffee, they gathered around the table in his office. Drew spread out a map of the area west of Cairns, including Lamb Range, which contained Davies Creek National Park.

'Well, Sir,' he said to Leslie, 'finding the car and seeing where it was found has extended our information but not solved the main problems – what happened to Odile Janvier and where is Michel? The only fingerprints in that car matching any database have been Janvier's, Danno Muphy's, Bugsy's and Sam's. There are others, but you'd expect that if Bugsy and Sam were swanning around in the car for a week before they lent it to Danno. There are also some prints that match the ones in the Earlville house that we think are Odile's. And, though the forensics have pulled the car apart, there's nothing at all to give us a lead on where Janvier is.'

Drew went on, 'I'm inclined to believe Bugsy's story about finding the car, although Mareeba will check the bush around there to see what Bugsy's growing. He's never struck me as a tree-hugger. We'll also never know how much ketamine was really there. He might not like the stuff himself but I'm sure he has friends who do.

'So we still have two broad possibilities. Either Michel killed her, possibly using ketamine to get her there and/or kill her, and then dumped the car and took off.

'Or somebody else, maybe more than one person, kidnapped them both, using ketamine, tied up Odile, killing her directly or indirectly, and did something similar with Michel which we haven't yet discovered. Like push him into that flooded creek. Let's have another look at our list of suspects.'

Drew opened his laptop. 'These are all the men who appeared on videos and in emails,' he said. 'All those who seem to have been paying up. We're working through contacting them all and checking their alibis. With great discretion. It's going to take days, if not weeks.'

Leslie nodded.

Drew peered at his list. 'We've got two cardiologists. Three GPs. Jim Hewitt and his son. A couple of other businessmen who maybe know Jim. Wilfred Lam – he's dead; we have to talk to his wife. That's going to be delicate. There's an orthopaedic surgeon. A plastic surgeon. A skin doctor, and a few more. Quite a lot have moved away from Cairns. Maybe to get away from the blackmail. If that happened Janvier probably stopped demanding the cash, but of course he would keep the evidence, and those doctors would go on being afraid …

'We've also got Henry Jolley and Arthur Mellish. They were around Cairns the whole time and what they were doing in that time is only partly confirmed by someone else. Mellish says he went up to the Tablelands to check on his property sometime on the Saturday afternoon before Yasi. He can't remember exactly what time and he says he saw a neighbour. The neighbour's not completely sure she saw him but says if she did it was about three in the afternoon. To get to that property he had to pass the Davies Creek turn-off. He admits he knows the private road and has been on it at times.'

Drew was on a roll. 'As for Jolley, he lives on his own. He says he was at home or in his office most of that weekend. He went to see some patients in the hospital both mornings, that's corroborated. But in the remainder of both days he had plenty of time to commit two murders and try to dispose of the evidence. Probably so did Wilfred Lam. He didn't work weekends.

'Especially interesting is where Jolley says he was on the Sunday evening, the 30th. He and the doc he works with, Tim Ingram, were in Jolley's office going through some files. Jolley's office is in the outpatient department and on a Sunday night not another soul was there. Just the two of them. For about four hours, he says.'

'Yes,' said Leslie. 'And Ingram didn't volunteer the information but did tell me that's what they were doing when I asked him. He did quite openly show me the calendar in his phone. And sounded plausible with the explanation. But we didn't get Jolley's statement about where he was until yesterday, whereas I spoke to Ingram on Saturday. They certainly would have had time, if they'd wanted, to get the two stories straight.'

'Well,' said Cass, 'four hours might be long enough to get hold of both Janviers, kill them and dispose of the bodies. Tim Ingram knew exactly where to get into that road. But dragging Odile Janvier in the dark and tying her up wouldn't have been easy.'

'If there were two of them,' said Drew, 'it wouldn't have been so hard. And Ingram himself might not have done the killing but might have thought it was OK to help Jolley dispose of the body because he was being blackmailed.'

Troy Barwen, who'd spent much of Monday afternoon googling ketamine use in dental practices, said, 'Either of them could have got the ketamine. And surgical gloves – they'd both be pretty skilled at managing things like injecting ketamine with their hands in gloves, so there'd be no prints anywhere. The same goes for all the other doctors – and for the dentist. Maybe even especially Lam. As a dentist he's entitled to use it. And he's originally from Hong Kong where we know ketamine's a big party drug.'

'Lam was certainly terrified of something,' Cass said slowly. 'But was it just of being exposed by the videos? Of his wife knowing? Terrified of what it would do to him professionally? That's a big factor for Jolley and Mellish. Or was Lam terrified because he murdered her? Or rather, organised her murder. I'm sure he didn't kill her himself, at least not alone. He wasn't physically capable of dragging

Odile Janvier from the road to where she was found, even if she was doped to the gills with ketamine.'

'Let's think that through,' said Drew. 'Lam decides he wants Odile Janvier dead so he organises one or more hitmen, maybe from overseas. They somehow find out where she lives – she's made that difficult but not impossible. Perhaps they just watch the unit for long enough to identify Michel then follow him home. They stake out the site at Earlville, then kidnap the two of them, take them up to the mountains full of ketamine, and kill her by some yet-to-be-established method. They do the same with Michel and dump him somewhere else that we haven't yet found.

'Problems with this scenario? There was no evidence of any kind of struggle in the house or of any break-in. Apart from the scarves. And I can't imagine the Janviers ever letting anyone in, not anyone who they were blackmailing, at least. And the person or people would have had to come with quite a lot of stuff – drugs, something to tie them up with and so on.'

'What about at the unit?' suggested Troy.

'No-one ever saw her there,' Cass pointed out.

'During the day,' Troy countered. 'Maybe she went there at night. To help make the videos. Send the messages. Count the money.'

'That would be an easier place to catch them,' Cass agreed. 'Also, all the suspects know the place. At least, they know the letterbox, even if they didn't make the connection with the front office, which was presumably why he set it up like that in the first place. Whereas, even if they did find the address of the house, they wouldn't know anything about who else might live there or the layout and so on. One of the things that's clear from all the men blackmailed is that none of them knew for sure the identity of their blackmailer, except the Hewitts. They all just knew it was somebody known to Odile Janvier. That's all. So even if they went down there some time and saw Michel Janvier in the front running a cleaning company, they wouldn't have known who he was or necessarily make a connection with the letterbox at the back.'

'And,' said Drew, 'if he was in the back and someone he didn't like turned up, all he had to do was not open the back door but go through into the front office, and slip away. He put a lot of thought into it all.'

'But, like the house,' said Leslie, 'there was no sign of a struggle at the unit. No sign of anything amiss when Barwen went there on Monday. If our supposed murderer went to the unit, you'd expect to see something more than we found there. Michel Janvier was a fit guy. He would have put up a fight.'

'There's also one big argument against it being hired killers,' said Cass, 'and that's the scarves. Hiring a killer, I think you'd want them just to do the job. Shoot her and dump the body in a hole in the bush. The same for her husband. You wouldn't want them to go prancing around the countryside with silk scarves.'

Troy Barwen looked serious. 'Yes,' he said. 'Cass is right. Those scarves are sending us a message. I'm just not sure what it is.'

Cass suppressed a snort.

Leslie said evenly: 'Troy, I think the message is that the killer was directly involved with Odile herself. I think Cass has a point about hired killers. Why would they bother with French scarves?

'But let's suppose that *Dominic* got someone to kill her – let's move on to that possibility. Dominic presumably knows nothing about his mother's … other activities, with the scarves or the blackmail. But he's suffered a lot in the past from being tied up by her. Now he wants her dead. Let's say because his brother wants to get married, buy a house. Dominic wants to help him and he's always wanted to get even with his mother. Getting rid of both his parents would mean the boys would inherit the house, which is worth enough for Dominic to help Damian and pay off the killer or killers. Dominic maybe doesn't feel too badly disposed towards his father so he gets taken somewhere quickly, shot and dumped, whereas Odile gets the slow death tied up in the bush. Tied up with scarves because that's what Dominic's ordered, to make the point to his mother that he hates her for what she did to them. The scarves might be a kind of symbol for him too. And Dominic probably has contacts who'd have no trouble getting hold of ketamine.'

Cass nodded. 'Yes,' she said, 'that sounds possible. But for the sons to benefit financially there have to be bodies found and identified. The parents can't just disappear. And if it was Dominic or Damian and they were counting on inheriting, the deaths shouldn't look suspicious, which Odile's definitely does. But … Odile's death could have been planned to look like Michel did it, and then Michel killed to look like suicide, except that Michel's body has disappeared, maybe in Yasi.'

'The other message that the scarves are sending us,' Cass added, 'is that at some stage the killer was at the Earlville house. He, or they, had to get the scarves. If she was grabbed somewhere away from the house she might have been wearing one. But not four.'

Troy's face brightened. 'Right!' he said, 'I hadn't thought of that. Something a woman understands!'

'One of many things only a woman would understand,' responded Drew.

'So, just going back to Arthur Mellish and Henry Jolley,' Cass said, ignoring this exchange, 'they both have a good reason to get rid of her but it wouldn't have been clear to either of them that killing her would stop the blackmail because they both believed someone else was involved.'

'I do have some reservations about Jolley,' Leslie said. 'Not on his own – but with Ingram's help. Jolley mentioned to me that there's a new woman in his life. This could be the trigger for him to finally do something about the blackmail, after putting up with it for years. Very likely Ingram is aware of this new development for Jolley; they work together. So

Jolley tells Ingram how he's being blackmailed and Ingram is so outraged he decides to help Henry get rid of her. And Ingram has the idea of using the scarves to make the point to her that she was getting the treatment she'd given Henry.

'Then,' he added, 'did Ingram stage his return to the tree to see if anything was obvious? And to check out the creek because he'd dumped Michel Janvier into it?'

'Well Sir,' said Drew, 'the thing is, that bridge really was broken and his car was in the creek. I saw it with my own eyes. He didn't stage that. And his wife was with him. And ... could they really have killed off Michel as well?'

'Perhaps. If they had to. But maybe I'm unduly suspicious of him,' Leslie answered. 'Then there's Jim Hewitt. He has men working for him who will stop at very little.'

'Though they're bloody incompetent!' retorted Cass.

'Agreed,' Leslie nodded. 'But there were no files on Hewitt or his son Aidan at Portsmith. Was this because Michel really did destroy the video when Jim's lawyer asked him to? Or because someone working for Hewitt went to the office at some time when Michel was there, kidnapped him, and took away the compromising videos? Videos which could have been more recent than twelve years ago, or could have involved Jim or other people he knows. Then they could have used Michel to get into the house, where they kidnap Odile as well, take her up into the forest, tie her up and kill her. Then take him somewhere else, kill him and dump the car. Only, again, we haven't found him yet.'

'Yes, that's plausible,' Cass agreed, 'because Jim is the only one of the blackmailed suspects who knew who Michel was.'

'And while it seems believable that he did want to make sure that after twelve years there was nothing left of that early video, it seems a bit excessive to send two guys to break into the place,' Drew said. 'OK, let's think about Michel again.'

A search at Earlville on Monday afternoon had uncovered a box containing two guns, deeply buried under the vegetable patch, as Damian had predicted. In good condition, well-oiled. A Lee Enfield rifle and a Queensland police-issue Glock 22, no doubt bought in a pub somewhere. Not loaded. Officers were still digging up the garden looking for other hiding places.

'I have to say I'm still not one hundred per cent convinced by Lyndall Symonds' belief that Michel was incapable of killing his wife,' Leslie said. 'So suppose he did tie her up and do the job … Let's think about that.'

'Then he stands next to his car by the road smoking cigarettes?' queried Cass. 'Why? Does he want to make sure she's dead?'

'Maybe they were smoked beforehand,' said Drew. 'Maybe he went and staked out the place first. Found the tree within a tree. Maybe even parked in the same place. Stood smoking while he made his plans. Of course, anybody who put her there might have done the same thing.'

'Would somebody else hang around the place where they'd killed his wife while Michel smoked multiple fags and told them the story of his life?' Cass asked.

'A kidnapper might let their victim smoke if they were trying to get information out of him,' Leslie pointed out. 'But anyway, putting the cigarettes aside, let's say that Michel kills her and then drives three kilometres away and parks the car as a decoy. Eventually it's going to be found, and he must have known that.

'Then he disappears.

'One scenario: he walks back to Davies Creek and passes through the picnic ground, which he could do without anyone there really noticing; he'd just have looked like a bushwalker. He makes his way up to the highway. Thumbs a lift from a driver who hasn't told us about it. And never goes home again. He could have hitched to Kalgoorlie by now. Don't forget he could have had a lot of cash with him. He's extorted several hundred thousand at least over the years, even if a lot of it was spent on Madame. Enough to get him to WA, or some other place far away, and set himself up with a new identity.

'Second scenario: he vanishes into the bush somewhere off the rainforest road, heading possibly across country and further south. Again with the idea of getting away from Cairns.'

'What about searching the bush even further around where the car was found?' Drew asked.

'We already have the men working their way through the rainforest in that area,' Leslie answered. 'And they've found not one single thing. Extending that search to a region half the size of Tasmania, which is what that state park is, seems to me a fool's errand. If he did kill her and dump the car, he could have walked clean out of the area and onto the highway in a couple of hours, leaving not a trace behind. We can mount a bigger alert for him across the country, particularly in North Queensland and the Gulf country, since that's where Damian says he's spent most of his time. But also right across to Perth and up to Darwin.'

'Talking of Damian,' said Cass, 'I should give him a call. It'll be all over the evening news that his father's car's been found and he should have heard it from us first.' She left the three men poring over the map.

In five minutes she was back.

'Kahlpahlim Rock,' she said. 'Otherwise known as Lamb's Head. Is that on your map there?'

'Um, yep,' said Troy. 'Right here. Highest point in the Lamb Range, it says.' He pointed to the red triangle marking the Rock.

'Damian says Michel took the boys there a couple of times when they were young. He thinks his dad might have been there by himself other times, and that where the car was found must be near the start of the track to the Rock. He thinks there might be two tracks, both going off the road.'

Leslie leant over and studied the map. 'I've been to the Rock once,' he said. 'It's beautiful but it's a helluva walk. Great view from the top.'

'I've been there too,' said Drew. 'When I was in high school in Atherton. It's a tough walk.'

With a finger he traced the trail from the road to the Rock. There were two tracks, as Damian had described. One led off not far from where the Mitsubishi had been found. The second began a bit more than a kilometre further on.

'There are probably old logging tracks from the other side of the Rock down to Gordonvale, to the main highway going south,' said Leslie. 'But it would be an extraordinary way to get away from the scene of the crime, if that's what he was doing. I think it's much more likely that he simply walked out past Davies Creek. If he walked anywhere at all.'

Cass looked thoughtful. She'd just been studying the clouds shrouding the mountains outside her window as she talked to Damian Janvier on the phone. Then she said: 'Maybe I'll just run an idea past Lyndall Symonds,' she said.

'What idea is that?' Leslie asked.

'Well, that Michel went to Kahlpahlim Rock,' she replied.

'If he went along the Kahlpahlim Rock trail at all it was about four weeks ago now,' Leslie said briskly. 'He's hardly going to still be there. It's rugged country. Even for experienced bushmen. It's still an important place for the Tjapukai people. There's no way we can search right through there.'

'Mmm ... but the idea did occur straight away to Damian that it was a place he might go.'

'Look,' said Leslie, indicating the map. 'He could also have walked down Bridle Creek Road past Copperlode Dam and down into Cairns. Which is what Doctor Tim and his wife were going to do by car. Much easier. He could have walked up to the highway and gone in any one of three directions. Damian himself told us he's had nothing to do with his father for years, the only knowledge he has of him is from years ago. We have to direct this search logically and with the best use of my resources. Which are finite.'

Cass nodded. All that was true. But she was captivated by the idea of the giant Rock, brooding high in the range, hidden in mist. She was determined to go there.

Kahlpahlim Rock, 12 March 2011

Cass and Lyndall set out early on Saturday morning. It had taken all of Cass's powers of persuasion to get Drew's approval for the expedition, which, he'd emphasised, she was undertaking in her own time and on her own responsibility.

The week had been devoted to the tedious business of interviewing reluctant suspects who'd had to be cornered between their operating lists and their consulting sessions, some of them in places far from Cairns. Almost all had unshakeable alibis for the critical period.

The two cardiologists had been at a conference in the States. One general practitioner had been on a walking tour in New Zealand, and another one in England. The dermatologist had been at his Gold Coast practice for two weeks including the crucial days. The gastroenterologist had undergone prostate surgery in Brisbane. The orthopaedic surgeon had been to a meeting in Florence and then on holiday in Italy ... The list of exotic alibis went on.

Jim Hewitt had spent the relevant time at his house in Port Douglas, where he had friends staying. He appeared to be covered, as did Wilfred Lam, whose wife, visibly distressed, swore he was at home with his family the whole weekend before Yasi, and whose receptionist Leanne produced the appointment book to confirm he had been fully occupied with the incisors and molars of his clients during the working week.

That left just Henry Jolley, Tim Ingram and Arthur Mellish with holes in their alibis. Jolley and Ingram said they'd spent the Sunday night together, which no-one else could confirm, and Mellish's neighbour remembered seeing him at the Tablelands house not far from Davies Creek, but couldn't say when, not even which day. Troy had been given the task of pursuing these gaps.

The only positive piece of news had come from Leah Rookwood, who phoned Cass to say that yes, ketamine in significant amounts had been detected in tissue samples taken from Odile Janvier's body.

'Leah must have special influence in Brisbane,' Drew said when he'd heard this. 'Normally it takes six weeks minimum for tox results.'

'I know,' said Cass. 'She leant on them heavily because there was no obvious cause of death at autopsy and it looked like murder. So they've confirmed ketamine. But no alcohol, cocaine, cannabis, other prescription drugs.'

In between these banal but necessary detective pursuits, Cass had enjoyed the respite of several long conversations with Lyndall, whom she was liking more and more. After checking with Drew, she'd told Lyndall about the ketamine, about where the car had been found, and then what Damian had said about Kahlpahlim Rock.

'I want to go to the Rock,' Cass said. 'I'd just like to go

and see it. I'm not expecting to find Michel Janvier.'

'Can I come with you?' Lyndall had asked immediately. 'I'd seriously doubt too that Michel would be there, despite what Damian says. I've been there once. The track's tough going for a couple of hours, but it's worth it at the top. You're fitter than me, not to mention younger. But I've been walking a lot in France.'

'Saturday?' Cass said.

Lyndall laughed. 'Yes, OK. Saturday. My jetlag's well and truly gone now. I can do it.'

Told of this plan, Drew was not impressed and did his best to dissuade her. 'Yes, you're due time off,' he said. 'You all are. But that should mean a day of relaxing at home, not a mad scramble up a difficult bush track. I can't spare anyone to go with you so you'll be there entirely as a civilian. And I can't believe you're going to find anything at all.'

'Well,' said Cass, 'at least we'll know.'

'Take plenty of water,' said Drew. *Aha*, thought Cass, *so I can go.*

'And make sure your mobiles are fully charged,' he said. 'Remember there's a helipad at the top, to service the mobile phone tower there, so there's mobile cover. But I can tell you, if I have to send a chopper to rescue you two I won't be amused.'

He gazed out the window in the direction of the range. Then he added: 'Diamond, I know you're a registered gun owner. You've got a weapon in your house?'

'A Glock. Same as service issue.'

'I think it'd be a good idea to take it with you.'

Dawn was breaking through the canopy as Lyndall drove along the road beyond the Davies Creek picnic grounds. This track now resembled the holding pen of a cattle market, so many vehicles had passed along it. As Lyndall splashed her Subaru Tribeca through a deep mud pool, the wheels spun then gripped again as she changed to a lower gear and the car inched forward.

'About eight k's down this road is the start of the ridge trail,' Cass said, peering at the guidebook in the half-light. Then she lifted her eyes to a break in the trees where a sunbeam lit up a flowering tree orchid. 'Oh!' she said, 'it's just beautiful here!'

Lyndall smiled and nodded, gripping the wheel as she steered the car across another muddy morass.

Five kilometres from the highway they came to police tape marking off the area where Odile Janvier had been found. The forest was very still, with only the occasional song from a bird waking high in the canopy.

The ridge trail's first section had once been an old logging track. Their plan was to climb up along this first trail and come back down the second track, then walk back along the road to Lyndall's car. The first trail was steeper, but it was also shorter. This would be the most demanding part of the walk and they planned to do it in the hours before the sun, and the temperature, rose too high.

Both women wore jeans and T-shirts and boots. Lyndall couldn't help noticing the bulge beneath Cass's T-shirt, even though the detective was off duty. But she said nothing. They each had a backpack with a water bottle, and Lyndall had brought sandwiches and a flask of coffee. All going well, they would make it to the top of the Rock by late morning and be back down at the road by mid-afternoon.

For a while the track followed a creek with sandy shores and stumpy palms. Then it crossed an old wooden bridge. Cass stepped gingerly onto this, remembering the sight of Tim and Chris's car in the creek on the day the corpse had been found. It held firm. The track widened out into the road loggers had made a hundred years earlier. Paperbark trees grew on both sides, much of their flaky bark peeled off by Yasi and lying in long sheets on the ground. Then the path began the steep climb to the top of the range. Parts of the route were defined by rough timber steps but it was still a demanding climb and they barely spoke for thirty minutes as they clambered upwards, grabbing at branches to steady themselves and sometimes crawling on hands and knees. Then the path levelled out onto a plateau.

'Wow,' groaned Cass. 'I need a break! Is it too early for coffee?' Sweat was running down her face and breasts and soaking into her T-shirt, and the knees of her jeans were thick with mud.

Lyndall laughed. 'Just have some water!' she said, unscrewing a bottle.

They sat on a group of small boulders as rays of sun broke through cloud above them, and looked upwards to where the track began to climb again and the eucalypts were replaced by purple-barked kauri pines. These huge trees were what the loggers had come to take.

They started up again. Coming to the start of the pines, Cass suddenly stopped and grabbed Lyndall's arm, pointing ahead. Lyndall peered at the path and saw what she thought was a dark purple kauri branch. Then the branch began to move and she saw that it was actually a large python, glistening purple in the sunlight.

'An amethystine python!' she said as they watched the snake slither away into the undergrowth. Fully stretched it measured at least four metres.

'They don't like humans,' she told Cass. 'They'll never attack if you just leave them alone. You can see how they get the name.'

Cass paid closer attention to where she put her feet after that; she had no intention of putting Lyndall's claim to the test.

They climbed through rainforest where ferns and palms jostled for space under the kauris and reached a junction marked by orange tape. Now the trail took a turn to the right and they began their approach to the Rock itself. Soon they could see a huge boulder that the guidebook identified as the first lookout along the ridge to the Rock. They staggered across and found footholds that took them to the top of the boulder. Cass looked around and took a deep breath. Even if they went no further, the climb had been worth it.

'It's fabulous!' she exclaimed and Lyndall nodded, panting from the exertion of the last few minutes. They flopped down on the warm surface of the boulder and looked around. Below them stretched the forest: grey-green and silver where the eucalypts grew further down the mountain, darker green with the glowing purple trunks of the kauris higher up. To the west they could see the broad plateau that was the Atherton Tableland, and in the distance the town of Mareeba starting to wake up to the day. A tiny bus was making its way down the distant highway, and a microscopic horse ambled across a field. Several hot air balloons were floating in the sky, orbs of gold caught by the morning sun. Near the Rock, a small cloud hung motionless above the dome like the froth on a glass of bitter.

'I'm beginning to feel less negative about Michel Janvier,' Cass said, unscrewing the thermos and pouring coffee into mugs, 'if he liked this place and brought his kids here.'

'Yep,' agreed Lyndall. 'I didn't meet him until years after he would have come here with the boys. It's good to think that he appreciated the bush and shared that with Damian at least. And he was apparently quite happy when he was out west. Before he met Odile. Although he was always inclined to fraud, to taking the easy option. That was in his personality long before he met her.'

'She does seem to have been a right bitch,' Cass said, watching a small grey bird with a lemon chest hop from branch to branch.

'The pale-yellow robin,' Lyndall identified, before saying of Odile: 'Yeah, she screwed up her husband, and her sons when they were kids, and it seems a lot of other people. She mightn't have been so destructive if she'd stayed in France with perhaps more help with the kids from Michel's family. They might have restrained her. That's not an excuse, just a comment.'

'Can I ask you,' Cass began, 'what Michel's attitude to you was, personally? As a man talking to a good-looking younger woman, about intimate sexual matters? How difficult is that, for a woman psychiatrist?'

'Well, thanks for the compliment,' Lyndall laughed. 'Actually he *was* difficult. Certainly male patients do hit on me, from time to time. But female patients do the same to male psychiatrists, I'm told. And gay patients, where a therapist is gay. I always felt wary about Michel. Not that he would make an advance, which I'm perfectly capable of handling. Rather that he would become emotionally dependent on me, or his idea of who I was, and seek masochistic gratification by being rejected by me. I always tried to keep a physical barrier, usually the desk, between us, to emphasise that there was always going to be an emotional distance between us. The relationship was always going to be a doctor–patient one, controlled by me, and I had to make that clearer to him than I need to do with most of my patients. Actually talking about sex, which is a regular part of my work, I don't find all that difficult with patients. About myself, though, with men, yes, it's difficult!'

Cass roared with laughter at this. 'Men!' she said. 'Talking to them about anything personal is hopeless. But I've given up on men anyway.'

Lyndall looked quite shocked. 'Surely not! At your age? What about the father of your son? He's not still in your lives?'

Cass gazed out towards Mareeba. 'Richie?' she said. 'No. He died when Jordon was not quite three. He hardly remembers his dad at all.'

'I'm sorry. You must have been very young when that happened.'

'Eighteen. Yes, it was terrible. Such a waste. I got pregnant when I was fifteen. Richie was seventeen. He didn't run away from it, though. He was very supportive. But we both dropped out of school and left home and travelled together. Right around New South Wales and southern Queensland. That was in 1993. We had a lot of relatives to put us up but we also worked. Picking fruit and things like that. And I admit, did some drugs, but not much. Jordon was born in Sydney.

'Then in 1995 my mother got sick. She'd just had my youngest sister, who's almost three years younger than Jordon. We were in Inverell. I took a train back to Newcastle with Jordon. Richie was coming with the van – we had this old, beat-up van. But he never made it. He was found unconscious in a back street in Taree and the van was missing. It was eventually found burnt out. No-one was ever charged for any of it. Richie spent six days in John Hunter Hospital but never regained consciousness.

'He was … funny, clever, he could have done so much. But the story of his death, it's totally an Aboriginal story. A young male Aboriginal story. The kind of story I don't want for my son. But the kind of story I wrote for my thesis.'

'Your thesis? In criminology?'

'Yeah. I did honours. I had ideas about being an academic. Successful Indigenous woman activist in criminal justice reform.'

'So is joining the Police a kind of positive action in that direction?'

'Funnily enough, it might be, although I never consciously thought that. My reasons for joining the force were much more personal. I was the classic case of the student who falls for her professor. In my case much older than me. And as it turned out I was not the only one, only, it took me a long while to realise. And it also had quite a bad effect on my son, for a while. Luckily my family helped a lot.'

After a moment Cass added: 'The prof, his name is Rufus Forbes, you may have heard of him.'

'Lord, of course I have. He's always on the radio, talking about social justice and Indigenous issues. He has quite a reputation.'

'Yep, he does. And what he has to say along those lines is mostly spot-on. He loves it. White fella left-wing hero, fighter for Indigenous rights. But in relation to women he's medieval. He wanted me because I'm Aboriginal. A trophy to display.'

'How long were you with him?'

'Two years. But not exclusively. I kind of knew that. But you know and you don't know.'

Lyndall nodded. Hadn't she herself used those exact same words?

'One day I came back early from fieldwork and found him in my bed with my flatmate. They were supposed to be babysitting Jordon, who was watching TV. He was ten.

'That's when I gave up writing the book of the thesis and the whole academic thing and decided to become a copper. Because I knew how pissed off he'd be. A lot of his public image is about exposing the police. And sure, a lot of it is justified. He's done some good things. But I joined the New South Wales force basically to spite him! It was only later that I discovered I'd made the perfect choice for me. I love what I do and yes, I do think it's possible to be a good cop and make a difference to some people. Though I wouldn't say that out loud in the station.'

'I'm sure you're right,' Lyndall said. 'I've done a lot of work in the courts, particularly with teenagers. There are good cops and bad cops, and the good ones can really make a difference; I've seen that happen, many times, where a cop decides not to press a charge and directs a kid into some program to help them. It's a pity that didn't happen to Dominic Janvier.'

Lyndall was silent for a moment, and then said: 'I understand about the whole infidelity thing. In a town as small as this, everyone knows. But no-one tells you. I spent days and nights wondering where Trevor was, agonising over it, when I was younger. Instead of just getting up and leaving, because that's hard to do with kids, but harder when I wanted to stay here, my work's here, my friends are here. It was only when the kids had finished school that I was able to leave.

'The kids know a lot. Give good advice. When I left Trevor, Nicola told me she wished I'd done it much earlier. Not for her sake; because I would have been happier, she said. And she was right.

'But, Cass, don't give up entirely on men. I've found a nice one in France. Although,' she added reflectively, 'I have no idea what he does when I'm not there. But I feel old enough to just live in the moment. And the moments have been good. I'm going back there at Easter.'

'I haven't come across anyone I fancy yet in Cairns,' Cass laughed.

'What about your colleague, Barwen? He seems to have taken a shine to you.'

'Troy. Yep. That's the case. I had to have some words with him. He's like a giant cocker spaniel, isn't he?' She rolled, spaniel-like, around on the rock, her tongue hanging out. 'I think I'm more of a whippet woman.' They both burst into laughter then gathered up their backpacks ready for the next stage of the climb.

Reading from the guidebook, Cass found the bower of a golden bowerbird beside the trail. The tower, two metres high, was woven from sticks around two saplings and decorated with forest flowers that the male bird had plucked. The bird himself, brilliant in his yellow plumage, hovered about protectively.

They climbed on through thick bush. The air was still very humid but at this height the temperature had dropped. They emerged onto bare rock, partly covered by cloud, then plunged again into a thick tangle of ferns and moss. Following the guidebook, they found a crevice between two boulders, slid down, climbed over a small tree, then up a steep path. Besides the ferns and mosses there were hundreds of orchids, white and pink and yellow, emerging from cracks in the rocks and feasting on tree trunks. Finally, they came to the saddle between the two highest points of the ridge, just as the hovering cloud moved away from the Rock.

Now there was just the hundred-metre climb to the helipad. Above them the silhouette of the mobile phone tower loomed in contrast to the beauty of the forest.

They dropped their backpacks on a patch of ferns and took stock of their newly found paradise. The top of the Rock was about eighty metres below them to the left. This was the very last bit of the walk. Leaving the packs they scrambled down the granite path and onto the lookout on the Rock.

The view was astounding. To the east they could see the whole of Cairns spread out by the Coral Sea, the hotels and the hospital like tiny pieces of Lego. The sea merged into the shimmering blue morning sky. The Barron River snaked its way across the country. A red and silver plane rose silently into the sky. Closer to their eyrie was the Copperlode Dam, cocooned in forest.

They sat on the Rock, warm in the mid-morning sun, sweat cooling their limbs. Everyday life and the pursuit of Michel Janvier seemed remote.

'I've looked out my office window at this place so many times,' Cass said, 'thinking that it's a magic place. Now I see that's true.'

They made their way back down to the helipad, sat down and unpacked their sandwiches. For a while they lay on their backs contemplating their surroundings, drowsy in the sun, which was now overhead.

Cass texted Jordon: *Fabulous views u must do it soon back pm fishpie in fridge mum.*

Lyndall texted Bernard: *on top of the mountain vraiment paradis sauf pour toi je t'aime L xxx* Then she got to her feet. 'Call of nature,' she declared.

'I have to wee too,' Cass replied. 'We can go between those ferns.'

'My needs are slightly more,' Lyndall said. 'I'll go behind those trees. I don't think I'm likely to run into anyone! Meet you by the start of the path down in a few minutes.' She indicated where the path back down began, at the far edge of the grass. She picked up her backpack and started across the grass, then disappeared behind the small trees.

As she undid her jeans and crouched down behind a shrub, Lyndall felt something slithering down her back. Peering over her shoulder, she realised that it was plant not animal – a long piece of lawyer vine had attached itself to the back of her T-shirt and jeans. She dealt with the purpose of her visit then carefully lifted the tendrils of vine off her clothes before doing up her jeans. This was taking time. Cass will be back on the path by now, she thought.

Back on the grass, though, there was no sign of Cass. Where was she? She should have been back sooner than Lyndall.

Suddenly, from the direction of the path leading to the Rock, there was a deafening noise. *BLAM! BLAM!* Two gunshots in rapid succession, very close by, the sound echoing off the Rock. And then Cass's voice, high-pitched and tense, coming from somewhere low down, out of sight, beyond the ferns: 'Lyndall, stay where you are!'

Lyndall let go of her backpack and ran back towards the trees. She threw herself down on her stomach and rolled into the protection of a hollow in the ground. Too bad if there were pythons in it! Her heart was thumping violently. It thumped even more when a squawking brush turkey rose from a mound in front of her. But the bird had been disturbed by her arrival in its territory and not the sound of shooting. It settled down again on the mound.

Lyndall was breathing hard, trying to make sense of what she'd heard. What the fuck was going on? Where was Cass? Had she run into Michel Janvier and had he fired shots at her, or she at him? Had he grabbed her? Was he holding her hostage? Was there some other person over there, armed and dangerous, who'd kidnapped Michel and now had Cass? This seemed unlikely, given the remoteness of the spot, but so did the idea that Michel was hanging out there with a gun or two.

After a few moments she cautiously raised her head. There was no sound at all. Her backpack lay abandoned on the grass. Over near where the path to the Rock began she could see Cass's backpack where she'd left it. She began to inch forward on her stomach towards it, staying within the protection of the trees that encircled the grass beside the helipad. She was trying to think of what she could say to Michel to calm him down. If he would listen to her before he shot anyone. If it was Michel doing the shooting.

Then, to her horror, she heard her mobile start to ring from within her backpack. Shit! The backpack was in full view to anyone in the forest straight ahead, or coming up the path from the Rock. But if it was someone from Cairns calling she could ask them to get help. Before she could decide what to do, the ringing stopped. And, again, there was not a sound.

The mobile rang again.

Lyndall got to her feet and ran across to the backpack, picked it up, threw herself back into the safety of her hollow and grabbed the phone from the front pocket.

To her utter astonishment she saw that Cass's phone was calling hers. God, she must be with someone who'd taken her phone. Lyndall pressed the green button and put the phone to her ear. She was so scared she thought she would vomit.

'Lyndall!' said Cass. 'It's me. Don't move, at least not forward on the track. I'm OK. Sort of. I fell partway down the side of the rock. A branch snagged my belt and saved me. I was dangling but now I've wedged my bum into the tree. But I'm going to need a rescue team and a chopper to get me out of here. Can you call Drew Borgese, tell him exactly where I am? And stay where you are – I've no idea how long this tree's gonna hold up, and I don't want you to fall by coming to help me. It's very slippery.'

'But …' Lyndall could barely get the words out, conscious that speaking would direct the gunman right to her. 'There's someone shooting,' she whispered hard. 'Trying to shoot you I think. Or me.'

Cass laughed. 'No, that was me! At first I couldn't reach

my mobile – it was in the back pocket of my jeans. But I could reach my gun. I didn't want to call out to you because I thought you might fall as well. There are ferns covering the edge of the rock wall. It's like a canyon. I didn't see it until I was already falling. So I fired off a couple of shots. I figured it would stop you in your tracks long enough for me to get hold of my phone.'

Lyndall could hear her breathing hard. 'Just hang in there, I'll call for help,' she said.

'One more thing,' said Cass. 'You can tell Drew they can stop searching. I've found Michel Janvier.'

Later, Lyndall would learn that it lasted sixty-five minutes. It seemed an eternity, yet passed in a flash.

She called Sheridan Street and Di put her onto Drew's mobile immediately. She did not mention the gunshots or the presence of Michel Janvier's presumably disintegrating corpse somewhere down in the bush below. Only that Cass was in peril on the side of a sheer cliff face. He reacted at once.

'So you're at the side of the helipad area? Is the helipad reasonably free of branches and other obstructions? Will the chopper be able to land there?'

'Yes it's clear and there's not much long grass.'

'And Cass is on the south side of the helipad?'

'As far as I can see, yes. A bit southeast, I think. I didn't actually see her fall.'

'Yep, I've got it. Right, I'm getting the rescue chopper up there. Hopefully it's in Cairns and won't take long. You stay exactly where you are, keep your mobile on and do what the rescue people ask you. Tell Cass they're coming.'

She ended the call and stepped to the edge of the helipad and called out: 'Cass, I'm going to shout because I've got to keep my mobile free for calls. I spoke to Drew and the helicopter is coming as soon as it can. I'm going to call out to you every minute, just so you know I'm here for you. Don't call back unless there's some change in what's happening. You need to save your energy.'

'OK,' Cass called back.

Lyndall looked at her watch. It was 11.55. Over the next seven minutes she shouted to Cass seven times. 'I'm here, Cass,' she told her, again and again, 'I'm still here and help is coming. You're going to be back down in Cairns in the hospital soon. You're going to get through this. Think of Jordon.'

At 12.02 her mobile rang. Drew.

'The chopper crew are just gearing up,' he said. 'They're at Cairns Airport. They want to know if they need to bring an ED doc?'

'She's fully conscious,' said Lyndall. 'I don't know how badly injured she is and I don't think she's going to tell me. Anyway it will take longer to pick up someone from ED. I'd say just send the paramedics.'

'Right.'

'Drew just called,' Lyndall shouted towards Cass. 'The helicopter's at the airport and the paramedics are coming. Very soon!'

At 12.09 Lyndall saw the tiny blue and red bumblebee that was a helicopter rise into the air above Cairns and head south across the sky. Then it turned inland towards the Rock.

At 12.12 her mobile rang.

'Doctor? Josh here from the rescue helicopter. We're on our way now. Can you see us?'

'Yes. Call me Lyndall. I'm on the edge of the helipad and I can see you in the air over Cairns.'

'OK – just move onto clear ground so we can see you easily when we get there. We're not going to land there straight away. We're going to see if we can see where Cass is and assess the situation.'

By 12.20 the helicopter and the sound of its engine grew larger as it approached.

By 12.23 the chopper was hovering above the cliff where Cass must have been. The noise was tremendous. Lyndall could just see the crew. Her mobile rang again.

'Lyndall? Josh here.' She could barely hear him above the roar of the engine. 'We can see Cass. She can see us. I'm going down with the winch to pick her up. Stand by.'

The door slid open and a figure in yellow, presumably Josh, stood on the brink. He was in full rescue gear, a helmet on his head, and strapped into a red harness. He waved to Cass down below. 12.28.

Lyndall held her breath as she saw him slide over the edge of the doorway and gradually descend as the winch let out the cable connecting him to the chopper. The noise of the chopper's engine drowned out all other sounds. 12.35. After a moment, as the cable was paid out further and further, he disappeared completely from view.

That was the most unnerving time for Lyndall. What if he dislodged Cass from her tree before she was properly strapped in the harness?

Then a second figure in yellow appeared at the helicopter door, and lowered what looked like another harness. It disappeared out of Lyndall's sight. What the hell was going on? Could they be bringing up Michel's body as well? Why? Surely that could wait. She could see the pilot working to keep the chopper in position and focused on the scene below him.

At 12.48 the cable began to move. Josh appeared with Cass in his arms. The harness didn't seem to be on her, but he was holding her tight. Lyndall could see that Cass's jeans were partly torn off by the fall and her thigh was badly grazed. Her left arm looked injured too. Some exotic leopard-skin underwear was on display. So that was what policewomen wore under their uniforms … Then Cass was carefully lifted into the chopper by the second paramedic. It was just 12.55.

Her phone rang again. Josh.

'Lyndall – can you see us? We've got her. Bit of trouble with the harness but we've got her. She says to tell you she's fine. Now we're going to pick you up and explain what's going on. Just stand back away from the downdraught. Phil's got to work out the direction of the wind.'

In a couple of minutes the helicopter was on the helipad. The door opened but Josh indicated that she should wait for the rotor blades to slow down before she came towards him. Finally they stopped and Lyndall began to run. He put down the stairs and she climbed up, and burst into tears of relief.

Cairns, 12 March 2011

At eight that evening, showered and changed, Lyndall made her way up the hospital stairs to Detective Diamond's room. Pushing open the door, she was rewarded with a wide smile from the detective, who was reclining on pillows, her left arm in a sling. At her right elbow was a bottle of Scotch and a glass was in her right hand.

'Lyndall! Thanks for coming in!'

'Hey, are you supposed to be drinking that stuff? Didn't you just have an anaesthetic?'

'Three hours ago. Just a short one to put this shoulder back in. Shit, I needed a drink. It's been a helluva day! Pour yourself one too. Not my usual tipple but my Inspector gave it to me. It's the good stuff.'

'I will. Yeah, you said it – you had the most miraculous escape,' Lyndall said.

'I did! But you tell me your bit first. Leslie's been in, he told me some of it, but I want to hear it from you. You got Michel? And he's alive?' Cass asked.

'Yes! He's in Intensive Care. I haven't decided when I'll go and see him. Or even if …'

When Lyndall had climbed into the helicopter she'd expected to flop down on the seat beside Cass and be flown back to Cairns, where Cass would get the medical attention she needed. Instead she found herself in the midst of more action.

Cass was strapped onto a stretcher but sitting bolt upright, her eyes wide with excitement. Her left shoulder was clearly dislocated, and she had a long laceration on her right thigh, to which the second paramedic, rapidly introduced as Sam, was applying a dressing. Cass was taking no notice whatsoever of these injuries.

'It's Michel, I'm sure it's Michel,' she said at once to Lyndall, 'lying at the bottom of that rockface, in a kind of hollow. I thought he was dead. But then, as I was being lifted up, I looked down, and saw his head move, and his eyes open. And Josh had a look at him too.'

'Yeah,' said Josh, 'we've just looked down from directly above him. I'd say he's injured, and not fully conscious. But definitely alive.'

'Then we need to get him out,' said Lyndall immediately.

'Yeah,' said Josh. 'Phil's just contacting the base. Cass has to go back to Cairns, obviously. But she only needs one person with her. And you know Michel. Cass says you're his doctor. Are you up to coming with me, to see if we can reach him? We think there's a way down on foot. Phil and Sam can go back to Cairns and bring back some more guys. Cass will call her boss.'

'I remember the map in the guidebook,' said Cass. 'You branch off from the trail down near the crevice with the little tree. Following down and around should take you to where he is.'

'OK,' said Lyndall. She looked at Josh: 'You'll bring some first aid stuff?'

He held out his emergency pack. 'I'm ready.'

'Then let's go.'

Lyndall hugged Cass. 'See you later – I hope!'

They climbed back out of the helicopter and Lyndall led Josh to the start of the trail. Behind them, they heard the roar of the chopper taking off, and watched it disappear across the sky towards the hospital. Lyndall and Josh began the climb downwards, stepping from rock to rock and clinging to branches and large ferns to steady themselves.

It was much quicker going down, Lyndall found. After ten minutes of steep descent they came to the track leading off to the left. Josh led the way. Suddenly he stopped and pointed.

Well concealed by a huge tree-fern was a small one-man tent. As they approached it, two bush rats ran out. The front flap was partly unzipped, and they could see that there was no-one inside. Rain had got in, there were puddles on the plastic ground-covering and a sodden sleeping bag. Tins of food, water bottles, a towel, were scattered around.

'He's been living here!' said Josh.

'Yes,' said Lyndall, 'but maybe not for the last few days, at least. It looks quite neglected.'

They continued their climb down, coming to a creek that ran along the edge of the Rock. Taking their direction from the mobile phone tower above them, they followed the creek bed to where it approached the hollow where the man was. Josh stopped for a moment, and pointed out a tree to Lyndall, forty metres above them, growing seemingly out of solid rock. This was the tree that had snagged Cass. It was now hanging by one straggling root.

'She was bloody lucky!' he said, taking Lyndall's hand and helping her across a wide stretch in the creek. Together they made their way around the wide border of the hollow in the rock.

The man lay on his back. There was an overwhelming stench of faeces and urine, and a cloud of flies rose from his body at their approach. Both his knees were buckled under him. His breathing was laboured, his skin purple. His face was obscured by a matted beard. But Lyndall knew at once that it was Michel Janvier.

She moved across to him, knelt down, touched his shoulder.

'Michel?' she said. He turned slightly, opened his eyes, but made no response. Rapidly she checked his pulse, limbs and trunk. Josh was unzipping his emergency pack.

'He's got a fever,' she said. 'And he's very dehydrated. I'd say he has pneumonia and probably septicaemia. Not surprising, looks like he's been here for days, if not weeks. Both legs badly injured and maybe the spine. We should leave him flat until we get your team here. Can you give him some fluids?'

Josh was already opening an IV pack. 'I'll put this up,' he said.

'Good,' said Lyndall. 'It's a very long time since I've put in a cannula!'

Josh leaned over. 'Michel, mate,' he said, 'I'm Josh. I'm going to help you. Going to give you some fluids. Into your arm. And we're going to get you out of here. Soon.'

The man gave a grunt and closed his eyes.

'Probably very affected by the fever,' said Lyndall. 'On top of whatever else has happened. There's no external sign of head injury and he's moving his arms at least.' She looked up. Sheer rock led up to a fringe of rainforest on the edge of the saddle. Did he fall, like Cass? Or jump? Or was he pushed?

Josh had the saline running in within seconds. He pulled out his mobile to call his base.

'Karen,' he said, 'we're here. He's alive but not well. Leg injuries, maybe spine, several days old at least. Pyrexia and pneumonia, the doctor suspects. I've got a line in with some fluids. We'll need splints, a stretcher, a couple more guys. He can be winched up from where he is I think.'

'Crowds are coming,' he told Lyndall when he'd finished the call. 'My people, and probably even more of Cass's people.'

The man on the ground gave another grunt and Lyndall squatted next to him again.

'Michel,' she said, 'it's Lyndall, Dr Symonds. We're going to get you out of here and to the hospital.' He grunted again and this time she understood what he said.

'Odile.'

No, she thought, I'm not saying one word about Odile. Not right now.

'Michel,' she said firmly. 'We're just working on getting you out of here. Soon. Everything else can wait.'

'We didn't have to wait long until we heard the chopper returning,' she told Cass as she sat at her bedside, sipping Leslie's favourite Scotch. 'There wasn't much more we could do for him until they arrived. They brought a stretcher and two more paramedics, and winched him up. It was very efficient. Drew was with them. And two uniformed men.'

'Scenes-of-crime officers,' said Cass. 'Although is it actually a scene of a crime, do you think?'

'There were quite a few things on the ground,' Lyndall said. 'He had a backpack and a knife. And there were empty ampoules of ketamine and a syringe. He must have given himself some. Two mobile phones. Empty biscuit packets. A water bottle. And – maybe you've heard – a Hermès scarf!

'There was also no shortage of water. Pools on the rock beside him. He could reach them and drink. That's what saved him. But he must have been rained on, every day he was there. He was sodden and stinking. No wonder he got pneumonia.'

'You were right about that,' said Cass. 'Leslie has been to the ICU. Bilateral pneumonia, they said. They reckon he's fairly aware of where he is and who he is. But he's not talking. Not at all. Won't say how long he was lying there or what happened. Maybe he really doesn't know. Won't answer questions about his wife.'

'Give him a few days,' said Lyndall. 'He's lucky not to have a head injury. He must have landed hard on his feet – both knees are dislocated and the tibias broken. That was his main problem. He couldn't move from where he landed. But tell me what happened to you!'

Cass had disappeared between some giant ferns to relieve herself, and was pulling up her jeans when she noticed a dramatic orchid nestling behind one of the ferns.

'I went over to look at it and found myself falling arse over tit,' she said. 'There's a kind of gully there, hidden by ferns, it's very slippery and it led directly to the edge of the Rock. I went straight down, but growing out of the rock was this tree which caught me. I was upside-down at first, not knowing what the hell had happened. Gradually I pulled myself up and realised I was truly up shit creek. Ten metres of sheer slippery rock above me and forty below and only the tree holding me. With all my weight held by its roots just growing out of the rock.

'I realised that if I called you there was bugger-all you could do,' she said to Lyndall, 'and anyway you might come down as well. Maybe you'd go straight to the bottom but maybe you'd knock me off my perch and we'd both go down!

'I wanted to get my phone but my shoulder hurt like hell and I couldn't reach my back pocket straight away. But I could reach the gun. So I fired twice. I did remember to shoot so I wasn't going to hit you or anything else that would make the shots ricochet and come back to kill me! Eventually I was able to wriggle around and get the phone out.'

'I've never been so scared in all my life,' said Lyndall. 'I couldn't decide whether to run out and grab the phone from my backpack and risk being shot by a lunatic gunman, or lie still and hope the lunatic wouldn't find me.'

'You were great, talking me through it,' said Cass.

Lyndall shook her head dismissively.

When Josh had reached Cass, he'd started to put the rescue harness around her, but with the additional weight, he saw that the roots of the tree were starting to give way. He'd grabbed a firm hold of her, but was unable to get the harness into place. So he'd called Sam, who'd dropped down another one but that hadn't helped, so finally Cass was winched up in Josh's arms.

'They're my heroes for life!' she grinned.

Cass had called Drew from the helicopter.

'I told you I wasn't going to be pleased, Diamond,' he said, but with great relief in his voice.

'Well, y'know,' she said brightly, 'I think I'm going to claim overtime for today. Because while I hung out on that tree I was working. I looked down and saw the body of a middle-aged male lying at the bottom. Alive but I'd say not very well. I'd bet millions that it's Michel Janvier.'

She was rewarded by a silence from Drew that lasted nearly ten seconds.

Then he said: 'Well done, Detective! Is he accessible by foot from the helipad? By climbing down around the Rock? I don't remember the geography well.'

'Yes,' Cass said. 'I'm sure he is. Lyndall and one of the paramedics have gone down to him right now. But they're going to need help to get him out and we're going to need men there, too. It's a lot easier getting there by chopper, I can tell you, than walking in!'

'I'll organise another chopper and some men and we'll get up there as soon as we can,' he said. 'You take care of yourself and I'll come to see you later on. It sounds like you're going to be in hospital a while.'

'Did they bring your car back?' Cass now asked Lyndall.

'Yes,' she answered. 'And Drew brought the things we found on the ground around Michel. The two mobiles both had flat batteries. Drew said they'd be recharged to see if they can give you any clues. He was also going to take a look at the tent. Seems like Michel had set himself up to be there for quite a few days.

'My first thought, when I saw the tent, was that Michel definitely killed her and then went bush. But Drew pointed out that he could have been kidnapped with Odile, but he managed to escape. He's very fit, or at least he was. He could fight off a couple of attackers even if they killed Odile.'

'Yes,' said Cass. 'Leslie also thought that was possible: Michel escaping after Odile was killed, and managing to take the car. Then abandoning it by the Rock trail, which he knew, and disappearing into that country that he also knew, which is too rugged to follow him into. And then maybe he went back to the tree, and his wife. To see if she was still there.'

'So,' said Lyndall, 'even finding Michel, if he can't or won't talk, you're not really much closer to knowing who killed her?'

'I think that's probably true,' said Cass, 'though Drew will be taking a good look at everything found up there, especially the ketamine.

'From what I could see,' Cass added, 'he was probably on the path down from the saddle when he fell. He was closer to the top lookout, the one we didn't get to. Or maybe he was taking a pee too. It's all really slippery up there.'

The door of the room opened and two people appeared. The first was a tall Aboriginal boy who Lyndall realised must be Jordon. He held out a hand in greeting, and then set down a steaming container of laksa for his mother.

'Thanks Jay,' she said, lifting the lid, 'they gave me the standard supper but I'm still starving.'

The second person was clearly an ED doctor. Dressed in scrubs, dark haired and in his early thirties perhaps, his gaze as he entered went directly to Cass. To Lyndall he seemed vaguely familiar.

'Hi!' said Cass. Rather warmly, Lyndall thought. 'This is Zak. He looked after me in ED. Zak, this is Lyndall. You already met Jordon, downstairs.'

'She was fantastic,' Zak told Lyndall. 'She stayed calm the whole time she was stuck out there – she even texted you, Jordon, and said she had a great view and would be back soon!'

Ohho, thought Lyndall. This is what happens when you turn up in ED rescued from a cliff face wearing very little apart from slinky animal-print underwear! But does he know she's *over men*? She tried to catch Cass's eye but her friend was busily tucking into her laksa.

'Would you guys like some laksa?' asked Jordon. I've got lots.'

'Actually, yes,' said Lyndall, 'I'm starving too!'

Jordon said, 'Zak?'

'Thank you, no,' replied the doctor. 'Take things easy there, Detective. I'll come back to check on you later on,' he added, in what Lyndall decided was a significant tone of voice. Cass was occupied with ripping the shell from a large prawn using her teeth and her one good hand and simply nodded at him.

When the door had closed Cass said through mouthfuls: 'I'm sure that man should have been off duty hours ago.'

'Someone should tell him it's a lost cause,' Jordon remarked to no-one in particular.

Cairns, 13 March 2011

Cass opened her eyes to see sunlight streaming through the slats in the venetian blinds. She felt delightfully warm and calm, and then remembered the painkiller she'd been given the night before. She lifted her right arm from under the sheet so she could see the face of her watch, which the nursing staff had transferred to that side. Eight o'clock! She must have slept for ten hours.

Hopefully Jordon would soon be here. He'd promised to come at eight with caffeine.

There was a soft tap at the door, which then opened a fraction. Not Jordon, though a vaguely familiar face. Then Cass realised it was that doctor Leslie knew – Henry Jolley – the one she'd chased the other night. She wriggled herself into a sitting position.

'Come in,' she said. 'Um, Dr Jolley, isn't it?'

'Yes. Ah, please call me Henry. I hope you don't mind my intruding, Detective. I really just came to see how you are. I was doing a round in the ward next door. You had a very lucky escape yesterday, from what I hear.'

'I did. The rescue team was fantastic. And my shoulder's back in place now too. When do you think they'll let me go home?'

'Well – shoulders aren't my area, but maybe later today or

tomorrow. I'm sure you're otherwise pretty healthy.'

He hesitated for a moment and then added: 'I heard you found … the woman's husband.'

'Yes,' said Cass. 'I guess it's all over the news. He was close to the Rock. He'd been there for some time, a few days at least. But it also seemed he'd been living in the bush up there. At least since the cyclone.'

'Your colleague, Detective Barwen … he told me a bit about it,' Henry nodded. 'He's been wonderful.'

Cass raised a surprised eyebrow. 'He has?'

'Yes. I understand that you … the police, Inspector Fernando … were suspicious, that Dr Ingram and I, we might have been covering for each other, saying we were in outpatients together that night. And I have to say, I did talk to Tim Ingram about Odile Janvier that night. He advised me to stop paying the money, and see what happened. I was still thinking about that when I heard she was dead. But anyway, Detective Barwen asked us if we were using hospital computers, and of course we were, and had we driven into the hospital car park, and gone through hospital doors with our passes, which we had also done, so he checked through all the electronic records and confirmed everything.'

Dogged persistence, thought Cass, *it really does pay off.*

A faint smile crossed Henry's face. 'And,' he added, 'I think he did the same for my surgical colleague, Dr Mellish. Tracked down all his movements in and out of the hospital with his pass and found he couldn't have been away long at all.

I ran into Mellish down at the police station yesterday. I would never have thought of *him* getting involved with that woman!'

'I can't really comment,' said Cass, also smiling slightly, 'but like a stinger jellyfish she had very long and poisonous tentacles. And traded on doctors' goodwill, as well as, umm, their human susceptibilities.'

Still Henry seemed to linger. Then Cass remembered the reason for the chase at Portsmith. The Controller.

'The husband's state of health will have to be assessed,' she said. 'We're still not sure what happened in regards to her death. But I'm sure you're wondering if he'll be charged with blackmail,' she continued.

Henry flushed, but nodded. 'Yes. I am concerned. And I'm sure I'm not the only one.'

'It will depend quite a bit on what his victims want. Do they want to press charges and provide information to us and proceed to what would be a trial in an open court?' said Cass.

'For myself, I'd just be happy to know that it's stopped,' Henry replied. 'I, er, as I explained to Inspector Fernando, I've met this wonderful woman. He told me that most people don't like blackmail, and he turned out to be right. I was in Sydney when I heard the news about the murder. I came back straight away because I was worried about the story becoming public. But now I've told … Susanna, and she was completely understanding. Appalled by what happened to me, actually. It wasn't a problem at all. I'd lived with this nightmare for years, and now it's over. That's all I want.'

There was a knock on the door. Breakfast was being wheeled in, and behind it Cass could see Jordon with a large paper cup. Henry held out his hand to Cass.

'I'll get out of your way,' he said. 'That's been really helpful. Thank you so much, I was worried about those things.'

'It's a pleasure,' Cass said. 'I'm sorry I chased you last week! I almost arrested you!'

'I deserved it! Get better soon.'

Henry left the room and walked out the main door of the hospital. He crossed the road and let himself into his private rooms. It was Sunday, there was no-one else there.

In his office he unlocked the bottom drawer of his desk and took out the two letters and the USB sticks sent by the Controller.

Back in the outer office, he hesitated for a moment.

Then he pushed the letters and USBs into a yellow plastic bag of the kind used for infectious pathology samples. He placed the bag into the dangerous waste bin in the sluice room at the back of the building. Later that day it would be churned up and spat out by the giant reprocessing plant at Portsmith. His relationship with the Controller was over.

With a spring in his step he headed to the Esplanade. There was time for a walk along to the Pier and back.

And later he had a lunch date at L'Unico. With Susanna.

At the same time, on the floor below where Cass was eating her breakfast, a man sat propped up in another hospital bed, watched from the door by two uniformed policemen. Two nurses were attempting to get the man to drink some juice. He was not cooperating.

Michel Janvier was not cooperating because his mind was wandering between morphine-induced sleep and semi-wakefulness, and the wakefulness was filled with images that he could not piece together.

He was in a hospital … that he knew at times. Dr Lyndall had been here … but now she was gone. At one point he thought he had seen her up in the bush, but that couldn't be right. At one point he thought she had been with him in a plane. Or a helicopter. But that couldn't be right either. He had wanted Dr Lyndall. He had wanted to talk to her. To explain everything. But his mouth was so dry and sore he could not speak. Then she was gone, and she had not come back.

Sometimes he saw Odile. Her lipstick was red and the bottoms of her shoes were red. She was in his arms and she was struggling, she kicked him and the red-bottomed shoe fell off and it was his fault. Then he could see her standing over him, her face grinning at him as she shrieked at him: Beg! Beg! You have to beg me for it. Then not Odile herself, but her head that was more a skull, the eye sockets empty, but still Odile's mouth, grinning at him. She was in the bush, in the rainforest. How did she get there? Had he taken her there? How could he do that? She would never let him do that.

He wanted a smoke but they would not give him one in this place. More than the smoke, he wanted the silk. Just to hold it in his fingers. That would be enough to ease the pain in his legs. He didn't want to drink. He reached out his arm and pushed the beaker away from his lips and shook his head. He could not find the English words to say that what he wanted was the silk. *Just give me the silk*, he thought.

'It's no use, Mandy,' said one of the nurses. 'Just keep the IV running today and give him more morphine so he stays quiet. The cops will have to wait to talk to him.'

Cairns, 15 March 2011

Cass ran a warm bath and poured in lemon bath salts. She was planning to soak her shoulder. When she was still it didn't hurt, but once she was up and about, even in the sling she'd been given, the joint ached. She was under strict orders from Leslie to rest up and not show her face in Sheridan Street for at least two weeks.

She climbed in, placing her mobile and her coffee cup on the side of the bath close to her good arm. She was reaching out her toes to turn on the tap for more hot water when the mobile rang. She sat up slowly and wriggled towards the phone. It was Lyndall. What did she want so early?

'Cass!' Lyndall sounded concerned. 'I'm sorry to call you at this hour. I know you're on leave. But I just discovered something, quite … well, something I think might shed some light on what happened between Michel and Odile.'

'Go on.'

'It's on my voicemail. Of a phone, quite an old phone, that I use only when I'm on call. I hadn't looked at it until this morning – I'm on call today, you see. I charged up the phone last night. And this morning I discovered a whole lot of messages from Michel. I must have given him the number when Dominic and Damian were first in court.'

'What kind of messages? When were they sent?'

'Messages to me. On the first and second of February. I think from a public phone. There's the sound of traffic in the background. He didn't have this mobile number; it's too new. I think he tried and tried to get me on the other number. But of course I wasn't here.'

'Right,' said Cass. 'I'm not supposed to be at Sheridan Street today. My only plan was to walk this new dog I seem to have agreed to take on; it's chewing up my backyard as we speak! But this changes everything. Can you come into the office in about, um, twenty minutes? I'll get Jordon to drive me in. I'm absolutely fine. Drew will be there. I know he's also got something they found yesterday, on Odile's mobile. Maybe we're going to understand the whole thing after all.'

'Yes, OK. It's eight o'clock now, that's fine. But I have patients booked in from 9.30.'

When Cass arrived at Sheridan Street, Lyndall was already there with Drew. He had brought up coffees for all of them.

'I decided I'd get you a double shot today,' he said to Cass, 'in view of your invalid status.'

'Thanks,' she said sweetly.

'Here's the phone,' Lyndall said, putting it on the desk between them. 'As you see it's an old phone, I don't use it much and the number's been the same for years. I only listened to the first two messages. I was a bit taken aback to find them so I called Cass straight away. There are five or six more.'

'Thanks,' Drew said, 'we'll listen to them in just a moment. First let me ask you, have you seen Michel Janvier since you helped the paramedics get him out?'

'Yes. I saw him yesterday in the hospital. You probably know, he's got multiple injuries to both legs. He's been moved out of intensive care. He's more alert now but still hardly talking. I think he's still very traumatised. And maybe his brain is affected by the septicaemia. I've made clear to him, as much as I could, and to everyone else, that he is no longer my patient. Given all the circumstances.'

'Yes,' Drew answered. 'I understand that. And what you've brought in to show us, and what we have to show you, may clear up how Odile Janvier died.

'He had mobile phones with him; we found both his and hers. But the batteries were flat in both, probably had been for weeks because he had nowhere to charge them.'

'Who was he going to call anyway?' asked Lyndall. 'He had no friends, no family he could talk to.'

Drew nodded. Then said: 'You saw that he had ketamine. So we presume he was able to self-administer that, until it was used up. Yesterday, by tracking down pharmacy records, we found he'd been prescribed some by a GP up on the Tablelands. That was twelve years ago. Michel was bushwalking by himself on Bartle Frere and fractured some bones in his hand. He found this doctor who patched him up under ketamine. It also seems that he got some more, illegally, somewhere in Cairns. Probably from contacts he'd met through Dominic. Maybe quite a lot over the years.

'We asked Damian about it. He had no idea but then we asked him to speak to Dominic and arranged that with Wellington. I gather Dominic wasn't prepared to say much even to Damian but he did tell him he knew their father had used ketamine at times and that he got a high from it.'

'Yes, said Lyndall, 'some people do. People with delusional tendencies would be particularly susceptible and that would include Michel.'

'It's possible Dominic put his father in touch with a dealer who got him the ketamine,' Drew said. 'It's also possible that Michel found his own dealer. It makes no difference.

'Several syringes with traces of blood were found in Michel's backpack,' he went on. 'All except one match his blood.

'We heard from the lab late last night that the last one matches Odile's. We assume this is the one that killed her, and that he gave it to her. He was still carrying it around. Together with the scarf.'

'So,' said Lyndall, 'Michel had used ketamine before. And I guess it's good that he still had some when he needed it at the bottom of the Rock. And Odile had ketamine before she died. That sounds to me like he gave it to her, maybe at the house, then took her up into the bush. But why? What pushed him over the edge? Was he intending to kill her with it?'

'We thought through all those things ourselves yesterday. And decided that all our other suspects could be ruled out.

And the answers to your questions, well they may be in your phone. At least partly. Would you mind playing the messages for us now?'

Lyndall she reached over and turned the mobile on. It gave several shrill rings. She pressed messagebank and found the first message.

'Doctor Lyndall.' Male; French accent. 'It's … it's Michel. I need to talk to you, I need to talk to you soon. Can you call me on this … *beep*!'

'There's only a ten second space for a voicemail message,' Lyndall said. 'I did that deliberately so I didn't get people leaving me long complex messages.'

'Doctor Lyndall, it's Michel … I need to talk, please call me … please … *beep*!'

'Doctor Lyndall, please, please, it's Michel … I need you … I …' Shouting now: 'Odile is dead … *beep*!'

Lyndall grimaced.

'Doctor Lyndall, Odile's dead … she's dead … I need to talk to you … I … Doc … *beep*!'

'Doctor Lyndall … you'll know I had to do it … she had to die … yes, yes, I had to … *beep*!'

Lyndall paused for a moment, looking at Cass, who nodded.

'Yes,' Cass said, 'seems like, one way or another, he planned to do it and he did.'

Lyndall scrolled down to the next message.

'Doctor Lyndall … Doctor Lyndall … it was because of Doctor Trevor … she shouldn't have … *beep*!' At this

Lyndall sat up straight. What on earth had Trevor got to do with this?

'Doctor Lyndall I had to punish her … she was going to show you the pictures … I said no … *beep*!'

Then a final message: 'Doctor Lyndall, I want, I want … I have to … to be with her …'

There was a series of beeps.

'The voicemail's full there,' Lyndall said. She put her head in her hands, thinking. Then, sitting up and looking first at Cass, then at Drew, she asked: 'How does Trevor fit into this? What's this about pictures?'

'Well, I was coming to that,' Drew said.

'As you know, the Janviers, both of them, were blackmailing a number of Cairns men over about the last ten years. Mostly doctors.'

Lyndall nodded. 'And – Trevor was one of them?' she asked.

'Not exactly,' said Drew. 'Umm … I know you're divorced. I also know from our records that your ex-husband was found dead in a motel in circumstances that suggested he'd been there with a woman. The woman had left precipitately and the staff had no idea who she was. But anyway there were no suspicious circumstances to the death itself.'

'No,' said Lyndall. 'He had a heart attack.'

'Yes,' agreed Drew. 'Well, I can tell you that we didn't find any film of your husband – ex-husband – with Odile Janvier, in Michel's collection.

'However, on Saturday after you found Michel, we took both the mobile phones, his and his wife's, and recharged them. There was nothing of any interest on Michel's phone. Nor was there much of interest on Odile's in regards to phone messages. But she had an iPhone, a new model. And she had recorded several videos.'

Lyndall took a sharp breath in. 'Yes?'

'I'm afraid they are of Odile having sex with your ex-husband, last year, up until the moment of his heart attack, when they abruptly stop.'

Lyndall let out a sigh. 'So it was Odile he was with when he died,' she said. 'How bizarre.'

She thought for a moment. 'So what you're saying is that whereas Michel was involved in all the filming with all the others they blackmailed, with Trevor it was Odile herself?'

'Yes, exactly. I talked to Cass about this last night. And she said you'd always been rather wary of Michel as a patient. That perhaps there was some, um, physical attraction, on his part. That led him to be protective of you.' Cass nodded.

'So possibly Odile wanted to try the blackmail on Trevor but Michel told her not to?' suggested Lyndall. 'Is that what you think?'

'Yes. And the voicemails confirm that, don't you think?' Cass asked her.

'Yes,' said Lyndall. 'I have to say that I was always aware that Michel had a kind of … fascination … with me. Well,

I could even call it an obsession. I kept it as controlled as I could. But I can imagine that if he'd told her he didn't want her being involved with Trevor, because he saw Trevor as some kind of extension of me, Odile would take great delight in persisting with it, to torment him.'

'Yes,' said Cass. 'That iPhone footage was all recorded in August and September of last year. Up until the day Trevor died. So we think that she'd been taunting Michel with this, perhaps over a few weeks. Then her plan came to an abrupt halt – in the middle of their meeting in the motel, Trevor suddenly died.

'So she was no longer going to be able to screw any cash out of him or threaten Michel with doing so. But she could see the effect of what she'd done on Michel. And she didn't like the fact that he had some feeling for you. So she threatened to send the pictures to you.'

Lyndall eventually said: 'Yes, that does fit what I know of him … and her. And that could have been enough to make him snap.'

She continued slowly, thinking it through as she spoke. 'So he decides he'll give her ketamine, which he has some experience of. And he'll take her out into the rainforest, which is an environment he feels comfortable in, but she doesn't. In fact, in a sense she was on his territory for once. And this time he'll tie her up. With her scarves.'

Cass said: 'You may not know that when her body was found, Odile's underwear was missing.'

Lyndall raised her eyebrows. 'That's interesting,' she said. 'So at some stage, when Odile was either unconscious or dead, Michel must have felt enough in control to take her pants off. Something he would never have done if she was alive and fully conscious.'

'And then,' asked Cass, 'could he have given her an even larger dose of ketamine? Enough to kill her?'

'If the pathologist isn't able to tell you that then it would be guesswork. I'm just a psychiatrist, it's not my area of expertise. But it would seem to me that a large dose of ketamine, or that plus exposure, would kill her quite quickly. He obviously knows a good deal about ketamine.'

'We think he must have left her there after she died,' said Cass. 'And maybe spent some time, maybe the night of 29 January, and other nights, in the car thinking about what to do next.'

'There were a lot of cigarette butts, by the tree and by the road,' Drew said. 'We think he probably went back to where Odile was, maybe several times, thinking about what to do. The scarves that tied her up were a bit frayed at the wrists. Perhaps he tried to untie her. Certainly if he'd wanted to he could have disposed of her body and it could have been a very long time before anyone reported her missing. If ever. Yet he chose not to do that.'

'I doubt he would have seen that as a choice,' Lyndall replied. 'The way I imagine he was thinking, he didn't foresee any consequences to his actions while it was all happening.

When she was dying. And once she was dead, I'm sure he was overcome with grief because she was the only person he'd ever really loved. You can see that from him saying he wanted to be with her.'

Then she added: 'At least, I'm sure that's how he reacted initially.'

'After a couple of days,' said Cass, 'he decides to call you. Just before Yasi. But the mobiles are flat so he uses a public phone. Maybe near Davies Creek, there is one there. Obviously he regarded you as someone who would understand. And in the phone calls he tells you he killed her, one way or another. Deliberately. And that he wants to die himself.

'But then at some point he decided to go to Kahlpahlim Rock. And apparently, to delay killing himself.'

'Just what I'm thinking,' said Lyndall. 'The Rock seems to have been important to him. Perhaps that whole area of the rainforest.'

'And then,' said Drew, 'he decides that instead of killing himself, with ketamine or some other way, that he'll take a tent and set himself up in the bush.'

'We know he didn't come back to the Earlville house after Yasi,' said Cass. 'And we've also heard, from the men who found his car in the bush, that there was quite a lot of food and camping gear in it.' Mareeba police had told Drew yesterday how Bugsy had suddenly recalled this information.

'So we're thinking,' said Drew, 'that maybe he spent the cyclone in the car, somewhere up there in the forest, close to the body. Maybe to protect it, if you see what I mean.'

'Then,' Cass said, 'there's a period of time in which he lives in the bush, he's still got the car, and he may even have gone into Mareeba or Kuranda for supplies. Because no-one knows he's missing, no-one's looking for him, he's just a bloke in a dirty four-wheel drive doing some shopping. And he's an experienced bushie, he's probably always kept camping gear in his car.'

'Things start to go pear-shaped when the car disappears,' said Drew. 'By then he must have had the tent camp up on the Rock. The car had been quite well concealed in the bush. He'd walk down from the Rock, maybe each day for a while, spend some time with the body, and possibly get a few supplies. But once the car disappeared, he wouldn't have known who took it and whether we'd found the body, or what was going on.'

Lyndall was listening intently to this. Now she said: 'This is what's described with *folie à deux*. Once the two people are separated, the one who was under the influence of the other starts to recover. So first of all Michel is overwhelmed with grief, and plans to kill himself as well. Probably next to Odile. But then she's no longer there telling him what to do, controlling him. Michel can see that, physically, more and more of her is disappearing every day. He has his own reality now. And he's got complete control of her, with her tied to that tree. He had a car, he had money, he's in the bush where he's been happy.

'It would have been quite a slow process. It would have been logical to dispose of the body deep in the forest, go back home, work out some story for the neighbours, start a new life. A more logical person might have done that. But a more logical person wouldn't have got into this situation in the first place.'

'So he doesn't kill himself after all,' said Drew. 'But then when the car disappears he retreats back up to the Rock and stays there.'

'Yes,' said Lyndall, 'that fits with everything that's been found, doesn't it? And no doubt he becomes more agitated about what he's going to do. Especially if at some stage he did try to go back to Odile, and saw that the police were there, and obviously she'd been discovered. Which leads to him ending up where he did. I'd say he fell, rather than deciding to jump. If he wanted to kill himself he would have used the ketamine. At least it seems clear no-one pushed him off the Rock.'

'Yes,' said Drew, 'it all fits. You know, we had a list of suspects as long as your arm but it comes down to what we were always taught as rookies. With homicide it's most often a family member. And more often than not, the spouse.'

Lyndall was silent, then said: 'You know, I'm glad he had the ketamine with him. It must have helped with the pain when he first fell. And obviously, he didn't use it all at once. He wasn't intending to kill himself, even then. He was still hoping to live. And even though he messed up so many people's lives, he didn't deserve a wife like Odile.'

'She certainly was a piece of work,' said Drew. 'And well out of the lives of quite a few citizens of this town. Of course, he'll go to prison for quite a while. And very possibly be in a wheelchair for the rest of his days, as I understand it. But he is still alive. And the younger son is coming back up from Hobart. He sounded quite concerned, on the phone, about his dad. So it's not all bad.'

'And the poor dentist?' asked Lyndall.

'There'll be a coronial inquiry. There was no suicide note, so probably there'll be a finding of accidental death, which will be better for the family than suicide,' Drew said, standing up. 'You'll be wanting to get to work,' he said to Lyndall. 'I'll get a car to drop you home, Cass.'

Lyndall nodded and stood up.

'Well, thank you very much for coming in,' Drew said. 'We'll keep the phone for a couple of days, if you don't mind.'

Lyndall decided to take the stairs rather than the lift, and walked slowly down, stopping for several minutes at the first landing to look out at the mountains beyond the town, now disappearing beneath the swirling clouds of a tropical morning shower. The mountains where Odile Janvier died. And, although she knew a doctor should always keep an emotional distance from her patients, she allowed herself a moment of understanding for Michel Janvier.

This evening, she would call Bernard.

Cairns, Thursday 17 March 2011

Claudine took Leslie's arm as they made their way down the brightly carpeted stairs of the Cairns City Cinema after the early showing of *Bridesmaids*. He was still laughing.

'You see,' she told him, 'you did like it! I told you so!'

'Yes,' he said, 'lots of wild women having fun. It certainly took my mind off the office. And I liked the traffic cop. He had a good attitude.' They had reached the foot of the stairs opposite the pizza bar. 'We could go there for Italian. Or would you prefer the Taj Mahal?'

'A good lamb curry is what I want,' she said firmly. 'Besides, see who's just gone in there. We might not be welcome.'

Peering through the window, Leslie saw Detective Cass Diamond, in jeans and silky top, with her left arm in a sling, in the company of a vaguely familiar dark-haired young man.

'And look who she's with!' said Claudine.

'Um, I know him, but ...'

'Heavens, Leslie! It's Zak! Zak Rookwood. Leah's son.'

'Zak? Isn't he still a medical student? He must be about ten years younger than she is.'

'He's thirty at least and a doctor in Emergency now. And I think both of them are well able to look after themselves. Come on, I'm starving.'

'Well she needs to come back to work soon,' Leslie

remarked as they headed out into the street. ‘She still hasn’t found out what happened to Wayne Buscati.’

Acknowledgements

Many people helped me in the writing of *Double Madness*, some by critically reading the manuscript, some by providing technical information, some by doing both. Jane Patrick, Jan Walker, Annie Chance, Michele Moore, John Timlin, my brother Richard Downes, my daughters Naomi, Viveka and Josephine, and my son Javed all read the manuscript as it evolved and helped develop the story and the character of Cass Diamond. Josephine provided tae kwon do moves, Naomi and Viveka directed me on Cass's likely musical tastes. My dear friend, the late Mary McCleary, explained the workings of New South Wales prisons, and Jonathan Carne gave me important information about *folie à deux*. My editors Kylie Mason and Deb Fitzpatrick helped enormously in improving the text.

I am indebted to Joshua Trevino for his thorough reading of the manuscript and advice about legal procedures, and to Detective Senior Sergeant Glenn Horan for guidance on police matters. *Double Madness* is a work of fiction and as such, does not seek to depict exactly how either detection or medicine are practiced. I can say though that wherever the legal or police details are accurate, Josh or Glenn are responsible; all inaccuracies are my own.

I thank them all.

THE CASS DIAMOND CRIME SERIES

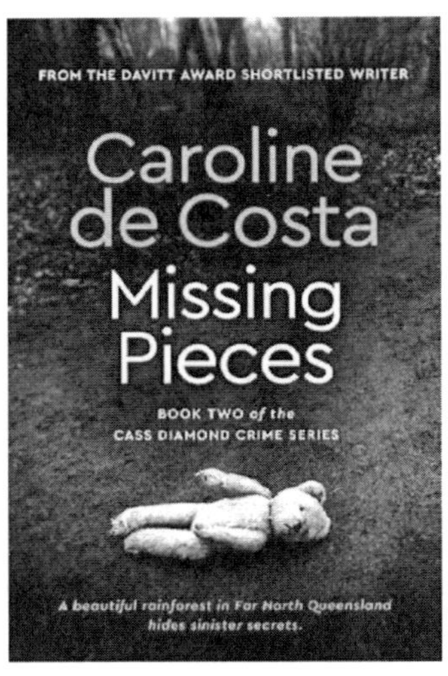

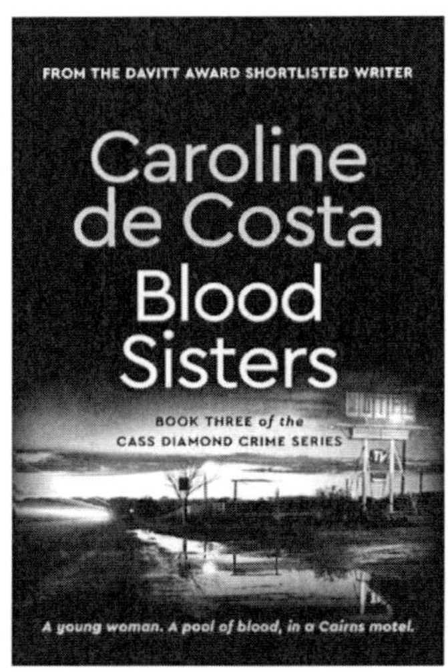